THE FRONTIERS OF
SPACE, TIME, AND LIFE—

The search for new frontiers has taken us into the exploration of genetic structure, on journeys into space, and searches to unlock the secrets of time. Now you can join thirteen of today's most imaginative authors on such exciting expeditions as:

"Traces" —When political and theological correctness insists there is no intelligent life but the human race, can any scientist's discoveries change that view of the universe?

"The Cutting Edge"—Nanosurgery had never been tried on a human. Was a near-hopeless case to be its first—and perhaps last—test?

"Ruins of the Past" —Driven by the desperate hope of saving herself from virtual enslavement, she dared the mountain heights from which no one in recent memory had returned alive. But would she find salvation amid the alien ruins or only a quick death?

FAR FRONTIERS

More Imagination-Expanding Anthologies Brought to You by DAW:

STAR COLONIES *Edited by Martin H. Greenberg and John Helfers.* From the time the first Homo sapiens looked up at the night sky, the stars were there, sparkling, tempting us to reach out and seize them. Though humankind's push from the stars has at times slowed and stalled, there are still those who dare to dream, who work to build the bridge between the Earth and the universe. But while the scientists are still struggling to achieve this goal, science fiction writers have already found many ways to master space and time. Join Robert J. Sawyer, Jack Williamson, Alan Dean Foster, Allen Steele, Robert Charles Wilson, Pamela Sargent, Mike Resnick, Kristine Kathryn Rusch, and their fellow explorers on these never before taken journeys to distant stars.

MY FAVORITE SCIENCE FICTION STORY *Edited by Martin H. Greenberg.* Here are seventeen of the most memorable stories in the genre—written by such greats as: Theodore Sturgeon, C. M. Kornbluth, Gordon R. Dickson, Robert Sheckley, Lester Del Rey, James Blish, and Roger Zelazny—each one personally selected by a well-known writer—among them: Arthur C. Clarke, Joe Haldeman, Harry Turtledove, Frederik Pohl, Greg Bear, Lois McMaster Bujold, and Anne McCaffrey—and each prefaced by that writer's explanation of his or her choice. Here's your chance to enjoy familiar favorites, and perhaps to discover some wonderful treasures. In each case, you'll have the opportunity to see the story from the perspective of a master of the field.

MOON SHOTS *Edited by Peter Crowther; with an Introduction by Ben Bova.* In honor of the thirtieth anniversary of that destiny-altering mission, mankind's first landing on the Moon, some of today's finest science fiction writers—including Brian Aldiss, Gene Wolfe, Brian Stableford, Alan Dean Foster, and Robert Sheckley—have created original Moon tales to send your imagination soaring from the Earth to the Moon. From a computer-created doorway to the Moon . . . to a unique gathering on the Sea of Tranquillity . . . to a scheme to get rich selling Moon rocks . . . to an unexpected problem at a lunar-based fusion facility, here are stories to fill the space yearnings of every would-be astronaut.

FAR FRONTIERS

Edited by

Martin H. Greenberg
and Larry Segriff

DAW BOOKS, INC.
DONALD A. WOLLHEIM, FOUNDER
375 Hudson Street, New York, NY 10014

ELIZABETH R. WOLLHEIM
SHEILA E. GILBERT
PUBLISHERS

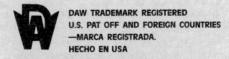

ACKNOWLEDGMENTS

Introduction © 2000 by Larry Segriff.

Traces © 2000 by Kathleen M. Massie-Ferch.

Star Light, Star Bright © 2000 by Robert J. Sawyer.

Chauna © 2000 by Alan Dean Foster.

Out of the Cradle © 2000 by Terry D. England.

The Cutting Edge © 2000 by Janet Pack.

Home World © 2000 by Marc Bilgrey.

Dreamlike States © 2000 by Kristine Kathryn Rusch.

The Last Bastion © 2000 by Lawrence Watt Evans.

Forgotten © 2000 by Peter Schweighofer.

Down on the Farm © 2000 by Julie E. Czerneda.

Set in Stone © 2000 by Andre Norton.

Ruins of the Past © 2000 by Jane Lindskold.

Angel on the Outward Side © 2000 by Robin Wayne Bailey.

CONTENTS

INTRODUCTION

Frontiers. There's something magical about that word. Something stirring in its echoes. Something that calls to us, that sets our blood singing, our pulse pounding, and our souls soaring. Frontiers are more than just that, however, more than just stirring action, compelling characters, and lives lived on the edge.

I've long believed that what our modern society needs most is a new frontier—something that would re-ignite a sense of patriotism and community, something that would help to channel our aggressions, something that would give us, as a nation and as a world, a sense of pride, a sense of productivity, a sense of progress. That's why I've been such a fan of the space program. It's also why, for the past twenty years or so, I've been so disappointed in our space program.

But space isn't the only frontier left open to us. It may not even truly be the final frontier. Some of my favorites include cities on the ocean floor, virtual reality, and perhaps the greatest frontier of all: death itself.

Come with us now as we invite some of today's top writers to take us on a personal tour of their own favorite frontiers.

TRACES

by Kathleen M. Massie-Ferch

Kathleen M. Massie-Ferch was born and raised in Wisconsin. She's there still, with a wonderful husband, two Scottie dogs, several telescopes, numerous rocks, and more books than she cares to count. She worked her way through college, earning degrees in astronomy, physics, and geology-geophysics. For the past twenty years she has worked for the University of Wisconsin as a research geologist. Massie-Ferch has made short fiction sales to a variety of places, such as *Marian Zimmer Bradley's Fantasy Magazine, Sword and Sorceress, Warrior Princesses,* and *New Altars.* She has coedited two historical fantasy anthologies for DAW Books; *Ancient Enchantresses* and *Warrior Enchantresses.*

"Which one?" I asked, but it was obvious which sample he wanted—my office wasn't that big. His dark eyes were wide with excitement.

"That pretty blue rock." Angshu pointed to the seven-inch-long assemblage of crystals. The five-year-old's dark and wild curls reinforced the determined set of his jaw.

"Of course." My arms strained under his weight, I had to set him down. "You're heavy, even in three-quarters G." I picked up the aggregate of beautiful blue crystals and pointed out several prominent marks. "See the lines that cross each side? Kyanite crystals break easily along these cleavage planes. I think your class will find this other rock much more interesting." I set the kyanite back on its padded resting place, despite Angshu's outstretched hand, and reached toward the dark brown rock from lower on the shelves. The intercom's chime resounded through my office.

My private code. Blast. Three swift steps brought me to my desk. Toggling the answer button silenced the incessant chime. "Geology section," I said.

"Dr. Sehkar?"

"Matt! Are you back already?" I glanced back around at Angshu, who watched the kyanite crystal as if it'd leap into his eager grasp.

"No, ma'am. We're still on the surface." Matt's labored breathing echoed off his EVA helmet and into the open comm link. His voice suddenly sounded older than his twenty-two years. "I'm still checking out this outcrop for you, but it's—well, the lava tubes aren't all that remarkable after all. The lava flows are in fact older than the cyanobacteria colonies offshore, as you suspected. But the beach is interesting. I think you should see it."

I suppressed a groan. Angshu tried to grab for the kyanite—well beyond his reach. I snapped my fingers. He stopped, although he refused to look at me. "Matt, I've got that prelim report staring me in the face. That's why I sent you instead of going myself, remember?"

"I know," Matt said. "I *need* your advice!"

I couldn't stop the groan. How I wanted to say no and finish my blasted report—but then nothing about Delta Pavonis Two went fast. "Aren't you even going to give me more of a hint?"

"No, it'll be more fun as a surprise. Remember, that's why you get paid the big bucks."

I almost didn't catch it. The keying phrase sent a shock through me. I could read a lot between those few words, and I played my part. "Watch your mouth, Matt." I checked my desk clock. "With travel time, mark it two hours from now. An hour, if possible."

"Thanks, boss." Relief eased Matt's voice back to its normal tone, although he was still breathing heavily. "I know it's your rec time—"

Time to change the subject.

"You sound out of breath." I punched in the proper code and my computer brought up his bio-vits and those of his team members. The stats looked reasonable; still, they could be wrong. "Have you checked your oxygen mixture recently?"

"It's fine. Just rough terrain."

"All right. Careful, Matt. I don't want any accidents."

"I know," he said, "no time for the paperwork."

"You've got that right!" I closed the channel and was about to call transport when I caught some movement at the edge of vision.

"No!" I yelled, too late. I lunged forward and grabbed Angshu in mid-fall. The chair he had been climbing on crashed against the shelves. The harsh sound of colliding chair and rocks echoed through the plastic and metal office and sent shivers through me. The lowest six of the ten shelves unhinged themselves and quickly dumped their contents.

"Oh-oh," Angshu said as he clung to me in dismay in the now silent room.

"Oh-oh is right. Look at this mess."

"They break pretty easy."

I sighed and hugged him. My heart thumped in my chest. The shelves weren't broken, only collapsible.

"If you had fallen among that—?"

"I'm sorry, Mommy."

I surveyed the pile of rocks and poliglas. "This will have to be cleaned up before we leave orbit. I don't have the hour it'll take just now." I squeezed him again before setting him down. I returned the chair back to its normal placement and snapped it into the floor locks, its secure position, then turned to my son. "As I said, you can take one rock to school today." I searched through the pile on my floor, setting aside several limestones sporting new scratches. My prized tholeiite from my very first planetfall—scuffed! I pulled out a fist-sized metallic rock. "Fortunately for you, most rocks are durable. Here, you can take this one, and only this one rock."

He wrinkled his nose at the dark-brown, irregular lump. "It's ugly!"

I forced it into his small hands. "True, but I've been to lots of solar systems and this is one of the oldest rocks ever found, anywhere. A meteoroid from Luyten 97-12. It's 5.8 billion years old."

"Wow!" Angshu examined the rock in awe.

"From an asteroid belt."

"Great-o!" He turned it over and over in his hands. "It's heavy! Did they find any dinosaurs there? Can we go there next instead of Beta Hidee?"

"Beta Hydri. No, we found only very simple life-forms, like we find everywhere. I keep telling you," I widened my eyes and pitched my voice lower, "we're the only spacemen."

The boy's smile vanished quickly. "But Airy told everyone at school you found spacemen. Where'd you find them? I want to see them, too."

I stiffened, the words stung. "Your friend, Airy, is wrong. When I served on the *JFK*—"

"Before I was born, right?"

"Yes. My associate and I thought we had found some fossils of a smart animal. Maybe smarter than a chimp. But the Theologians proved me wrong." I stooped to look him directly in the eye. "There is only one God and one intelligent species, just like they teach you in biology class. It's very important you remember that. Be sure to tell Airy I said so." This conversation would require more attention, between planets. Now I had to get planetside, and soon. I toggled the flight hangar and asked for a landing pod.

"Sorry, ma'am," Flight Chief Nolan answered. "The physical science department already has all my one-passenger pods out. Most everyone else is finished by now. Are all your people loners today?"

"No, it's just a big watery planet with widely spaced outcrops of dry land."

"You've got to settle for a four-pod. I've one left." I

waited, hoping for another answer; Nolan's chuckling filled the silence. "Dr. Sehkar, they're not *that* much bigger, but if you want, I'll round up a pilot for you."

"No, thanks, Chief. You do realize what happens whenever I have extra room?"

A hearty laugh answered me. "Yes, ma'am. Just try to contain yourself this time and leave some rocks for the next survey team." He paused briefly. "Hmm. You'd better hurry, Doctor. XO just made a request for a four-pod for some last minute underwater bug hunting. The next smallest is a ten-pod—"

I interrupted him. "I'm on my way. I want that four-pod. Don't you dare give it to Exobiology!" I was up, grabbing my field pack and rushing out of my office, with Angshu in tow, before the echo of the hangar chief's voice faded.

We were immediately assaulted by the noise of the crowded corridors. The buzz of tense conversation— even some arguments—and hurried footfalls bounced off the brightly painted walls of the *T.C. Chamberlin*. The sounds hugged me like a scratchy wool sweater. The only time more people moved about was the day before the ship set orbit. Then there was an air of anticipation and excitement. Now people simply rushed from labs and offices, comparing survey results and hastily finishing their preliminary planetary reports. I dodged a distracted crewman and in the process bumped into old man Greg Greely from Astrophysics.

"Sorry," I mumbled.

"It's always a pleasure seeing you and your handsome son. Hi, Angshu."

"Hi, Dr. Greg. See my rock!"

"And a nice meteoroid it is."

"Can I look through your telescope again, Dr. Greg?"

"Of course, anytime. Praise be, Angshu, you've grown since I last saw you. Can it only have been a week?" He patted the boy's head, then looked at me. "Dr. Sehkar, perhaps we three can have dinner again soon?"

"After we leave orbit," I answered. "I'll make dinner and then you men can go look through your telescope. Let's plan later. Now I'm going planetside one more time."

"Oh? That'll get Ops excited," he stated dryly. "Why so late?"

"Later," I dismissed his many unspoken questions. His hand on my arm stopped me.

"Will this upset the Theology Council?" His words were soft and meant only for my ears.

I hesitated, remembering Matt's voice. "I don't think so. Just an outcrop my tech can't explain away."

"Good."

I grabbed my son's hand again as Greely moved away. Angshu and I hurried through the crowded hall. It took barely a minute to get him settled in school; half-destroying my office still had him intimidated—a small blessing—then I made for the hangar access tube.

"Dr. Sehkar!"

I ignored the first attempted distraction—maybe he'd go away—but the insistent voice edged closer.

"Dr. Sehkar!"

I continued walking, partially turned, and waved. Commander Nichols, Ops Chief, increased his stride to catch up. It took too few steps.

"What's on your mind, Commander?" I asked when his steps finally matched mine. He was so tall that I never got used to his size. He seemed twice my own height of 158 centimeters. Maybe if I saw him more often, I'd get used to his towering form. I'm glad I didn't have to. His water-blue eyes, long nose, and angular chin were all perfect, but when summed together they gave his face too strong and brutal a look for a man of the cloth, and that left him with an anger which never diminished. You could feel it like a cold wind.

"My last status report shows you still have five people down below."

I stopped at this corridor's connecting access hatch and punched in the code. The latch circuit clicked open. "Actually, I think you'll find I have seven people planetside, and I'm on my way down to supervise the last sampling." I pulled on the large door so perfectly balanced even a child could open it.

Commander Nichols followed me through the hatch into the air lock and secured the door latch behind us. We both started removing the outer soles of our boots, exposing the magnetic, inner soles. The latch cycled closed with a comforting click. We went through the next hatch.

"I'd like to see things wrapped up soon. Do you anticipate a delay, Dr. Sehkar?" He paused ever so slightly before using my title.

I opened the next seal, and kept my voice neutral. "You sound as if I typically cause delays. On the contrary, since I've been on the *Chamberlin*, I've always finished my reports on time, if not early."

"You mistake my concern for criticism. Your work is theologically sound."

"Thank you."

"If only your husband had been so meticulous."

"I don't have a husband," I replied evenly, despite the chill in my chest.

"Excuse me, your son's father. Martin Tilton."

"Dr. Tilton is not a part of my life anymore," I whispered tartly, even though no one would have heard us if I had screamed the words.

"He isn't? Are you sure?" Nichols' voice had just a hint of disbelief in it.

"According to the Council's ruling, Dr. Tilton does not exist and never has. You'll find no evidence of him in any school yearbook or scientific journal. I was never married. He is not part of Angshu's life either. And I'd thank you not to bring any hint of disgrace into my life or my son's, or I'll report you to the Theological Family Council."

"Of course." He was all smiles and sweetness, as if he could be trusted.

"I mean it. *Ill words will only cause harm.*"

Nichols inclined his head slightly. "You know your code."

"Just as well as you do, I suspect. What is the purpose of this conversation? You waste your time if it's meant purely for insult. Or are you trying to threaten me?"

"Threaten you?"

"Yes, by bringing up a heretic's name. Linking him with me. I know there is no record of Dr. Tilton in *Chamberlin*'s computer. I could demand to know how you came about your information."

"It was not my intent to threaten you."

"I hope not." I didn't believe him, and he knew it, too.

"The Captain wants us back on schedule soon. We've several days to make up."

We entered the spiral access tube that led to the heart of the *Chamberlin*. Perhaps he wanted an argument; I didn't. I let the tension flow from me as I set a pace comfortable for my shorter legs. We walked the spiral pathway that was at a sharp angle to the busy corridor we had just left. Our pace would also minimize the effects of the walk that began at three-quarter G and proceeded to zero-G at the center of our rotating, cylindrical ship. Even so, my stomach protested. I always felt as if I climbed an endless ramp. I concentrated on the clicking our boots made on the metal floor. The sound distracted from the sensation of losing Gs and helped me avoid thinking of my stomach's strengthening protests. Nichols' presence always left me feeling combatant.

"Hmm, several days?" I repeated as if I didn't believe his statement. "There is one small problem in exploring new worlds. Timetables don't allow for unpredictability. That's why the Science Council, of which I am a member, runs this vessel and not the flight crew."

"Just so you know—"

I stopped, more to ease my stomach's protest than anything else. The pervasive hum of the ship's circulation motors seeped through the soles of my feet. I loved that soothing rhythm. It was as if the ship was alive. "This is my fifth planetfall with the *Chamberlin*. I'm not that green, Commander."

He shook his head. "I know that. If you can use this corridor at this pace and not get sick to your stomach, you're better than half my crew." We continued walking.

I couldn't stop the smile. He could be so charming when he wanted. Did he notice the irony? No, not him. He just thought he was all charm. "It's all in the diet," I said. "My people have iron stomachs."

Nichols returned a slight smile, hidden mostly by his blond mustache. "I was going to guess it was because you're so short. They say short people have less trouble with Sim-gravity." He stopped by an adjoining hatch at one-quarter-G level—the service crew section and Operations. "Also, I suppose your experience on the Explorer-class ships helps."

"Again you tread on ice. My past is past, so the Family Council decreed." I forced the bitterness out of my voice. Why was it there? I was over the past, wasn't I?

Nichols paused a moment, obviously phrasing his words carefully. "For your son's sake, I hope so. It would be unfortunate if he lost both parents to the justice system. What I intended to say is, there are no ghosts and therefore no need to chase them."

No, the bitterness was still there, simmering just below the surface. He knew it, and knew how to trigger it, too. Damn.

"Ghost chasing? I've heard my work on the *Kennedy* described many ways, but your phrasing is—inventive. I never majored in Theology as you did, Commander, but my theology teachers failed to discuss that life-form. The next time you give a sermon on that topic, let me know. I'll be sure to attend the service." His back stiffened and his smile vanished, but he said nothing. Good. I took two more steps away. "I'm a scientist. I try to keep an open mind on my new research. My old research, too, for that matter."

"If that's true, you'd be the first researcher I've met who can. Scientists easily deceive themselves into thinking otherwise. I often wondered how much of your husband's work was really yours. You were the better student. If you hadn't been pregnant—"

"Commander, you are out of line!"

He shrugged. There were no words of apology in his vocabulary—never had been, never would be. "The Captain asks you to please hurry your work. We're behind schedule and get worse with each new solar system. If we don't make up time before returning to port, we may have to skip the last scheduled system until after we pick up the next group of interns."

"Which means some of our current interns will be short of credits for graduation. Understood, Commander."

"God bless your path, Doctor."

"God bless," I returned evenly as I continued on my way.

Matt scribbled on his notepad and held it up for me to read. *We shouldn't have found this rock!* He then wiped the pad clean.

"I know," I said over the open comm link. "I know." Sweat trickled down the center of my back as I stood in my EVA suit, staring at the base of the cliff. The terminus of an old lava flow towered above us. Matt and I stood on an even older flow. Its broken and spiny surface, weathered to a dull red in many areas, now served both as a pod landing area and a beach leading to the ocean thirty meters behind us. Steam drifted in from the water and across the barren landscape; it was caused by a new lava flow spewing molten rock into the ocean a few hundred meters up the beach. From the base of the cliff protruded an old lava tube, in which I could have easily stood. A black river of popcorn-shaped lava flowed out the tube, forever frozen in place despite the warm, 35-degree Celsius day. Near the tube was a light green-gray outcrop, partially enclosed in lava. Matt's crew of three intern students continued using chisel and rock hammer to remove more of the black lava still encasing the hexagonally shaped boulder.

A cold shiver walked my spine. There was no way I could explain this outcrop. We could just walk away from this now, and never look back. Sometimes I wondered if never knowing wasn't best. Ignorance being bliss and all. But could I just walk away? Or maybe I was getting carried away! There could be a simple answer. This young world had yet to even develop land plants and animals; it was too young to have evolved higher intelligence! Therefore it had to be a simple answer, somewhere. I shrugged, more for my own benefit than anyone else's, and exchanged glances with Matt again. His fair brow was still furrowed. Walking away into darkness wasn't my style.

"I love volcanic rocks. Relax, Matt. It isn't going to bite you or the students." He finally attempted a smile as I contacted the hangar facility. "Nolan, does XO still want a four-pod?"

"Yes, we do," interrupted an unfamiliar voice over the comm's open link.

"You on your way back already?" Nolan asked.

"No. If they can bring me that ten-pod, I'll trade them."

"Yeah, and what you gonna do with my pod after that?" The amusement was clear behind the mock sternness in Nolan's voice.

I cringed. I wouldn't hear the end of this one for a long time, maybe never. Nolan would exaggerate the whole story. *You should see the size of Somita's rock this time! It's bigger than she is!* Thank God the next holy day was one of fasting and not feasting.

"I found this rock I want to bring back."

"Just one?"

Matt's timid smile turned into a full grin. He'd give Nolan even more color to add to the tale. Then again, that might actually help by softening the oddity of this rock. People loved a good yarn.

"Yep, one's enough right now," I said, playing along.

"Should I warn ship's storage about this?" Nolan asked seriously, but no less amused.

"Naw, just get them to put a small lift in that ten's cargo bay."

"While I'm at it, should I warn the bridge crew we need to increase our orbit?"

"Nolan, it's not *that* big a rock!"

"Yes, it is!" Matt added.

Nolan chuckled again. "Just checking. XO wants to see your latest toy. They should be by in forty minutes. Hmm, Dr. Sehkar, could you run a confirming check on your people's oxy mix and supply while I've got you on-line?"

I waited as Matt checked the readouts of the landing crew, wishing I could scratch the sweat trickling down my back. Matt showed me the stats. "Nolan, we're all fine here, between 40 and 80 percent full. I've more in mine and we all have spare canisters."

"Great, that checks with my readouts. Nolan out."

By the time the ten-pod arrived, we had the boulder completely free from its lava encasement. I watched the newly arrived Bio team exit the ten-pod; following the two XO team members in their orange EVA suits were two other people. One person I recognized as my chief assistant, Tom Fremen. No one else would dare wear theology class patches—left over from his Boy

Scout days—on his EVA suit. The other person wore a yellow crew suit.

I glanced at Matt and silently mouthed. "Who?"

The technician mouthed back, "Nichols," and quickly went to wait beside the boulder.

I spoke first. "Tom, you've finished that geophysical database already?"

"Not yet. Nichols thought you needed my help."

"I would have requested it, if I had. You can work a longer shift tonight, and perhaps tomorrow, to compensate for joyriding."

"Isn't it a little big?" Nichols interrupted as he indicated the boulder. The rock was surrounded by people; there was no mistaking it now.

"Depends." I started toward the others.

"Why waste your time? It's just a hunk of rock."

"No. It's hexagonal, fine-grained, light in color and it doesn't belong on this beach, and certainly not in the middle of a lava flow."

"Really?" he asked.

Blast!

As soon as I finished, I wanted to take back my words. I didn't have to justify anything to him!

"So, one of those marine critters XO's been telling me about put it here."

A biotech cut in. "There's at least one species that collects oddities, much like Earth's crows. Perhaps a proto-nest complex. Water levels fluctuate. This was a subaqueous flow, wasn't it?"

"It's not that old a flow—so it could be a critter," I easily agreed. I didn't have a clue. The biotech's rea-

son was as valid a guess as any other. "Admittedly biological factors wouldn't be my first assumption. My
theology classes concentrated on fossil identification."

"Cut off a small piece and let's be on our way."
Nichols's suggestion was almost an order. He really
was trying to get under my skin! I kept my tone easy
and natural.

"Too hard to break up. This is not a safe environment in which to use torches. Just a few meters offshore is a cyanobacteria colony. A big one. If that
colony decides to burp again, in unison, and a rare
pocket of O-two comes breezing by, we'd get a
firestorm that I'd rather not be near, thank you. Unless
you're volunteering for the job." I didn't wait for an
answer. "And don't suggest using a handheld diamond
corer. No time. The most efficient approach is to drag
the entire rock to my lab where I can sample it to death
and be done with it."

"All that weight? It must be ten tons!"

"Closer to twenty. The pod's lift will tell us exactly.
But this rock will end up as so much space junk when
we're done with it."

"Right! Your rock collection is the largest teaching
collection in the whole fleet. Since when do you dump
samples?" Nichols asked dryly.

"All the time. I only keep pretty rocks."

"You don't have to sample every planet."

"This isn't your decision. You've been trying to
needle me all day. Why?" I kept my voice even, almost
mild, but I had his attention.

"Just your imagination."

"I don't think so. Any more hassles and I'll report you to the Science Council. Understood?"

He only nodded in response.

"Good. Since you're a better pilot than the rest of us, you can fly us back to the *Chamberlin* when *I'm* ready to leave."

"At your service, Doctor. Nolan thought you'd need help flying a loaded ten-pod."

"I'll have to thank him for his concern," I answered. Oh, he'd get a thank you, all right. "Now, unless your extensive theological background can correctly ID the biological process that deposited this sample, do something useful, like getting out that lift." I glanced around and then headed toward Matt.

The pale, gray-green stone block stood three-and-a-half meters tall and just over one meter wide. Matt and I had a devil of a time getting it up to the lab. But the cargo holds were too busy this time of any planetfall to examine the rock there. Something about this sample left me uneasy. I set up a ladder near one of its six sides. Its muted color blended in with the steel-gray walls of the lab. Counters, filled with securely anchored optical microscopes, compu-tabs, electron microscopes, and probes ringed the room. Tables, once secured to the floor where the block of stone waited, were now pushed off to the side.

The intercom chimed. "Open link. Yes?" I asked.

"Doctor," Matt began. "I've gotten the first two scan runs compiled and in the database. Everything

looks good. No inconsistencies. Do you want me to
stop and help you, or continue?"

I couldn't help but smile. "I know your love for
compiling data, but I want it all in the database before
we leave here tomorrow. No more screwups. I don't
want to find out two weeks from now we need just one
more pass over the Southern Ocean." I glanced at Tom,
but he was wisely looking elsewhere since it was his
screwup that lost the first set of compiled records. If he
had lost the raw data, I'd have spaced him myself.

"No problem," Matt answered.

"Close link." I patted the rock and addressed Tom.
"Let's start. I've always been amazed by what hot volcanic waters can do to normal minerals. And this watery world has its share of active volcanoes."

Cold laser-torch in hand, I climbed the ladder, adjusted my coveralls so I could sit comfortably on the
ladder's top, then dialed the desired energy setting. A
small blue circle touched the rock's surface, then filled
the deepening crack as the energy beam cut the material. I carved sheets of fine-grained rock from the
upper surface and laid them like slices of stale cake on
a tray. The laser worked well with minimal heating.
Still, it left the air smelling as dry and dusty as a desert
at noon. Finally the automatic sensors detected the
changes and kicked in additional cooling and filtering
for the lab. One vent, directly over my head, blew cool
air down my neck. Delightful! A relief after so much
time in an EVA suit. I wanted a bath. A long soaking
bath! I'd have to wait weeks for that simple pleasure.

"I heard you and Nichols talking," Tom said.

"You like Nichols, don't you?"

"Sure, don't you?"

"Oh, he's *very* handsome."

"You two were talking about the fauna. I thought there were only small animals here. Nothing big enough to move this."

"You didn't watch the video-synopsis XO gave last week?"

Tom frowned. "I started to."

"The reports are produced to enhance your education. Besides, XO always does a class job of it."

"But they never find anything interesting. Sometimes you think they plan it that way."

They're not smart enough! or *That's just PR!* would have been typical responses from me, if this were Matt and we were alone. Tom wouldn't understand the joke. "The most unusual critter," I switched into my best lecture voice that was sure to put him to sleep, "they found was a rather simple, but strange arthropod."

"Arthropod?"

"Similar to your favorite trilobite, but much more primitive than that sample from the Cambrian Burgess shale I gave you. This planet is still in the Precambrian phase. But these arthropods grow really big. They've found some that are five meters long. Picture that! A five-meter-long kleptomaniac moving this rock."

I finished cutting off another slab and nodded to the tray. "That's a start. Could you have Carrie work on these right away? Beginning with the second slab. I want to see the thin section as soon as it's done. Then she can scan it with the Jacob's scope and the Baush."

"Both?" Tom asked.

"We're assigned to evaluate the equipment. I can't recommend one piece of equipment over another if there isn't a fair test."

Tom left. Alone with my own thoughts, my mind wandered to my conversation with Nichols. I had lied to him; I still considered Martin my husband. If the Theological Council found out—I tried to push Martin from my mind. I had my job, and right now that needed my attention.

I kept working while waiting for my technician's reappearance. Tom wasn't returning. I could feel the tension creeping up my arms and residing in my neck as I sliced sections off the rock. Where was that man? And more importantly, what was he doing? He finally came back looking as if he had only been gone the five minutes the job should have taken instead of thirty. He could have done most of the thin sections himself.

"You checked on your report, I assume?" I asked.

"No, I got a personal call." He avoided looking me in the eye—a bad sign.

"We're on a tight schedule. I'd appreciate your keeping your mind on your duties."

For a moment Tom looked like he was going to justify his actions, make up some excuse; instead he answered, "Yes, ma'am."

Perhaps he was reporting my old-fashioned ways—my insistence that "real" thin sections be made, as if I didn't trust the scanners. I didn't. Scanners had a place in the lab. They could accurately give mineral content—quartz, more k-spar than plag, some muscovite—the answer had to be a granite, or was it a rhyolite? The day a scanner could consistently distinguish between rhyolite and granite, would be the day I— It'd never happen on my watch.

Only a few minutes more passed before a soft buzzer interrupted us. It was Carrie's signal telling us the samples were ready. By the time Tom returned, I had cut ten centimeters into the rock. I stopped, climbed down the ladder, and waited as Tom inserted a thin section into the microscope and displayed the sample's image on the half-meter-square view screen.

What had been grains too fine to see with the naked eye were now pale green to clear fibrous crystals cutting through and surrounding colorless orthorhombic crystals. I set the torch down and turned the scope's stage, rotating the picture on the screen. I put in the polarizing lens and turned the stage again, then removed the lens. I moved the thin section around, examining the entire sample.

"I don't know that one, Doctor," Tom said as he pointed to the screen.

"It's olivine altering to chrysotile asbestos. Serpentine. And I'd have to bet that there wasn't a metamorphic rock within a thousand klicks of that site."

Tom shrugged. "Maybe a storm surge washed that hunk up on the beach or a shoal during or just before the last eruption."

"Have to wait until we've time to examine the geophysical logs from the sea floor to find a source rock. The seismic profiles should scream out the change from oceanic basalt to a serpentine." Now if the data hadn't been lost, I wanted to say, but didn't. I moved the slide around again, bothered by what I saw. "This is why visual inspection is useful, Tom. A probe would indicate serpentine and leave it at that." Given enough time, I might turn even Tom into a decent technician. Might. "This doesn't show the usual macroscopic fibers of natural chrysotile. The fabric is uniformly amorphous, an igneous texture, yet the mineralogy says metamorphic."

"Maybe we should cut deeper, beyond the worst heating effects from the molten lava?"

"My thoughts exactly. Let's cut off this corner we've been working on."

With laser in hand, I adjusted the beam. At the top of the rock I started a cut about thirty centimeters from the outer edge and moved down about thirty centimeters and over to the other edge. The laser encountered varying densities of rock, slowing the process as I adjusted the beam several times. As we lifted the severed corner away, something fell to the floor with a solid thump. I stared openmouthed at several chunks of red granite; other pieces lay inside a cavity in the original rock.

"Mother of Heaven!" Tom said.

I squelched my excitement, and practically dropped the corner piece into Tom's grasp, then retrieved the closest piece of granite from within what I now saw was an asbestos shell. I turned the granite over in my hands, then felt the inner surface of the asbestos rock. "Now how in Heaven's name can this be?" I tried to sound confused, and found it wasn't too hard as a gnawing began in my stomach. Tom would report my every word.

Scowling, I got down from the ladder, walked around the rock again and picked at a small chunk of lava that stubbornly clung to the outer surface of the lighter-colored rock. Dry salt from the ocean still coated the rock, adding a rich smell to the ship's filtered air.

"Granite pieces inside a hollow piece of asbestos!" I shook my head in a scholarly fashion. "Geologically impossible."

Tom picked up another piece of granite from the floor. "Asbestos can be made into different objects, right?"

"Sure," I agreed. "It was used extensively in the past by weaving the fibers, much as you'd weave cotton. It was also made into a type of felt."

"Paper wasps use wood to build their nests. Could these proto-trilobites use asbestos in their nesting?"

I looked at the slide still in the scope. "Inventive, Tom." And meant it. "Theologically sound." Another good point in his favor. "I can't think of a better explanation. It'll make Nichols happy." Tom didn't notice my sarcasm. "There's a problem in that there is no life on this planet anywhere near as advanced as wasps. Also why put granite inside?"

Tom shrugged. "Their own eggs were destroyed or they just liked pretty rocks? I mean, look at this. Fresh, unweathered red, feldspar crystals and silver mica, some pyrite." He moved the sample in the lab's bright light. "Look how it sparkles. Anyone would like this, even Commander Nichols."

I restrained my comments, tossed my rock sample into the air and caught it again. "An age curve would tell us how long ago the lava encased it. The heat should have penetrated even this thickness of asbestos and changed the lead values from their base." I indicated the rock he was holding. "Have Carrie get me a ratio curve."

"Yes, ma'am."

I fished around in my coverall pocket for a hand lens and looked at the granite sample more closely. "Tell her to try zircon, then a sphene separation for dating; both minerals are present in high enough quantities. That'll give us a cross-check. I want to know how long it's been since that lava flow's heat changed the time curves. Then we'll compare that with the actual potassium-argon date from the lava flow."

The graph glowed on the computer screen. The lead 206-uranium 238 age ratio was plotted against the lead 207-uranium 235 age ratio. In a perfectly closed system the two age ratios would be equal and the rock's correct age would lie on the *concordia*—the curved line that gently arced across the screen. But nothing was a closed system and, as I expected, the lava encasing the asbestos and its enclosed granite had caused a thermal resetting of the granite's lead-uranium ratio. Its age now plotted below the *concordia* curve, on the straight line: the *discordia*. I stared hard at the graph.

The lava had encased this asbestos rock for some 8,000 years. I engaged the intercom.

"Astronomy Department, Greely here."

I got the old man himself. He must be bored. "Dr. Greely, this is Dr. Sehkar. I've some rocks that I'm trying to date. Do you have the primeval lead ratio from this system's asteroids yet?"

"This about your new monolith?"

"What?"

"Between Nichols and Tom, the whole ship has heard about your new rock."

"Thanks for the warning," I replied dryly. "You'd think they'd have better things to do than talk about my work habits. As if no one has ever collected a rock before!"

The older man laughed briefly. "You tend to bring bigger samples home and more of them than most researchers. People notice and, sometimes, are even infected with your passion for rocks."

"Yeah, right."

"It'll take only a minute to get the lead ratios for you."

I waited in silence, staring at the graph, trying to get it to answer my rising number of questions.

Greely's voice broke my concentration. "I've attached a file of values for you to your home directory. As expected, this planetary cloud had a compositional makeup very similar to Earth's. We've found an absolute age of two-point-four times ten-to-the-ninth years with the standard error deviation."

A chill crawled down my spine. "Are you sure?"

"Yes. In fact, you could use Earth standard ratios for lead isotopes, and I suspect for uranium and strontium too, and still be accurate within an acceptable error band. As accurate as you can get with this data set, anyway. Why? You sound troubled."

I sighed. Where did I begin? "I am. We ran some tests on a granite found inside my monolith. I plugged the ratios with Earth's values, expecting that that would suffice, but I got eight times ten-to-the-ninth years."

"Three times too old! That's some error. You use zircon?"

"Zircon and sphene. Both methods produced the same age. And the potassium-argon date for an encasing lava flow matches the discordia curve of the granite. What does the solar spectrum say about this system's sun?"

"Let me recheck my values. I'll get back to you."

I waited and reran the numbers through the model. It wasn't long before the intercom sounded.

Greely sounded younger with his enthusiasm. "Dr. Sehkar, I reevaluated this star's spectrum. For a G6, this sun's at the early stages of main sequence. If it were eight billion years old, the spectrum would show a buildup of heavy elements. I don't see that. This sun's just beginning to live. It's nowhere near the helium burning sequence."

"Which means I've got a significant error somewhere. These samples look fresh enough, as if they were taken from the middle of a pegmatite, not something found at the surface, or in a lava field. It's hard to believe these rocks are even half their age."

"I can't think of many answers, and none the theologians would like."

"Ouch, how you talk, and over an open channel! There must be an error, somewhere." Knowing I wasn't convincing either Greely or myself.

"God will provide the answer." That was better language. "I'd say someone was pulling your leg and gave you a bogus sample, except the oldest system any of our ships have been to is Kapteyn's star and its dinosaur planet. That's only six-point-two billion years old."

"I wouldn't call Kapteyn's fauna dinosaurs," I said patiently.

"You geologists are too fussy, as bad as theologians. Warm-blooded lizards are dinosaurs! I don't care about their hip joints."

"I bow to popular consensus, Doctor. I'll just have to check my equipment. If you find any errors . . ."

"I'll call. Greely out."

I returned to the monolith to empty the interior samples into a storage bin. My hand shook slightly. I was glad to be alone. All the rock samples were near fist-size, each had rough sides, and sported lighter-colored marks. Other rocks bore recent scars from my cold-laser knife. The bulk of the samples were red granites with some grays. There were a few basalts and garnet schists. The monolith's chamber was small, about one-third of the overall size, with the bottom being a smooth serpentine layer. I ran a handheld penetrating

radar down the monolith's side. It showed varying
densities in the rock, but in a regular pattern. I'd bet
there were a total of three distinct chambers! The other
two would be just like this one at the top. I set up a
suction-mounted laser drill in the middle-third of the
monolith, and attached an airtight shield over it with
monitoring devices.

It took the drill only a few minutes to punch a small
hole into the asbestos side. The inner gases were composed of oxygen, with small amounts of argon, neon,
nitrogen—breathable air, but dead air, no microbes—
nothing like the atmosphere existing on Delta Pavonis
Two now, or anytime in the past. I repeated the process
on what I suspected would be the lowest of three seg-
ments. Same air chemistry. Both gas samples would be
saved for climatology. Maybe Greely knew someone
from that department who could do a detailed analysis
without talking too much.

With the laser, I enlarged the middle hole and found
numerous fossiliferous carbonates and marbles, and
kimberlites.

"Damn, the find of a—damn," I muttered. I had to
have a plan before Nichols showed up. Was I just
that lucky, or were finds of this nature so common-
place that other scientists ignored them out of self-
preservation? Had to be, but I had never even heard
a single rumor!

Angshu!

Nichols would start with rumors about signs of intelligent life and then try to trap me in heresy charges.
No, I was smarter than that, wasn't I?

I adjusted the laser beam and moved down to the lowest portion of the rock and sliced off the lava still clinging to the main rock. I cut a round hole some twenty centimeters in diameter through the serpentine sides; its thickness matched above. A spot glance at the interior's contents indicated several varieties of sandstones, conglomerates, and quartzites.

I returned to the second chamber to remove the contents, and found I was examining a fossiliferous carbonate. No, I would examine everything further between planetfalls, when I had time; right now, the sooner they disappeared into cabinets, the better. Keep Tom busy elsewhere. Still, as I carefully placed each sample into a storage bin, I identified them, trying to determine where on this watery planet I could find the outcrop. I stopped unloading when I found a piece of black slate. I turned it over and found a perfectly preserved trilobite the size of my thumb. If I were in graduate school, I'd call it a Cambrian *Ogygopsis*. How would an XO theologian explain such a similar species on so young a planet—only 2.4 billion years old! It had taken Earth nearly 4 billion years to produce such a species.

They'd find a way.

I gently wrapped it in protective padding. Every subtle detail of that fossil was important; I dare not chance another rock damaging it now.

Next I found a pure white, finely crystalline marble. Light danced off the crystal faces as I turned the piece. I caught my breath. The marble contained a fossil of a jellyfish-like creature twelve centimeters long and five centimeters wide. Under the bulbous upper portion extended three tentacles that terminated into claws. The soft tissue was wonderfully preserved!

Tingling ran from my toes to my scalp. I rushed into my office and knelt by my private rock collection—still decorating the floor. I sorted rocks until I found a specific light gray marble; the fossil consisted of two tentacled claws, below which was, perhaps, a rounded shell. I held the pieces side-by-side. My private specimen's fossil was incomplete, but both fossilized creatures were the same species in the same type of rock, probably from the same rock formation. I had collected my sample from a massive asteroid belt circling Ophiuchi 36—many light-years away from this small planet we now orbited.

The vision of Ophiuchi's tri-suns swam in my thoughts, as I had last seen them, each an orange-yellow globe in the black velvet of space, ringed—even as Saturn was, but on an infinitely larger scale—by two halos of rubble.

The only planets that had orbited the K-type, trinary star system had broken up some 5,000 years ago. Now each ring was slowly coalescing into another, smaller planet. The inner debris uniformly showed that the original planet had once been thriving with life. That planetary system had begun the changes in my life. But it hadn't been till the next planetfall that my familiar life would be forever lost because of a planet which orbited a sun too small to even show up on my great-grandmother's star charts. Ophiuchi BD-12 had sent my husband to jail and me into virtual exile from the heart of science and the Explorer Program into the backwater of the Survey Program. The *JFK* had been the Science Council's shining star, the *Chamberlin*'s was old and past prime.

How could things have been handled differently? How should we have handled it better? Could I have changed things? Time slipped away as I daydreamed.

A waste! The past could never be recaptured. My gaze strayed back to the jumble of rocks still on my floor.

"Well, this is one problem I can fix." I reached over and buzzed Angshu's school.

"Child care," Betty Saari said.

This woman always sounded chipper and on top of any situation—no mountain too high, no storm too dangerous. "Betty, this is Somita Sehkar. How's Angshu behaving himself?"

"Hello, Doctor. He's been an angel, as always." There was mirth in Betty's voice that caused me to chuckle, wondering what my son had been up to this time.

"Earlier he was a bit more mischievous and as a result my office needs straightening before we leave orbit. Is there a sitter available to bring him here and supervise him while I finish my report?"

"I've got a twelve-year-old boy I can spare. Will he do?"

"Perfectly."

"They're eating at the moment. I'll send them over after they've finished."

"Great! Thank you."

"My pleasure!"

I cut the comm link and again knelt by the rock pile. With a brief snap, the first disarrayed shelf was back in its operational mode. One shelf followed after another. I was about to snap the last collapsed shelf into place when I froze. Ophiuchi 36's tri-suns swam before my mind's eyes.

My gaze moved ever so slightly to rest on the rocks at my knees. A limestone on top of the pile still had the lighter colored percussion marks on one edge where my hammer had struck the rock to break it into a smaller sample.

I saw again the samples from within the monolith. Many of the granite pieces contained such marks—crushed crystals, almost white against the darker colored minerals. Of course I hadn't paid attention before now! One never sees the common, everyday things. But the rocks from within the monolith weren't supposed to be hand samples. Not for me anyway; not for the Theological Science Council on Intelligent Life.

The answer was so simple and splendidly clear. Two rock hounds, eight thousand years apart!

How were we different? What had the other—

The intercom's soft chime interrupted me.

"Sehkar here."

"This is Ops, Dr. Sehkar. You haven't answered our request for clearance to leave orbit in two hours. Is your department all clear?"

I toggled the computer and found several calls logged in and waiting attention. I looked at my hand samples again. Nichols would jump all over my decision.

"Doctor?" the crewman asked.

"No, we're not," I answered in as firm a voice as I could muster. "We have problems with our equipment. I don't want to leave orbit until I'm sure of our data's validity."

There was a slight pause. "Understood. Astronomy has requested a ten-hour delay. Will that meet your needs?"

That man was a saint. Greely knew I'd need more time before I'd commit. And two requests for delay couldn't be refused. Ten hours? I had a feeling I'd want to go planetside again. "Make it fifteen hours," I said.

"Does this concern the rock your assistant has been spouting off about?"

"I can't imagine what Tom's been saying, but I'd ignore him. He can't tell the difference between rhyolite and granite."

There was a slight pause before the officer responded. "Navigation says we might as well wait a full day."

"I hate to lose that day, but it's necessary to compile this data."

"How do you want these placed again?" Matt asked. He floated before the control panel of the cargo bay's lift and worked the sensors that maneuvered the storage containers.

I pointed to each box in succession. "First, second, and third." Matt was smart, but when it came to moving equipment in zero g, nobody could beat Tom. The man was truly skilled in operating a null-g forklift. But I couldn't risk Tom being here.

"We've got company," Matt said softly, not looking up from his work.

Moments later Dr. Greely pulled himself over to us. He carried a small box and next to it he carried a small electronic device mostly concealed by his large hand. He flipped a switch, activating it, and then concealed the device in his overall pocket. I merely exchanged glances with Matt. I wanted to ask where the hell he had gotten a scrambler, but it was best not to know. Only a few public places were openly monitored and this was one of them. How long would it take anyone who might be listening to realize we hadn't stopped talking, that something was wrong with their equipment, and they came looking?

"I've found those meteoroids from the Eta Cassiopeia system," Greely said. "I had accidentally mislabeled the sample drawer, plus I have a sample from Sol's system."

"Excellent! Your two plus mine means we have samples from fifteen systems." I took the box.

"I stopped by XO," Greely said. "They have an answer."

"And?" I suppressed my excitement.

"That fossil is definitely an *Ogygopsis* trilobite. They're ninety-nine percent certain."

I kept my voice low. "I knew that rock came from Earth! I bet I could even take you to the outcrop. It's one of Earth's most distinctive formations."

"I wonder what they thought of our home?" Greely mused.

Matt looked at me, clearly not liking the bent of this discussion, scrambler or no.

I shrugged. "Not much, if they left without leaving any traces behind."

"What if this monolith was not left deliberately? Eight thousand years is a very long time. They may not be able to return."

"I honestly don't think it was planned," I began. "Not as we've planned our leavings. Some survey team, like ours, needed to conserve weight. Perhaps they landed their whole ship and then unexpectedly needed to dump weight to achieve escape velocity. Maybe their ship is at the bottom of the ocean. Or is just another asteroid in this system. Or they made it home and forgot this little world."

"But if anyone else comes back this way," Matt added, "they'll know they're not alone."

"That's my hope. Nichols thinks— No, what he thinks doesn't matter. I'm conserving weight and making an exchange—one collection for another."

"And what if they like their isolation?" Greely asked.

"Like humans," I said.

"Us?" Matt asked.

I nodded and went on. "We're terrified we might not be alone. That we might not be God's only children. This monolith was left by spacefaring people who have been to some of the same worlds as us. That likely means they're neighbors of ours, but since this is the first evidence we've found, it also means they've been very cautious."

"It's been 8,000 years," Greely said. "Not much from any of our survey outings would survive that long! Before today, we deliberately tried to leave each world untouched."

"What will the theologians say?" Matt asked. "How will you tell . . . ?"

"Nothing," I answered. "They'll say nothing because I'll say nothing. This find will never be made public. I've a child and a promise to protect."

Greely touched my arm, stopping me from moving away. "You're not writing a paper? This is proof! They have to consider evolution a viable theory. That intelligence isn't only a gift from our God. We've proof!"

"Proof doesn't change anything. The Theory of Evolution and the Theory of God's Work are not mutually exclusive. One or the other. They never have been. Besides proof is not important. It never has been. No, I'll not say one word. No one will!"

"But?" both men said in unison.

"The life-forms on Luyten 97-12 were advanced beings. In a few thousands years maybe they would have reached for the stars. An intelligent species wiped out by our purest, holiest citizens. God's chosen children are murderers, pure and simple. And what about the fossils on Ophiuchi BD-12? Stop staring at me as if I've lost my mind, Greely. I was only wrong in saying what they were. The purpose of the Explorer and Survey Programs isn't to find other life-forms. It isn't to prove the theologians wrong."

"What is it for?" Matt asked. I waited for him to answer himself. He soon nodded slowly. Even the young learn. "It's to prove how wonderfully advanced man is as a species, isn't it?"

I nodded. "We've never expected space to be so full of life, yet so lonely at the same time. And many people pray and pay to see that it stays that way. And it will."

Matt looked around the pod bay. "If the Council finds out what we're about to do, they'll pull our contracts, if we're lucky."

"They're not going to find out. Only the three of us know. I can't afford another blemish on my tarnished record. I was kicked out of the Explorer program. If I get kicked out of the Survey program, they won't even let me teach college, and high school will be out of the question. They won't let me near my own child, let alone anyone else's. Out here I'm isolated. They can't stop my work, not if it stays in my head."

"In the meantime we just twiddle our thumbs?" Matt asked.

"No, we work, and we keep our mouths shut. Years ago I had a theory," I told both men. "Because of our son, my husband took the blame and was first branded an outcast, then a criminal. Now he doesn't even exist." I pushed all the feelings back as far as I could. No matter how much experience I had, it still hurt. Suddenly I realized Greely's hand was on my arm. I had stopped talking and was staring into the past.

"He doesn't exist," I repeated. "No amount of supporting evidence will change that. Ever. Nothing will release him from prison and bring him back to me. But Angshu does matter."

"If we change our tactics?" Greely interrupted softly. "Low-key, cleverly worded news reports. Some people will come to the proper conclusion without you saying a word."

I smiled again. "You're a bigger fool, or should I say dreamer, than me. You want change? So do I, but until we meet a race with bigger guns to force us to play nice in the universe, nothing will change." I took a deep breath. "Planets are fragile. I think someone should explore the asteroid belt of Ophiuchi 36 much more carefully. Maybe we are alone, now."

"Don't hold your breath. Look how long it took us to learn that many dinosaurs were warm-blooded and that some made tools. And that was on our own planet!"

"But dinosaurs died out sixty-five million years ago. We're only talking about eight thousand years here."

"Governments do change," Greely said.

"Not enough. I'm out of this game. End of discussion!"

He paused. "Think about it. If we can unquestionably identify each solar system where those rocks in the monolith came from, we might be able to trace their journey back to their home world. One ship alone can't do that. I know others who would help sift and winnow for the truth. We wouldn't be alone in this."

I smiled, recognizing his quote. I couldn't bear to sift anymore; it cost too much. "I don't have the stainless background you have. My God, you taught theology for years. I wish I had known you sooner, and taken your lead. Maybe I wouldn't have gotten into so much trouble."

"You like trouble, Somita." His gaze went past me for a moment, and then his shoulders stiffened. "Argue with me!" he ordered softly.

I squashed the desire to turn around and instead complied. "You're a fool." My voice rose in volume, but not too much. "That's the silliest theory I've heard in years. I've got better things to do with my time than listen to this prattle."

Out of the corner of my vision I saw several service-crew members enter the bay.

"Prattle? I was serving in the Explorer program while you were still in diapers. Prattle! Just because you became the youngest member ever named to the Science Council doesn't mean you're as smart as you think. I've a few brilliant moments left!"

"I've got work to do. Don't bother me until you've gotten a grip on your mind, old man." With that, Greely pushed away and pulled himself over to the hangar door. Part of me was worried why Greely wanted it believed we were not on good terms anymore.

I waited next to the ten-pod as Matt worked the lift again. The magnetic soles of my boots kept me securely in place. Still, I held onto one of the many hand supports fastened to the ceiling, floor, and walls around the bay.

Matt had the three storage containers stacked and

secured together. The finished product looked much like the original monolith still in my lab in pieces and in hiding.

"These containers," Matt said, "are very heat resistant."

"Place them directly in the flowing lava."

"What if the lava isn't hot enough to affect the rocks inside? How would anyone date this event?"

"Good point. Take some of the molten lava from closer to the source and drape it inside the upper container. Encase a piece of granite with the lava."

"Clever."

"It's a shot in the dark," I answered.

"Most of these samples are your personal property. How long did it take you to assemble this collection?"

"A career, such as it is at the moment," I shrugged and met Matt's green-gray gaze. "It'll give me an excuse to find others. The ancients tried to turn lead into gold. Little did they know that lead was more precious."

Matt's smile widened. "Only if you're a scientist and you want to know how old things are."

Carefully Matt moved the replacement monolith into the ten-pod's cargo hold. I walked slowly inside, each step carefully placed. The monolith was just about stowed away when Nichols and another serviceman entered the cargo bay and propelled themselves over to us. My wish that Nichols would hit his head on the ten-pod's side went unfulfilled. I hastily threw webbing over the monolith and Matt helped me secure it.

Nichols held onto a suspended hand support and stared into the ten-pod's hatch. "You're wasting our time with this trip back to the planet's surface."

I sighed as I snapped the last webbing anchor into place. Matt went over to his EVA suit and started shrugging it on. The serviceman who would pilot Matt to the surface sailed past me and to the pilot's chair. His movements were sure and exact. I left the ten-pod.

"The Captain wants—"

"You spend a lot of time speaking for the Captain, Mr. Nichols. Does he know this about you?" I brushed away his retort. "I answered his objections at the Science Council meeting last night. The mission stands."

The pilot signaled ready, so I propelled myself away from the ten-pod, caught a handrail—thank God—and pulled myself out of the cargo bay, impressed with my agility. It pays to get angry, now and then. Nichols followed me to the hangar's observation booth. The ten-pod launched quickly. I wondered if Matt was rushing the pilot. Nichols was a tense presence beside me.

"What are you doing?"

I answered a safer question. "We are trying to maintain this planet's ecobalance and leave it as close to how we found it as possible. Or think of it as being nice to critters."

"Rubbish. How long was that rock in the lava flow before you found it? The critter is long dead."

"Probably. XO made this request to me, and the Science Council backed my decision to return the monolith to its natural state."

"How long did it take you to talk XO into making the request?"

"I've better things to do." I started to pull away and out of the observation booth, using the handrail.

He grabbed my left arm. "I'm going to report you to the full Theology Council when we return to port."

"Go ahead, make a bigger fool of yourself because there's nothing to report." I gripped the handrail even more tightly and pulled my arm free.

"What were you and Doctor Greely arguing about?"

"Don't you have something better to do than spy on me? If you think you'll make Theology Council by walking over me and my career, think again. It'll never happen." I then casually propelled away, but stayed within reach of a handrail.

"Heretic!" His accusation reached me, but he had no proof. Thank God.

After the *Chamberlin* left Delta Pavonis Two's orbit, I fielded more questions about my celebrity rock. Tom kept talking it up until I pointed out how sinful arrogance was and how many sins he was committing. The visual portion of my report mentioned nothing of the monolith; my published report mentioned only a bit more, although I did help the Theology department and XO prepare their reports. Even I half believed the species we named was in fact the one responsible for creating the monolith. Once that report was published, Tom stopped his remarks. No one listened to him anymore.

We never did make up our lost flight time, nor did we skip any planets. The department heads, led by Greg Greely, screamed loudly to the onboard Science Council and louder at the Service crew. Someone on the Council found a loophole in the Service contract, forcing them to maintain the original course plan and not skip any planets. When we returned to port, lawyers would take up the battle. All in all, I thought things were going well when we finally returned to University Station—the multibillion-dollar space habitat out near Uranus' orbit.

The day we got back, I took Angshu to the park. Refitting the *Chamberlin* for the next voyage could wait a few days, though I would have liked it if Greely had answered his comm link that morning. It was almost as if he had been avoiding me lately, and then his cryptic message this morning was too odd to even begin to understand. Still, being off the ship was wonderful.

I stood under a white pine tree near the middle of Freedom Park. Angshu played on the park equipment. The air smelled delicious. Angshu had been born on the station and had never been closer to Earth than this park. We came here often when in port.

There had been some changes. A plaque had once been the focal point of the park. Greely and I had once discussed the words contained on the costly bronze. The words were worth far more. They were replaced by playground equipment, including a huge slide.

The plaque had been a replica of one at the heart of my alma mater's campus. Both celebrated the trial and acquittal of a scholar over 230 years ago. I tried to remember the words.

". . . *Should ever encourage that continual and fearless shifting and winnowing by which alone truth can be found.*"

Had I come here looking for the plaque when I couldn't find Greely? Maybe. There had been comfort in its silent presence. Had the original been removed, too? Most likely. So now *they* could no longer even face their lies. It suddenly felt darker and colder in the universe.

Angshu never noticed as he climbed on every pole and crosspiece, swung on each swing, and insisted on going down the highest slide. The slide didn't look the safest for someone as young as Angshu, even at three-quarters G, so we went down together. Then we returned to sit under the pine tree again for some cookies and juice. The plaque, or rather its absence, shadowed me.

"Angshu, remember when we talked a few weeks ago about God and man's place in the universe?"

"Yes, I remember. There is only one God and one smart species."

"Good! Why can there be only one truly smart species?"

"Because we're human and are made in God's image and he has only one image."

"Now if someone asks you about whales being just as smart as humans, what would you say?"

"They're wrong."

"Why?"

"God's not a whale or dolphin or ape. He's just like us."

"Very good." I hugged him and Angshu returned to play, but I didn't feel very proud of myself.

Everything I told him was theologically correct. The politically correct information would protect him, but it was a lie. All of it. Someday I would tell him the truth. When he was old enough to keep silent. I wondered what age that would be.

Yet he knew about his father, and even when taunted by playmates, never voiced this secret. But then, if he did talk about his father, the little he knew could be passed off as learned by gossip. No, Angshu was still too young for the whole truth.

I leaned back against the tree trunk. Before too long, Matt's familiar figure approached. As he sat down nearby, I held out a bag of juice, which he declined.

"What's wrong, Matt? You look upset."

He raked fingers through thick locks. Then he carefully pulled something from his pocket and placed it in my hand. I put the object in my own pocket. Without looking at it, I knew what it was by feel. My pulse raced—one of Greely's best scramblers!

"Greely made me promise to give you one. He thought you would need it. I destroyed all the others. I had to, too dangerous now."

"Why? What's going on?"

"Doctor Greely was arrested an hour ago by the Station's Theological Council on charges of capital crime."

My heart was a lump in my throat. I managed to ask, "Why? What crime?"

"Divine slander, for a start. The charges are expected to escalate with the inquest. He published a paper entitled, 'Cosmology, Evolution, and Alien Intelligence.'"

"Why would he do something so foolish?" My voice was an angry whisper.

"He thinks a public trial of a leading theologian will open some eyes."

"He's wrong. I've lived through such a trial! Ninety percent of what he has to say will never be made public. And the rest will be distorted and altered so no one will recognize the truth behind the words." I restrained myself from moving, although I wanted to run to Greely and beg him to recant. "That explains the cryptic message I got this morning. He said, *'There are more important things than being safe.'* I didn't understand what he meant."

"He said there is no way you, or I, could be dragged into this mess."

"Easy to say, but reality? Nichols will—"

"Do nothing. Somehow Greely listed Nichols as coauthor. I don't know how Greely got the proper electronic signature to do it, but Nichols was arrested, too. They stand trial together. It looks ironclad."

I was too stunned to laugh or cry. My thoughts skipped from the past to the now at random. We waited in silence for a few minutes before Matt spoke up.

"I've got to go. My flight for Earth leaves in two hours."

"What? But I thought you were accepted at—"

"My acceptance to North American came through last night."

"Greely's school?" I whispered.

Matt shrugged. "You don't have much time either. The *Van Hise* leaves day after tomorrow."

"So?"

"You're on it. You've been transferred by order of the Science Council. Carrie is packing your lab even as we speak. She's been transferred, too." He shrugged off my unasked questions. "The *Chamberlin* is grounded with most of her crew, science or service staff, to stand as witnesses at Greely's trial. Not all the crew, though. Tom's been transferred to an Explorer class ship."

"He'll wash out," I mumbled.

"Doesn't matter. He won't be accessible at the trial. Some of the *Chamberlin*'s XO staff have also been transferred. Everyone to different ships or Earth posts."

"Damn, Greely is thorough."

"Or his friends are. I left a few other messages and notes for you with Carrie. She's good. You can trust her. I do."

"I'm going to miss you, Matt. You're the best student I've ever had. You're going to do well."

He nodded, then smiled. "Yeah, I think so. I've a lot to thank you for, most of all for teaching me how to keep an open mind on research."

"Can you hide that quality? You'll need to be able

to control your feelings in front of strangers, especially if you want to pass your doctoral exams."

"Yeah, I think so. I'll just have to remember how your eyes change when you talk about your husband's trial. I'll never doubt the power of the Council again. Maybe we'll serve together on the same ship someday after I finish school. It'll be three years at least. I plan to take a heavy theology load."

"You're smarter than I was. Take care, Matt."

"You, too, Somita." We stood and he gave me a hug, and then went over to hug Angshu good-bye. I watched Matt's receding back as if the whole world had collapsed around me. I was afraid that I'd see him arrested and then the police would be here next. They'd make Angshu a ward of the state and turn him into a darker version of Nichols. I shivered despite the warm air. Maybe no matter what I did that would happen. I envisioned the plaque back where it belonged. . . . *Fearless shifting and winnowing* . . . It was not fearless, not now. Not for a very long time to come, if ever. Angshu had to know the truth and I had to teach him how to hold that truth deep within his heart and mind where it would remain safe. So he would always be safe, despite whatever might happen to me.

I had to leave to help Carrie pack, but I couldn't make myself move. It felt safe here.

When Angshu came back for more cookies, I told him we were going to be leaving soon on another ship. He didn't mind. Space was in his blood, just as it had been in Martin's.

"Angshu, why are whales so smart?"

"God made them that way."

"Maybe, maybe not." I didn't know how much I wanted to say just now, but I knew I could not let my son grow up to be another Nichols. I could almost hear the prison doors closing around me as they had closed around my husband. Maybe Greely was right; there were more important things than being safe. Maybe. There was such a fine line to walk between truth and reality, between fearful and fearless.

STAR LIGHT, STAR BRIGHT
by Robert J. Sawyer

Robert J. Sawyer's novels *The Terminal Experiment,*
Starplex, Frameshift, and *Factoring Humanity* were
all finalists for the Hugo Award, and *The Terminal Ex-*
periment won the Nebula Award for Best Novel of the
Year. His latest novel is *Calculating God.* He lives
near Toronto. Visit his web site at *www.sfwriter.com*.

"**D**addy, what are those?" My young son, Dalt, was
pointing up. We'd floated far away from the ancient buildings, almost to where the transparent dome
over our community touches the surface of the great
sphere.

Four white hens were flying across the sky, their little wings propelling them at a good clip. "Those are
chickens, Dalt. You know—the birds we get eggs from."

"Not the *chickens,*" said Dalt, as if I'd offended him
greatly by suggesting he didn't know what they were.
"Those lights. Those points of light."

I squinted a bit. "I don't see any lights," I replied.
"Where are they?"

"Everywhere," he said. He swung his head in an
arc, taking in the whole sky. "Everywhere."

"How many points do you see?"

"Hundreds. Hundreds."

I felt my back bumping gently against the surface; I pushed off with my palm, rising into the air again. The ancient texts I'd been translating said human beings were never really meant to live in such low gravity, but it was all I, and countless generations of my ancestors, had ever known. "There aren't any points of light, Dalt."

"Yes, there are," he insisted. "There are thousands of them, and—look!—there's a band of light across the sky there."

I faced in the direction he was pointing. "I don't see anything except another chicken."

"No, Daddy," insisted Dalt. "Look!"

Dalt was a good boy. He almost never lied to me— and I couldn't see why he would lie to me about something like this. I maneuvered so that we were hovering face-to-face, then extended my hand.

"Can you see my hand clearly?" I said.

"Sure."

"How many fingers am I holding up?"

He rolled his eyes. "Oh, Daddy . . ."

"How many fingers am I holding up?"

"Two."

"And do you see lights on them, as well?"

"On your fingers?" asked Dalt incredulously.

I nodded.

"Of course not."

"You don't see any lights in front of my fingers? Do you see any on my face?"

"Daddy!"

"Do you?"

"Of course not. The lights aren't down here. They're up there!"

I touched my boy's shoulder reassuringly. "Tomorrow, we'll go see Doc Tadders about your eyes."

We hadn't built the protective dome—the clear blister on the outer surface of the *Dyson* sphere (to use the ancient name our ancestors had given to our home, a term we could transliterate but not translate). Rather, the dome was already here when we'd come outside. Adjacent to it was a large, black pyramidal structure that didn't seem to be part of the sphere's outer hull; instead, it appeared to be clamped into place. No one was exactly sure what the pyramid was for, although you could enter it from an access tube extending from the dome. The pyramid was filled with corridors and rooms, and lots of control consoles marked in the script of the ancients.

The transparent dome was much larger than the pyramid—plenty big enough to cover the thirty-odd buildings the ancients had built here, as well as the concentric circles of farming fields we'd created by importing soil from within the interior of the Dyson sphere. Still, if the dome hadn't been transparent, I probably would have felt claustrophobic within it; it wasn't even a pimple on the vastness of the sphere.

We'd been fortunate that the ancients had constructed all these buildings under the protective dome; they served as homes and work spaces for us. In many cases, we could only guess at the original purposes of the buildings, but the one that housed Dr. Tadder's office had likely been a warehouse.

After sleeptime, I took Dalt to see Tadders. He seemed more fascinated by the wall diagram the doctor had of a human skeleton than he was by her eye chart, but we finally got him to spin around in midair to face it.

I was floating freely beside my son. For an instant, I found myself panicking because there was no anchor rope looped around my wrist; the habits of a lifetime were hard to break, even after being here, on the outside of the Dyson sphere, for all this time. I'd lived from birth to middle age on the inside of the sphere, where things tended to float up if they weren't anchored. Of course, you couldn't drift all the way up to the sun. You'd eventually bump against the glass roof that held the atmosphere in. But no one wanted to be stuck up there, waiting to be rescued; it was humiliating.

Out here, though, under our clear, protective dome, things floated *down,* not up; both Dalt and I would eventually settle to the padded floor.

"Can you read the top row of letters?" asked Doc Tadders, indicating the eye chart. She was about my age, with pale blue eyes and red hair just beginning to turn gray.

"Sure," said Dalt. "Eet, bot, doo, shuh, kee."

Tadders nodded. "What about the next row?"

"Hih, fah, roo, shuh, puh, ess."

"Can you read the last row?"

"Ayt, doo, tee, nuh, tee, ess, guh, hih, fah, roo."

"Are you sure about the second letter?"

"It's a doo, no?" said Dalt.

If there's any letter my son should know, it should

be that one, since it was the first in his own name. But the character on the chart wasn't a doo; it was a fah.

Dr. Tadders jotted a note in the book she was holding, then said, "What about the last letter?"

"That's a roo."

"Are you sure?"

Dalt squinted. "Well, if it's not a roo, then it's a shuh, no?"

"Which do you think it is?"

"A shuh . . . or a roo." Dalt shrugged. "It's so tiny, I can't be sure."

I could see that it was a roo; I was surprised that I had better vision than my son did.

"Thanks," said Tadders. She looked at me. "He's a tiny bit nearsighted," she said. "Nothing to worry about." She faced Dalt again. "What about the lights in front of your eyes? Do you see any of them now?"

"No," said Dalt.

"None at all?"

"You can only see them in the dark," he said.

Tadders pushed against the padded wall with her palm, which was enough to send her drifting across the room toward the light switch; the ancients had made switches that were little rockers, instead of the click-in/click-out buttons we build. She rocked the switch, and the lighting strips at the edges of the padded roof went dark. "What about now?"

Dalt sounded puzzled. "No."

"Let's give your eyes a few moments to adjust," she said.

"It won't make any difference," said Dalt, exasperated. "You can only see the lights outside."

"Outside?" repeated Tadders.

"That's right," said Dalt. "Outside. In the dark. Up in the sky."

Dalt was the first child born after our group left the interior of the Dyson sphere. Our little town had a population of 240 now, of which fifteen had been born since we'd come outside. Dalt's usual playmate was Suzto, the daughter of the couple who lived next door to my wife and me in a building that had clearly been designed by the ancients to be living quarters.

All adults spent half their days working on their particular area of expertise, which, for me, was translating ancient documents stored in the computers inside the buildings and the pyramid, and the other half doing the chores that were needed to support a fledgling society. But after work I took Dalt and Suzto for a float. We drifted away from the lights of the ancient buildings, across the fields of crops, and out toward the access tunnel that led to the pyramid.

I knew that the surface of the sphere, beneath us, was curved, of course, and, here on the outside, that it curved down. But the sphere was so huge that everything seemed flat. Oh, one could make out the indentations that were hills on the other side of the sphere's shell, and the raised plateaus that water collected in. Although we *were* on the frontier—the outside of the sphere!—we were still only one body-length away from the world we'd left behind; that's how thick the sphere's shell was. But the double-doored portal that led back inside had been sealed off; the people on the interior had welded it shut after we'd left. They wanted nothing to do with whatever we might find out here, calling our quest for knowledge of the exterior universe a sacrilege against the wisdom of the ancients.

As we floated in the darkness, Dalt looked up again and said, "See! The lights!"

Suzto looked up, too. I expected her to scrunch her face in puzzlement, baffled by Dalt's words, but instead, near as I could make out in the darkness, she was smiling in wonder.

"Can—can you see the lights, too?" I asked Suzto.

"Sure."

I was astonished. "How big are they?"

"Tiny. Like this." She held up her hand, but if there was any space between her finger and thumb, I couldn't make it out.

"Are they arranged in some sort of pattern?"

Suzto's vocabulary wasn't yet as big as Dalt's. She looked at me, and I tried again. "Do they make shapes?"

"Maybe," said Suzto. "Some are brighter than others. There are three over there that make a straight line."

I frowned. "Dalt, please cover your eyes."

He did so, with elaborate hand gestures.

"Suzto, point to the brightest light in the sky."

"There're so many," she said.

"All right, all right. Point to the brightest one in this part of the sky over here."

She didn't hesitate. "That one."

"Okay," I said, "now put your hand down, please."

She drew her arm back in toward her body.

"Dalt, uncover your eyes."

He did so.

"Now, Dalt, point to the brightest light in this part of the sky over here."

He lifted his arm, then seemed to vacillate for a moment between two possible choices.

"Not that one, silly," said Suzto's voice. She pointed. "This one's brighter."

"Oh, yeah," said Dalt. "I guess it is." He pointed at it, too. I couldn't see anything, but it seemed in the darkness that if I could draw lines from the two children's outstretched fingers, they would converge at infinity.

Dr. Tadders was an old friend, and with both Suzto and Dalt seeing the lights, I decided to join her for lunch. We grew wheat, corn, and other crops under lamps here on the outside of the sphere, and raised chickens and pigs; if you wanted the eggs to hatch, you had to put low roofs over the hens, because they needed to be in constant contact with their clutches, and their own body movements were enough to propel them into flight; chickens really seemed to love flying. Tadders and I both knew that we'd have had more interesting meals if we'd stayed inside the sphere, but the ancient texts said that although the interior was huge, there was still much, much more to the universe.

Most of those on the interior didn't care about such things; they knew that the sphere's inner surface could accommodate over a million trillion human beings—a vastly larger number than the current population—and that our ancestors had shut us off from the rest of the universe for a reason. But some of us had decided to venture outside, starting a new settlement on our world's only real frontier. I didn't miss much about the inside—but I did miss the food.

"All right, Rodal," Dr. Tadders said, gesturing with a sandwich triangle, "here's what I think is happening." She took a deep breath, as if reviewing her thoughts once more before giving them voice, then: "We know that a long, long time ago, our ancestors built a double-walled shell around our sun. The outer wall is opaque, and the inner wall, fifty body-lengths above that, is transparent. The area between the two walls is the habitat, where all those who still live on the interior of the sphere reside."

I nodded, and kicked gently off the floor to keep myself afloat. We drifted out of the dining hall, heading outdoors.

"Well," she continued, "we also know that there was a war generations ago that knocked humanity back into a primitive state. We've been rebuilding our civilization for a long time, but we're nowhere near as advanced as our ancestors who constructed our world were."

That was certainly true. "So?"

"So, what about that story you translated a while ago? The one about where we supposedly came from?"

I'd found a story in the ancient computers that claimed that before we lived on the interior of the Dyson sphere, our ancestors had made their home on the outer surface of a small, solid, rocky globe. "But that was probably just a myth," I said. "I mean, such a globe

would have been impossibly tiny. The myth said the
home world was six million body-lengths in diameter.
Kobost—" a physicist in our community "—worked out
that if it were made of the elements the myth described,
even a globe that small would have had a crushingly
huge gravitational attraction: five body-lengths per
heartbeat squared. That's more than ten thousand times
what we experience here."

Of course, the gravitational attraction on any point
on the interior of a hollow sphere is zero. When we
lived inside the sphere, the only gravity we felt was the
pull from our sun, gently tugging things upward. Here,
on the outside of the sphere, the gravitational pull is
downward, toward the sphere's surface—and the sun
at its center.

I continued. "Although Kobost thinks human muscle could perhaps be built up enough to withstand such
an overwhelming gravity, his own studies prove that
the globe described in the myth can't be our home
world."

"Why not?" asked Tadders.

"Because of the chickens. There are several ancient
texts that show that chickens have been essentially the
same since before our ancestors built the Dyson sphere.
But with an acceleration due to gravity of five body-
lengths per heartbeat squared, their wings wouldn't be
strong enough to let them fly. So that globe in the myth
couldn't possibly have been our ancestral home."

"Well, I agree that's puzzling about the chickens,"
said Tadders, "but wherever our ancestors came from,
you have to admit it wasn't another Dyson sphere. And

the inside of a Dyson sphere forms a very special kind of sky. Remember what it was like when we lived in there? Wherever you looked over your head, you saw—well, you saw the sun, of course, if you looked directly overhead. But everywhere else, you saw other parts of the sphere. Some of those parts are a long, long way off—the far side of the sphere is a hundred and fifty billion body-lengths away, isn't it? But, regardless, wherever you looked, you saw either the sun or the surface of the sphere."

"So?"

"So the surface of the sphere is reflective—even the dull, grass-covered parts reflect back a lot of light. Indeed, on average the surface reflects back about a third of the light it receives from the sun, making the whole sky glaringly bright."

People in there did have a tendency to float facing the ground instead of the sky. I nodded for her to go on.

"Well, our eyes didn't evolve here," continued Tadders. "If we did come from a rocky world, the sun would have been seen against an empty, nonreflective sky. It must be much, much brighter inside the Dyson sphere than it ever was on the original home world."

"Surely our eyes would have adapted to deal with the brighter light here."

"How?" asked Tadders. "Even after the great war, we regained a measure of civilization fairly quickly. There was no period during which we were reduced to survival of the fittest. Human beings haven't undergone any appreciable evolution since long before our ancestors built the sphere. Which means our eyes are

as they originally were: suited for much dimmer light.
Of course, the ancients may have had drugs or other
things that made the interior light seem more comfortable to them, but whatever they used must have been
lost in the war."

"I suppose," I said.

"But you, me, and everyone else in our settlement
who has lived inside the sphere—we've damaged our
retinas, without even knowing it."

I saw what she was getting at. "But the children—
the children born here, on the outside of the sphere—"

She nodded. "The children born here, after we left
the interior, have never been exposed to the brightness
inside, and so they see just as well in the dark as our
distant, distant ancestors did, back on the home world.
The points of light the children are seeing really do
exist, but they're simply too faint to register on the
damaged retinas we adults have."

My head was swimming. "Maybe," I said. "Maybe.
But—but what *are* those lights?"

Tadders pursed her lips, then lifted her shoulders a
bit. "You want my best guess? I think they're other
suns, like the one our ancestors encased in the sphere,
but so incredibly far away that they're all but invisible." She looked up, out the clear roof of the dome
covering our town, out at the uniform blackness, which
was all either of us could make out. She then used one
of the words I'd taught her, a word transliterated from
the ancient texts—a word we could pronounce but
whose meaning we'd never really understood. "I
think," she said, "that the points of light are *stars*."

* * *

There are thousands of documents stored in the ancient computers; my job was to try to make sense of as many of them as I could. And I made much progress as Dalt continued to grow up. Eventually, he and the other children were able to match the patterns of stars they could see in the sky to those depicted in ancient charts I'd found. The patterns didn't correspond exactly; the stars had apparently drifted in relation to each other since the charts had been made. But the kids—the adolescents, now—were indeed able to discern the *constellations* shown in the old texts; ironically, this was easier to do, they said, when some of the lights of our frontier town were left on, drowning out all but the brightest stars.

According to the charts, our sun—the sun enclosed in the Dyson sphere—was the star the ancients had called Tau Ceti. It was not the original home to humanity, though; our ancestors were apparently unwilling to cannibalize the worlds of their own system to make their Dyson sphere. Instead, they—we—had come from another star, the closest similar one that wasn't part of a multiple system, a sun our ancestors had called Sol.

And the *planet*—that was the term—we had evolved on was, in the infinite humility of our wise ancestors, called by a simple, unassuming name, one I could easily translate: Dirt.

Old folks like me couldn't live on Dirt now, of course. Our muscles—including our hearts—were weak compared to what our ancestors must have had, growing up under the stupendous gravity of that tiny, rocky world.

But—

But locked in our genes, as if for safekeeping, were all the potentials we'd ever had as a species. The ability to see dim sources of light, and—

Yes, it must be there, too, still preserved in our DNA.

The ability to produce muscles strong enough to withstand much, much higher gravity.

You'd have to grow up under such a gravity, have to live with it from birth, said Dr. Tadders, to really be comfortable with it, but if you did—

I'd seen Kobost's computer animation showing how we might have moved under a much greater gravity, how we might have deployed our bodies vertically, how our spines would have supported the weight of our heads, how our legs might have worked back and forth, hinging at knee and ankle, producing sustained forward locomotion. It all seemed so bizarre, and so inefficient compared to spending most of one's life floating, but—

But there were new worlds to explore, and old ones, too, and to fully experience them would require being able to stand on their surfaces.

Dalt was growing up to be a fine young man. There wasn't a lot of choice for careers in a small community: he could have apprenticed with his mother, Delar, who worked as our banker, or with me. He chose me, and so I did my best to teach him how to read the ancient texts.

"I've finished translating that file you gave me," he said on one occasion. "It was what you suspected: just a boring list of supplies." I guess he saw that I was only half-listening to him. "What's got you so intrigued?" he asked.

I looked up, and smiled at his face, with its bits of fuzz; I'd have to teach him how to shave soon. "Sorry," I said. "I've found some documents relating to the pyramid. But there are several words I haven't encountered before."

"Such as?"

"Such as this one," I said, pointing at a string of eight letters on the computer screen. "'*Starship.*' The first part is obviously the word for those lights you can see in the sky: *stars*. And the second part, *hip*, well—" I slapped my haunch—"that's their name for where the leg joins the torso. They often made compounded words in this fashion, but I can't for the life of me figure out what a 'stars hip' might be."

I always say nothing is better than a fresh set of eyes. "Yes, they often used that hissing sound for plurals," said Dalt. "But those two letters there—can't they also be transliterated jointly as shuh, instead of separately as ess and hih?"

I nodded.

"So maybe it's not 'stars hip,'" he said. "Maybe it's 'star ship.'"

"*Ship,*" I repeated. "Ship, ship, ship—I've seen that word before." I riffled through a collection of papers, searching my notes; the sheets fluttered around the room, and Dalt dutifully began collecting them for me.

"Ship!" I exclaimed. "Here it is: 'a kind of vehicle that could float on water.'"

"Why would you want to float on water when you can float on air?" asked Dalt.

"On the home world," I said, "water didn't splash up in great clouds every time you touched it. It stayed in place." I frowned. "Star ship. Starship. A—a vehicle of stars?" And then I got it. "No," I said, grabbing my son's arm in excitement. "No—a vehicle for traveling to the stars!"

Dalt and Suzto eventually married, to no one's surprise.

But I *was* surprised by my son's arms. He and Suzto had been exercising for ages now, and when Dalt bent his arm at the elbow, the upper part of it *bulged*. Doc Tadders said she'd never seen anything like it, but assured us it wasn't a tumor. It was *meat*. It was muscle.

Dalt's legs were also much, much thicker than mine. Suzto hadn't bulked up quite as much, but she, too, had developed great strength.

I knew what they were up to, of course. I admired them both for it, but I had one profound regret.

Suzto had gotten pregnant shortly after she and Dalt had married—at least, they told me that the conception had occurred after the wedding, and, as a parent, it's my prerogative to believe them. But I'd never know for sure. And *that* was my great regret: I'd never get to see my own grandchild.

Dalt and Suzto would be able to *stand* on Dirt, and, indeed, would be able to endure the journey there. The starship was designed to accelerate at a rate of five body-lengths per heartbeat squared, simulating Dirt's gravity. It would accelerate for half its journey, reaching a phenomenal speed by so doing, then it would turn around and decelerate for the other half.

They were the logical choices to go. Dalt knew the ancient language as well as I did now; if there were any records left behind by our ancestors on the home world, he should be able to read them.

He and Suzto had to leave soon, said Doc Tadders; it would be best for the child if it developed under the fake gravity of the starship's acceleration. Dalt and Suzto would be able to survive on Dirt, but their child should actually be comfortable there.

My wife and I came to see them off, of course—as did everyone else in our settlement. We wondered what people in the sphere would make of it when the pyramid lifted off—it would do so with a kick that would doubtless be detectable on the other side of the shell.

"I'll miss you, son," I said to Dalt. Tears were welling in my eyes. I hugged him, and he hugged me back, so much harder than I could manage.

"And, Suzto," I said, moving to my daughter-in-law, while my wife moved to hug our son. "I'll miss you, too." I hugged her, as well. "I love you both."

"We love you, too," Suzto said.

And they entered the pyramid.

I was hovering over a field, harvesting radishes. It was tricky work; if you pulled too hard, you'd get the radish out, all right, but then you and it would go sailing up into the air.

"Rodal! Rodal!"

I looked in the direction of the voice. It was old Doc Tadders, hurtling toward me, a white-haired projectile. At her age, she should be more careful—she could break her bones slamming into even a padded wall at that speed.

"Rodal!"

"Yes?"

"Come! Come quickly! A message has been received from Dirt!"

I kicked off the ground, sailing toward the communication station next to the access tube that used to lead to the starship. Tadders managed to turn around without killing herself and she flew there alongside me.

A sizable crowd had already gathered by the time we arrived.

"What does the message say?" I asked the person closest to the computer monitor.

He looked at me in irritation; the ancient computer had displayed the text, naturally enough, in the ancient script, and few besides me could understand it. He moved aside and I consulted the screen, reading aloud for the benefit of everyone.

"It says, 'Greetings! We have arrived safely at Dirt.'"

The crowd broke into cheers and applause. I couldn't help reading ahead a bit while waiting for them to quiet down, so I was already misty-eyed when I continued. "It goes on to say, 'Tell Rodal and Delar that they have a grandson. We've named him Madar.'"

My wife had passed on some time ago—but she would have been delighted at the choice of Madar; that had been her father's name.

"'Dirt is beautiful, full of plants and huge bodies of water,'" I read. "'And there are other human beings living here. It seems those people interested in technology moved to the Dyson sphere, but a small group who preferred a pastoral lifestyle stayed on the home world. We're mastering their language—it's deviated a fair bit from the one in the ancient texts—and are already great friends with them.'"

"Amazing," said Doc Tadders.

I smiled at her, wiped my eyes, then went on: "'We will send much more information later, but we can clear up at least one enduring mystery right now.'" I smiled as I read the next part. "'Chickens can't fly here. Apparently, just because you have wings doesn't mean you were meant to fly.'"

That was the end of the message. I looked up at the dark sky, wishing I could make out Sol, or any star. "And just because you don't have wings," I said, thinking of my son and his wife and my grandchild, far, far away, "doesn't mean you weren't."

CHAUNA

by Alan Dean Foster

Alan Dean Foster was born in New York City and raised in Los Angeles. He has a Bachelor's degree in Political Science and a Master of Fine Arts in Cinema from UCLA. He has traveled extensively around the world, from Australia to Papua, New Guinea. He has also written fiction in just about every genre, and is known for his excellent movie novelizations. Currently, he lives in Prescott, Arizona, with his wife, assorted dogs, cats, fish, javelina, and other animals, where he is working on several new novels and media projects.

"Mr. Bastrop, we're looking for something that doesn't exist."

Slowly, painfully, Gibeon Bastrop lifted his gaze to meet that of the master of the *Seraphim*. It was a gaze that had once struck those upon whom it had fallen with awe or fear, envy or unbounded admiration, or a host of other strong emotions. Nowadays, it most often inspired only pity. Inwardly, Gibeon Bastrop raged. He could only do so inwardly. It had been nearly two decades since he had been physically capable of expressing extremes of emotion.

He was not even sure how much of him was the original Gibeon Bastrop anymore. So many parts had been replaced: cloned, regrown from his own reluctant tissues, or where necessary, replaced with synthetics. The brain was still all Gibeon Bastrop, he felt, though even there the physicians and engineers had been forced to tweak and adjust and modify to keep everything functioning properly. They were very good at their work. Gibeon Bastrop could afford the best. If you couldn't, you were unlikely to live to be one hundred and sixty-two—next April, Bastrop mused. Or was it May?

"Mr. Bastrop?"

"What?" It was Tyrone, badgering him again. Always wanting to give up, that Tyrone. Give up, turn around (although they were so far out now that "around" no longer had any real meaning), and go home. A fine Shipmaster, Tyrone, but easily discouraged. How long had they been searching now? Barely two years, wasn't it? The youth of today had no patience, Bastrop reflected. None at all. Why, Tyrone was barely in his eighties: far too young to be complaining about time. Let him reach triple digits; these days, you had to earn the right to complain.

"Mr. Bastrop." Contrary to the owner's belief, the Shipmaster possessed considerable patience. He was exercising some of it now. "The Chauna doesn't exist. It's bad enough to take us chasing after a fairy story— but an *alien* fairy story?"

"It is not a fairy story." Gibeon Bastrop might no longer be capable of raging, but he could still be adamant. "The Cosocagglia are insistent on that point."

Shipmaster Tyrone sighed. Outside, beyond the great convex port that fronted on Gibeon Bastrop's ornate stateroom, stars and nebulae gleamed in other-than-light profusion. There wasn't a one among them the Shipmaster recognized, and he had been journeying among the starways for more than half a century. The Old Man was taking them farther and farther into the void, closer and closer to Nowhere.

"The Cosocagglia are an ancient species existing in a state of advanced decline. Now if the Vuudd, or even the redoubtable Paquinq, had vouchsafed the existence of the mythical Chauna, I would be more inclined to grant the remote possibility of its existence." He smiled in what he hoped was a sympathetic manner. "But the Cosocagglia?"

Gibeon Bastrop's voice dropped to a mutter. He was tired, even more so than usual. "The Cosocagglia were a great race."

"Once." Tyrone was no longer in any mood to coddle his employer. Like the rest of the crew, he had been too long away from home, was too much in need of blue skies and unrecycled air. "That was tens of thousands of years ago." He sniffed scornfully. "They no longer even go into space. They have forgotten how, and travel between worlds only when they can book or beg passage on a ship of one of the younger species, like the Helappo or ourselves. They have hundreds of legends from those days. The Chauna is just one of many."

He felt sorry for the Old Man, marooned in his motile, no longer able to stand erect even with the aid

of neurorganetics. For a hundred years, the name of
Gibeon Bastrop had been one to be reckoned with
throughout the sapient portion of the galaxy. Inventor,
engineer, industrialist, megamogul; his influence and
his fame were known even on nonhuman worlds. Now
he was a shadow of the self he had been: mentally
slow, weak at advanced cogitation, unable to survive
more than a few days at a time without an immoderate
amount of medical attention. The provisions and personnel he had brought with him on the *Seraphim*
would have equipped a hospital big enough to serve a
good-sized conurbation. It was all for him. Everything
and everyone on the ship existed to keep Gibeon Bastrop happy and his every need looked after.

What must it be like, the Shipmaster mused, to live
out your last days knowing that being the richest
human being alive no longer meant anything?

"The Chauna is not a fancy!" Bastrop pounded the
arm of his motile with a sudden surge of strength. "The
Chauna is real!"

"Far more so the people on board this ship, sir.
They have lives, too. And families, and careers, needs
and desires. All of which they have left behind so that
you could follow this whim of yours."

"They were paid to allow me to do so."

"Well paid." Tyrone was willing, as always, to con-
cede the obvious. "But I'm afraid that's no longer
enough, sir." Taking a step forward, he gestured at the
port and the shimmering magnificence of the drive-
distorted star field beyond. "They've been away from
home for too long. We're not talking a month or two.

Past two years in Void is enough to drive anyone crazy."

The hoverchair hummed softly as Bastrop pivoted to face the sweeping galactic panorama. "I haven't changed—but then, you all thought I was insane when I began this expedition. Why should you think differently of me now?"

The Shipmaster's tone was kindly. Like nearly every other member of the crew, at heart he genuinely liked the Old Man. It was Bastrop's obsession that was hated, not the individual behind it. Nor was great wealth, as it so often is, an issue. Gibeon Bastrop was admired for starting from nothing and acquiring his mammoth fortune through the astute application of exceptional genius and plain hard work.

"We don't think you're crazy, Mr. Bastrop. Just in thrall to an idea."

Gibeon Bastrop looked up at the younger man. "Is that a crime?"

"No, sir," Tyrone replied patiently. "But you must realize that your particular obsession is not shared by your crew. Initial enthusiasm gave way first to tolerance, then to grudging compliance, and most recently to exasperation. I have worked hard to keep it from progressing to the next step." He leaned toward the intricate, elaborate floating chair that not only kept Gibeon Bastrop mobile, but alive. "Word that we have finally struck for home would immediately alleviate any potential problems and eliminate growing tension."

Bastrop nodded tiredly. Even his enfeebled voice,

when he finally replied, was one that could still command fleets and minions. "We've come to find the Chauna. We will continue to search until we have done so."

Tyrone's lips tightened. His response was devoid of insolence, but firm. "At the risk of voicing a cliché, sir, money can't buy you everything. It can't buy you people."

"No, but it can damnwell rent them for me," Bastrop declared confidently.

"It can't buy you a myth."

"That still remains to be seen. You are dismissed, Mr. Tyrone."

The Shipmaster nodded tersely and bowed out. Wakoma and Surat were waiting for him on the bridge.

"What did he say?" Surat was small and dynamic, like a puppy perpetually kept on a too-short leash. She was also the finest navigator Tyrone had ever worked with. "Did you make your point?" Her expression was no less eager than Wakoma's.

"I made it." The Shipmaster brushed past them. "And he promptly ignored it. Standby for downslip." He settled into place in front of his bank of readouts. They, at least, would respond to him.

Crestfallen but far from surprised, the two seconds-in-command parted, off to see to their own stations. Tyrone's words meant that more weeks, maybe more months, of pointless wandering lay before them. Like the rest of the crew, they were beyond homesick. If this kept up, the "home" portion of their worsening condition would begin to drop away for real.

"Maybe he'll die." Wakoma struggled to concentrate on his work. Like everyone else on board the *Seraphim*, he was an exceedingly competent professional.

"Not likely." The tech seated alongside him kept his voice down. "There's enough advanced medical technology on this ship to allow an amoeba to operate a *torkay* projector. With the medics' watching his carcass twenty-four-seven, I'll bet the old bastard's got another ten years left in him."

The ship plunged out of OTL to emerge in the vicinity of Delta Avinis. It was the forty-third multiple star system the *Seraphim* had visited since leaving home. According to the elaborate Cosocagglia mythology, the Chauna was only to be encountered in multiple star systems. No one knew why this should be, not even the Cosocagglia themselves. It didn't matter, Tyrone grumbled silently as coordinates were checked and confirmed, because there was no such thing as a Chauna. They might as well be searching single-star systems, or dark wanderers, or the ghostly gray stone spheres known as stuttering molters.

"Something beautiful." That was how the Cosocagglia legends identified the Chauna. A stellar phenomenon that was supposedly unsurpassingly beautiful. That was about all the fable had to say about it, too. Tyrone had seen the translations, laboriously performed by the xenologists who worked with nonhuman species like the Cosocagglia. Where the Chauna were concerned the Cosocagglia could supply reams of adjectives but nothing in the way of specifics. A Chauna was no more, no less, than a Beautiful Thing.

The phenomena had been encountered but rarely, millennia ago, when the Cosocagglia had been in their prime: a youthful, expansionist, vital race. To see a Chauna, it was said, was to be blessed forever with knowledge of what real beauty was. Any individuals so consecrated by the vision were held up to be the most fortunate of travelers. But for all its supposed wonder, there remained in the crumbled lore of the species not a single description of the Chauna itself.

If that was the case, then how exceptional could it be? Tyrone mused. Even if it existed, it was hardly likely to be a previously unobserved phenomenon. In the course of the past thousand years humankind had identified an enormous range of stellar objects and events, from x-ray bursters to miniature ambling pulsars to Möbius black holes. Some were so esoteric the always busy astrophysicists had not found time to name them. Some were even beautiful, like the tornadic nebulae and the gamma-ray ropes. But none, according to the Cosocagglia who had been shown imagings of them, were Chauna.

Delta Avinis was an impressive, but not unprecedentedly so, double star system. There were half a dozen planets, all sere, all lifeless. Their orbits were erratic, their gravitational grip on continued existence uncertain.

As soon as he was confident that downslip was finalized and that the system held no surprises, Tyrone rose from his seat, formally relinquished control of the

ship to Wakoma and Surat, and announced that he was
going on sleeptime. Two months ago, such announce-
ments by the Shipmaster had been greeted with unified
protest. Now people simply muttered to themselves in
his absence. Everyone was too tired to demonstrate
loudly. Resigned to a seemingly interminable fate, they
had not yet decided what to do about it, or what to do
next. That eventuality might manifest itself at the next
star system, the Shipmaster knew, or the one after that.
He would keep things going as long as he could. It was
part of his job.

Surat waited for several minutes until she was sure
her superior was gone before rising from her position.
"I'm going to talk to Gibeon Bastrop."

One of those who served under her looked up in
alarm. "Are you sure that's wise, Anna?"

The navigator shrugged slim shoulders. "What can
the Old Man do—fire me? I'm not refusing to perform
my duties. Maybe later, but not yet. Not today." Such a
refusal, they both knew, could result in a Hearing
Board denying recompense to the perpetrator. Angry
and frustrated as they were, no one aboard the
Seraphim wanted to sacrifice two years' superior pay
in order to make a point.

No one challenged Surat as she made her way
through the ship toward the Old Man's quarters. The
Seraphim was a sizable vessel, with a crew of several
dozen. Everyone was too busy or too apathetic to con-
front her. They knew they had arrived at yet another
system. There was no sense of excitement, no joy of
discovery. Next week, the procedure would be re-

peated. As it had been now for more than twenty-four months. As it might be for another. No one wanted to think about it.

Well, Anna Surat was thinking about it, and she intended to give full voice to her thoughts.

There were guards posted outside Bastrop's quarters. They had been there since Tyrone had mobilized them four months ago, when the first serious rumblings of discontent had begun to make themselves known among the crew. Everyone on board knew that if Gibeon Bastrop died, his crazed quest across the cosmos would die with him, and they could all go home. No one had tried to hurry the process along— yet. Surat knew that they were hoping time and accumulating infirmities would do for them what none of them could do in person.

She was admitted without having to wait. Depending on his mood and health, Gibeon Bastrop liked company. Long journeys in Void were lonely matters at best.

She found him seated before his dog. At the moment, the obedient sphere was taking dictation. Bastrop pivoted his motile to greet her. As he did so, he essayed the shadow of a smile. Once, that expression had charmed millions. Now it was all the Old Man could do to induce the muscles in his face to comply with the most basic of physical demands.

"You're looking well today, sir." The polite mantra fooled neither of them.

Bastrop waved the dog away. It drifted off to sulk in a corner, powering down as it did so. "I'm always up for a visit from an attractive woman, Anna Surat. To what do I owe the pleasure of your company?"

When was the last time he had had a woman, she found herself wondering perversely? Does he even remember what it was like? So old—he was so *old*! If not for the dozens of doctors and millions of credits at his beck and call, he would have been dead thirty or forty years ago. Instead, he had bought himself an extra lifetime. And for what? So he could spend it like this, visibly decomposing in an expensive hospice motile that every month had to take over more and more of his own failing bodily functions? She resolved never to allow herself to be placed in such a situation. Not that she really needed to worry about it. She was about a hundred million short of qualifying for that level of health care.

"Mr. Bastrop, I know that Shipmaster Tyrone has been to see you . . ."

At her opening words his expression fell. His voice dropped to a more familiar, aged, raspy whisper. "Oh. That again. I was hoping . . ." His words trailed away.

Hoping what? she wondered. That I came her for the pleasure of your selfish, semi-senile company? She forced herself to smile engagingly, wondering even as she did so if he was capable of responding to such gestures.

"You can't subject us to this any longer, Mr. Bastrop. It isn't reasonable. It isn't fair."

From the depths of memory the parchmentlike substance that covered his face twisted into a semblance of a grin. "The search for beauty is never reasonable or fair, my dear. Being beautiful yourself, you should know that."

Damn him, she cursed silently. She had determined before entering that nothing the decrepit industrialist said or did was going to affect her. But even the shadow of that smile was capable of sparking something within her. It was no comfort to know that it had done likewise to thousands who had come before her.

"You can't distract me with words, sir."

"Pity." He turned slightly away from her. "There was a time when I could have done so effortlessly. Long ago, that was."

Feeling sympathy in spite of herself, she advanced to rest a hand on his shoulder. Beneath the synsilk lay very little flesh and much angular bone. She wanted to pull her hand away but did not.

"You are unloved here, sir. I realize you know that, and don't care. I can't change that. Not even you can change that." Her words came a little faster. "But by turning for home now you can regain their respect! You can conclude this in a way that will be remembered with pride instead of animosity."

He turned back toward her. Not by pivoting the chair this time, but by making an actual physical effort to rotate the upper portion of his remaining body. "And what about you, Anna Surat? Do *you* hate me for what I've done?"

"No, Mr. Bastrop. I don't hate you. I'm not the hating type. I just want to go home. I have a husband, you know. At least, I hope I still have a husband."

"You are a starship navigator. He knew what he was

getting into when he married you. Everyone knows. I've been married myself, so even if you think otherwise, I do understand. Outlived most of them." He shook his head slowly. "They were all comely, in their own way. But they were not the Chauna."

Surat knew she shouldn't have spoken harshly to her admittedly generous if stubborn employer, but the time for overindulgence was past. "*Nothing* is the Chauna, Mr. Bastrop! They say that you were once accounted the smartest man in all the civilized worlds. What happened to that person? Did he . . . ?"

"Get senile?" Gibeon Bastrop chuckled. "I don't think so—but then if I was, I wouldn't know it, would I? I don't think the pursuit of ultimate beauty stamps me as mad, Anna. I think it marks me as sane. Saner than most, I should say. Ultimately, what else is there but beauty? Beauty of discovery, beauty of thought, beauty of soul. It's one thing I've never been able to buy, Navigator. Now it's all I want. The last thing I want. No other human being has seen it. We will be the first."

"Many old myths are very alluring, Mr. Bastrop. Seductive, even. But in the end they're only myths. Isn't the loveliness of legend enough?"

"Maybe the Chauna is a world, Anna Surat. Have you thought of that?" Excitement danced in eyes that had been thrice replaced. "A world so wonderful even the Cosocagglia have no words for it. Can you imagine the reaction such a discovery would produce? A world even more captivating than Earth, empty and waiting for us. Or maybe it's a gas giant with multiple rings that glow like gold in the light of triple suns. But most likely it's something we can't imagine."

"Neither can the Cosocagglia," she responded, "because it doesn't exist. Anything of absolute beauty has to be imaginary, or it ceases to be exceptional and becomes just one more cataloged item in the always expanding stellar pantheon."

He started to reply, stopped, and began to wheeze softly. She ought to call somebody, she knew. She ought to summon help. Instead, hating herself, she stood and watched, silent and hopeful. No such luck. The hospice motile did things with tubes and probes, and in less than a couple of minutes the Old Man was breathing normally again. Shallow, but normal.

"That was uncomfortable." His eyes met hers. "You really think I'm being unreasonable, Anna Surat? To want, after more than a century and a half, this one last thing? To view beauty that no one else has seen?"

Her resolve began to melt. He was working his wiles on her, she knew. A hundred years of practice gives a man certain skills. But she could only be manipulated to a limited degree.

"No, Mr. Bastrop. It's not unreasonable to want such a thing. But it *is* unreasonable to want to see that which does not exist. If you would only . . ."

A voice entered the room via an unseen synthetic orifice. "Mr. Gibeon Bastrop. Mr. Gibeon Bastrop, sir!" She recognized Tyrone's commanding tones. What was he doing awake? Sleeptime was precious to every crewmember, from the lowliest to the Shipmaster. What had brought him back to alertness? "Are you awake?"

She responded for him. "Yes, he's awake."

"Navigator Surat? What are you . . . ? Never mind. Mr. Bastrop, I'm rotating the *Seraphim* on its axis. Please look to your port and viewers."

"Why?" The transformation that abruptly overcame the Old Man was astonishing to behold. Suddenly, he looked barely a hundred. "What's happening?"

"Something—we're not sure, sir. An energetic transmutation of a level— Berowski and her people are working on an evaluation, but the field changes and fluctuations are . . ."

The Shipmaster broke off. Perhaps he was too busy to continue. Or perhaps he was simply, like everyone else on board the *Seraphim* who was at that moment in a position to view the event, too overwhelmed to continue.

The enormous expense of the two-story high port polarized automatically as the twin suns of Delta Avinis revolved into view. Nearby, one of the dead planets that orbited the twin stars took a shadowed, heavily-cratered bite out of the Void. Anna wondered at the Shipmaster's words until the second, lesser sun slowly hove into view. Then she pointed, and her lips moved slowly.

"Oh! Look at it. Just look at it!"

Gibeon Bastrop had displaced the hovering chair forward until it could no longer advance. It floated right up against the material of the port, pressing against the thick transparency. Had Bastrop been able to continue forward, the navigator had no doubt he would have done so, right out into the vacuum of space itself.

"Look at what, Anna Surat? At that? At the Chauna?"

Something had materialized *between* the two suns. Hitherto invisible, the extraordinary ephemeral shape was rapidly becoming visible as it drew energy from the nearest star. One gigantic jet of roiling plasma after another burst from the surface of the smaller sun to be drawn across many A.U.s into the larger. Each jet was several hundred times the diameter of the Earth, infinitely longer, with an internal temperature rated in thousands of degrees centigrade.

And each time a violent, spasming plasma jet erupted between the two stars, a portion of it illuminated the Chauna. The legend of the Cosocagglia was not a wandering planet, or a lost ship of profound dimensions, or a streak of natural phenomena as yet unidentified by science. It was at once something less, and much, much more.

"My God," Anna Surat whispered in awe, "it's *alive!*"

There were two wings, each ablaze with lambent energies of a type as yet unstudied. They rippled and flamed across the firmament, faint but unmistakable, like bands of energized nebulae ripped loose from their primary cloud. Nearby stars were clearly visible through them, but they were substantial enough to retain color. With each massive emission from the smaller star, the Chauna partook a little of the enormous energies that were passing between the two suns. The central portion of the event (creature? . . . spirit?) was sleek and slightly less pellucid than the wings. No other features were visible: no limbs, no face, no projections of any kind. No other features were necessary.

"It looks," an awestruck Anna Surat observed almost inaudibly, "like a butterfly. But what's going on? What is it doing?" She had to strain to make out the Old Man's reply.

"It's feeding, Anna. Though it's millions of kilometers across, it's too fragile a structure to draw energy from a star itself. So it waits for one star to drift near enough to another for all that massive gravity to do the job for it. When it senses what's going to happen, it places itself between the two and filters what it needs from the fleeting eruptions of plasma, like a great whale feeding on plankton. Neutrinos, cosmic rays, charged particles—who knows what it ingests and what it ignores? How would you, how could you, possibly study such an entity? We can only watch and marvel. In the process, it apparently acquires throughout its substance a little ancillary coloration."

"A little!" The tenuous but vast extent of the Chauna was already greater than both suns. She continued to stare—what else could one do?—even as the *Seraphim*'s instruments methodically registered the immense strength of the repeated solar outbursts while her screens fought to shield her frail, vulnerable, minuscule occupants from the effects of all that energy being blasted out into space.

On other worlds, instruments would register the

pulsarlike outburst and place it in the proper category of celestial disturbances. They would not note the presence of a third object drawing upon a tiny portion of the expelled energies. Though of unimaginable size, that object was far too ephemeral to be perceived by distant instruments.

The feeding of the Chauna was an infrequent event, or it would have been noticed before. Clearly, the Cosocagglia had noticed it, in their thousands of years of spacefaring. Now it was, at last, the turn of humans to do so. The myth had been made real. And it was a discovery that could be shared, and supported, and categorized. The *Seraphim*'s battery of recorders would see to that.

When those incredibly attenuated sun-sized wings *moved*, there was a collective gasp among the crew of the witnessing vessel. Nothing like a Chauna had ever been seen before, and nothing like a Chauna in motion had ever been envisioned. It was beyond imagining, past belief, a magnificent violation of known astrophysical doctrine. With that movement, no one questioned any longer if the phenomenon was alive. It was visible for another minute or two, a colossal undulation of energized color rippling against the star field, a million billion times vaster than any aurora. Then it was gone, the life-sustaining solar energy it had assimilated dispersed throughout its incomprehensibly vast incorporeality.

For a long time the navigator stood staring out the lofty port, aware she had been witness to one of, if not *the* greatest, sights the galaxy had yet revealed to humankind. Then she was reminded that her hand was still resting on the sharp-boned shoulder of the man who had made it possible for her to experience the inconceivable wonder. The man who had continued to insist all along that it was real, that it existed, and that the tiny, wandering creatures called humans might actually be able to descry such a marvel. Who had insisted despite the protests and disapproval of his fellows.

Suddenly she understood a little of what had made Gibeon Bastrop the singular individual he was. Suddenly she understood something of the source of his remarkable ability, and drive, and power. It made her wish she could have known the *man,* and not simply the pitifully weakened and superannuated husk that presently occupied the motile.

"You were right, Mr. Bastrop. You were right all along. You and the Cosocagglia. And everyone else was wrong. Mr. Bastrop?" Her hand slid gently along the shoulder until it made contact with the leathery neck. The head reacted by falling forward, stopping only when the strong chin made contact with the all but exposed sternum. The neck did not pulse against her hand. When she shifted it, no air from the open mouth moved against her palm. She drew her hand back slowly.

"You were right," she repeated. "It *was* beautiful. As beautiful as you hoped it would be. And so, I see now, were you."

OUT OF THE CRADLE

by Terry D. England

Terry England is the author of a novel called *Rewind*. He has been a journalist for more than twenty years, and also has written for *New Mexico* magazine. This is his second published story. He lives and writes in New Mexico.

Pain seared across his face, pulsing in synch with the waves of heat roiling from the magma hole. An odd, tiny movement pushed into a corner of his vision. A blister, swelling slowly, a last-ditch defense against the relentless heat.

He locked his gaze back on the glowing lava, mesmerized by the undulations of color and heat: radiant shades of red, touches of blue, an occasional yellow flare, weaving together in a hypnotic blend. . . .

He tried to flex his fingers, but they wouldn't obey. His hands were foreign objects, no longer under his control. Skin and synth-dermal sleeve melted into each other, colors of both lost into a grayness slowly spreading. He dragged his left leg forward; some of the melted overboot pulled away and remained behind, an artificial footstep in the bleak gray and black of the new lava. Hot slivers shot up his thighs and arrowed up his back.

His vision swam and he fell to a knee, scream scraping out of a parched throat as thigh skin split open, exposing quivering muscle.

"Choc—choco—" His lips refused to move, his voice just a whisper. He fell on his side.

A bulbous object bounced into view, stopping directly overhead. He screamed again as metallic talons wrapped around his torso and yanked him off the ground. Cooling sprays washed over smoldering skin; his last conscious sensation was the diminishing of the pain as the black overtook him.

He sat up on the narrow table, ran his hand across his chest, abdomen, along his thighs. Skin stayed taut over muscle; penis, toes, fingers where they should be, pink and flexible; muscles bunched and stretched with each movement. He swept a hand through thick, dark hair; it had been the first to go, melting and dribbling across his scalp. He'd almost turned back right then.

He leaped off the table, ran vigorously in place for ten seconds, dropped and did ten quick push-ups, sprang to his feet and broke into a rhythm of side-to-side stretches.

"Lincoln Jones, Cradle NA210," a neutral voice called out. "Live comm. Accept?"

"ID, please."

"Quasi Alham, Cradle NA210."

"Accept."

"Please drink fluid in red cup on table. Discharge denied until substance ingested."

Lincoln picked up the cup and looked at the greenish stuff. It smelled like too-sweet guava juice and had the consistency of tomato paste he had seen once in an Out-World restaurant. Plus, there was a lot of it.

"So, my sib, Pele won, didn't she?" Quasi's voice, this time using a young-man old American Midwest flat accent, came out of a speaker on the wall.

Lincoln swallowed some of the substance, grimaced. "She lost. I'm still alive."

"But for the miracle of modern medicine. You know, most 'zekes sample Hawaii for surf and sea, soft breezes under swaying palms, and the gentle caresses of shapely synth-Polynesians steeped in datalore of ancient sexual rites. Not Lincoln Jones, the sensualist. Damage?"

Lincoln got half of the liquid down. "I'll check." He tapped a button on the table; words formed on the wall. "Near-collapse of cardiopulmonary system from ingestion of gases. Reproductive system damaged to nonfunctionality—hmm, didn't notice that one—nose tissue burned to nonfunctionality. Epidermal layers down to muscle fiber of right hand and fingers fused, ten percent of left hand had sloughed off. Eighty percent skin burned to second degree; twenty percent to third degree. Trauma factor 44, survival factor 3, overall score, 92."

"Almost half baked. Did you wait or did you call?"

"I tried to call." Lincoln swallowed some more of the fluid. "Waited too long, but the medi-ship controller heard enough of the call to determine I was in big trouble."

"Hmmpf. Trouble, indeed. The TerraSphere can

sensate the lava flows of Kilauea for you without risking you dying."

"Pixel fantasies. I *felt* all that heat. It was *real*." He drained the last of the substance. His stomach felt bloated.

"Nor be forced to drink two liters of goop."

Lincoln looked at the empty container. "That is the only positive I can see—"

"While I see another speech coming. I'm sliding out. Until your next adventure, you twisted sensualist. Ciao."

Lincoln studied himself in the mirror. Brown hair, brown eyes, wide face, mouth set in a smirk. He erased that, continued to study the body, trying to detect changes, a spot where the nano-bugs made an error, slipped up, gave him a mole or left a scar. Well, if there had been a slip, he couldn't find it. To do a detailed exam, he'd have submit to a cellular scan, but he didn't want to take the time. Moot point, anyway. Changing one's body was as easy as changing one's clothes, so worrying about every little cell being exactly right was unnecessary. This physique still had an overwhelming resemblance to the Lincoln Jones who'd arrived in Hawaii two days ago, the Lincoln Jones formed by DNA combinations donated by his Parental DNA Donors. Sometimes he wondered which feature came from whom, but that also was a useless line of inquiry. The PADDs had met, given up some DNA, then departed, perhaps together, perhaps not, perhaps in the last act before giving up their original 'zekes for good in order to Cross Over. Or perhaps they'd already

Crossed Over and simply selected the code from their personal records. His gestation came in an artificial womb and he was born into a Cradle, a group home designated NA210, operated by State contractors. His 11 Cradle siblings comprised his family, all spending their childhoods in the flesh, all looking forward to the day when they Crossed Over themselves into the TerraSphere as distinct but formless entities, freed from flesh. Forever.

Except him.

And that was causing problems within the Cradle.

He turned from the mirror, ordered a bluish kilt, interlink vest, and sandals on the processor, then took a water shower, letting the liquid flow down his skin in sensual streams. The garments were waiting in the repromatt locker when he finished, and as he wrapped the kilt around his waist, he realized the bloated feeling had passed. He slipped his sandals on, then the vest, carefully aligning the link connections in the collar with those in his neck, and left.

Back in the room of the only surviving hotel on Waikiki Beach, Lincoln kicked off the sandals and settled onto the couch, fingering the control buttons on the vest.

"News, WNN. Continuous cast," a voice said.

Visual: A building burning, flames reaching into the sky, two persons watching. Julie Cotton, the artificially created but beautifully sculpted TerraSphere newswraith, intoning in the background. ". . . called the Harry S. Truman House located in Independence, Missouri, which caught fire early this morning. Town officials were taken by surprise and could not get enough corporeals together to fight the blaze, so the House burned to the ground. Federal Park Service officials said the House had been left untended because few corporeals visit the site any more. In fact, the records show the last corporeal visitor was six months ago. It would seem, then, dear watchers, that Mr. Truman's old house won't be missed very much—"

The image blinked and Lincoln faced a man with olive skin, slanting eyes, and thin face.

"Cracker?" Lincoln said.

"Only to talk to you," the face said.

"To sell something, to get me to donate high chips to some cause, to enlist me in some scatterbrained enterprise."

"My name is Fortuna and I represent the Orion Foun—"

"Forget it." Lincoln cut the connection. Always someone trying to ram in and make one pitch or another. He sighed, sat back, slid his feet along the carpet until something hard hit his left big toe. He plucked a small metal object out of the nap. Lincoln stared at a small, brownish metal disk. A bearded man's profile dominated one side, with the words "In God We Trust" along the edge over the head. Just behind the man's neck was the word "Liberty" and in front was "1999" and a "D" below that. He flipped the disk over and found, below a representation of a building of some kind, the words "ONE CENT." Above the building, along the edge again, "UNITED STATES OF AMERICA." Between the words and the building's roof, more words, E PLURIBUS UNUM. The history-immersion lessons filtered up through his memory until he realized he and the bearded man shared a name, that this was a token for cash money, one cent out of a hundred. He drew a blank on the building, though, and the odd words above it, so he tabbed his linkvest again.

"The building represented on the reverse is the Lincoln Memorial," came the even voice of the Historian of Archives. "The penny, as it is called, honors Abraham Lincoln, the sixteenth president of the United States, links top left. Inside the memorial is a statue of Mr. Lincoln seated, with excerpts of speeches carved on the walls, links right. The Lincoln-head cent was designed by Victor David Brenner and the coin was issued in nineteen-oh-nine to mark the one-hundredth anniversary of Mr. Lincoln's birth. The first design had wheat ears on the reverse, but the memorial replaced the wheat in nineteen-hundred fifty-nine. This penny design was in use until the denomination was eliminated in twenty-twenty-one. The metallic content of the coin—"

Lincoln jumped the lesson, picking the odd phrase with a twitch of eyeball. "The words are Latin, an ancient language derived from the ancient country Latinum, links above, where the city of Rome was established in what is now called Italy. The language was spread by the rise of Rome as a military and cultural power, links left. The words mean Out of Many, One. It is the motto of the United States of America—"

Lincoln cut off the droning historian but continued to gaze at the disk. Odd how the hotel cleaner-bots could miss something this big. He tossed the disk up, caught it, leaned back, tossed and caught it again, this time snapping his thumb so it spun. Whoever dropped it likely is lamenting the loss of something valuable, something just over 150 years old. In that age, people didn't live very long. Now, they lived far longer.

At least, in their minds they do.

A white garment like a Greek chiton wrapped itself tighter around the girl on the platform as a lanky man with red hair and beard wearing a tuxedo with top hat clamped heavy cuffs on her ankles. A slight breeze rippled the garment and her long brown hair. She stared out over the edge of the bridge, down the dry riverbed where it turned at the base of a granite cliff. A pyramid of grassy berms had been piled fifty-four meters below where the woman now stood.

"All righty-o," said Top Hat. "Set."

The girl—late teens, Lincoln guessed—turned languidly toward Top Hat. "The cord is right?"

"Guaranteed." Top Hat flashed a toothy grin, stepped back.

The girl turned back without a sound. She stood easily, though her eyes were unfocused.

"She's gathering karma," piped up a tousled-haired teenager in skintight pants swirling with every color in the spectrum in a constantly changing pattern.

"Is it difficult?" Lincoln's sarcasm was answered with a smirk.

The girl lifted her arms straight out, then fell forward, sailing off the bridge in a graceful arc. The cords whined as they slid over the edge, then snapped. The girl hit the top right of the berm pile; her body jerked in the return flex of the cords, then hung limp, one arm at an odd angle.

A bulbous medi-ship leaped skyward from a bluff west of the bridge and swooped down to her. It grappled her inside and let the cords fall free. Then it rose, halted at bridge level.

"Massive trauma to the head and neck," a mechvoice intoned. "Fracture on right side of skull, jaw dislocation. Fracture and displacement of spinal cord at third and forth cervical vertebrae. Collapse of right lung but full trauma to digestive and cardiopulmonary organs not assessable at this time. Damage to skull suggests concomitant damage to brain. Death probable within fifteen minutes. Score: Trauma factor forty-five, survival factor seven, overall score, eighty-four."

"Yabba!" the teen blurted as the medi-ship zipped away. "Her best yet. If she survives, of course. Doesn't count, otherwise."

Lincoln leaned over the railing. Top Hat and another youth in a shapeless white jumpsuit were pulling the cords up. Below, a crew readjusted the berms the girl had knocked askew.

"That's it, then?" he said.

"Well, yeah. You can die instantly if you hit the berms wrong. The idea is to do damage, but live to crow."

"Ummm. I suppose there's buzz there. It just seems so—lackadaisical."

"Ain't you a little old for this, anyway?"

Lincoln eyed the teen, who glared back with a half-challenging, half-amused look.

"You have a problem with that?"

"No. Just we rarely see someone past First Score here. Are you an Incorrigible?"

"No." Lincoln turned, brought one foot up flat against the rock balustrade, crossed his arms and leaned back. "I just haven't Crossed Over yet."

"You're an Incorrigible. Name's Slaben, by the way."

"Lincoln Jones."

"Yabba. Three more years, then freedom. Cross-Over comes, I'm gone. No more constraint." He thumped his bony chest. "When I shuck this, it'll be in such bad shape, no one'll want to use it again."

Indeed, the young body bore a lot of scars, as if he'd stopped remolding past a certain point. Lincoln had heard of this, a sort of a mark of bravery, a rite of passage the way hunts for dangerous animals once marked the line between child and adult. It didn't matter, of course, because remolding could fix any body, change it, make even Slaben's scarred carcass into something sleek and perfect.

"You're so eager to become a wraith."

"Mind without body—oozin'. A life of sliding, yabba." He grinned. "Want to go next? I'll shuck my place."

Lincoln shook his head. "I'll pass. No challenge." It

wasn't the pain that bothered him—that was the idea, after all—but something seemed to be lacking.

The teen shrugged. "You'll be back, Mr. Jones. I know your type."

"Do you, now. A man of the Out-World, wise beyond his years."

Top Hat made a backward dive off platform, keeping the headgear in place until he hit the berms.

"I just know. You Incorrigible 'zekes are pretty much alike. All body, no mind."

The train hurtled down the track, locomotive roaring, connecting rods and drive wheels just a blur. The train, twenty flatcars loaded with steel I-beams, gained more speed, and soon Lincoln, strapped to the front of the locomotive, saw the wall rising above the horizon. The wind tore at his face, puffing his cheeks and forcing his lips back in a rictus. He watched the wall grow until it dominated everything before him. In the last seconds, he noted the rectangular pattern of the bricks before they smashed into his face, the momentum from the locomotive behind doing its best to ram him through the entire wall.

After a moment, "Boy, that was stupid," a voice said into the darkness.

Six minutes later, "No zap, eh?" Quasi, his wraith in the form of a young man with a ponytail and dark skintight covering, was sitting on a green lawn.

"Cartoons," Lincoln said, his proto-self resembling him except for the jeans and shirt. In the darkened connector booth, his body was wrapped in a gauzy layer.

"Excuse me?" Quasi added an Old-South lilt to his voice.

"Cartoons. You know, animated movement—"

"Oh, sure. They're all over the Spher—"

"Not those. I'm talking about the old two-dimen hand-drawn and painted films they projected on a wall."

"Oh, yeah, yeah. Timmons was interested in those. Kinda boring, actually."

"Then you can understand when I say being driven into a wall in a TerraSphere interactivity is like an old cartoon. No matter how horrendous the crash, or heavy the falling piano, or the force of the blast of the stick of dynamite they were sitting on, those old characters would walk away, instantly ready for the next gag. See? In here, you cannot push beyond preset limits in the program. I did not feel a thing when the locomotive hit the wall. The Sphere safety parameters saw to that. If I did it Out-World, I would feel exquisite pain in the brief seconds before I died."

"Exquisite pain? You sound like one of those sados in the Marat Province."

"Even they don't feel real pain."

"Who wants to? That's one reason nearly everybody being born now eventually Crosses Over—we can shuffle off that mortal coil and live without pain, suffering, disease. Why would you ask anyone to give it up?"

"Because they're addicted to the easy life."

"Addicted? Aaaagh." Quasi stood up. "You don't

know what you're talking about. Why'd you turn down that Out-World body-banging bit?"

"It's missing zip. You fly off, fall fast, smash into ground, and bounce a bit. I saw a girl break her neck, and a kid labels it her personal best. Nothing of substance behind it, though."

"You actually passed on sensual gratification? You virused or something?"

"No, no. If I get desperate, maybe. The kid said I would."

"What kid?"

"Some wise-guy teener. Banging his body until he's freed, as he calls it, in Cross-Over."

"Sound like he's got his balls in the right place. You oughta take a lesson from him."

"In body banging? No, thanks."

"Don't be a zero. You could take a cue from him. In fact, maybe you should."

Lincoln looked at Quasi. "When I need counseling, I sure won't go to a teenager. Or you, either."

After disconnecting his body from the booth, Lincoln returned to the mountain cabin he was renting. He stepped out on the back porch which, by virtue of the cabin having been built on the edge of a ravine, overlooked the small stream splashing below. He took a deep breath, let it out slowly, letting tenseness flow out with the air. Before him stretched a deep forest of muted green, evergreens of all shapes and sizes; real trees, bending in the breeze that blew against him, penetrating shirt and trousers and cooling his skin. His eyes rose along the flanks of the far mountains, following their rumpled forms skyward where the season's first snow had coated the peaks.

He could pinpoint the exact moment he deviated from the cultural norm. During Cradle NA210's eighth year of existence, they'd physically traveled to Michigan district, North American Commonalty. Winter had arrived in full force. None of the children had experienced snow, none cared. Except Lincoln. He stepped outside one night to watch the flakes tumble down in thick profusion, tickling his nose and cheeks. A drift had formed against the back fence. He touched it first with a gloved hand, then pulled the glove off and touched it again. The coldness of the feathery crystals astonished him. He pulled up his sleeve and buried more arm. Then the coat came off; soon after the shirt. Before long, he stripped off everything and jumped in. Just as the cold started to become painful, a beam of light caught him. The Schoolmaster and Cradlenanny, both temporarily corporeal, looked down at him from above the light tube.

"Controller help us," the Schoolmaster had said. "We have a sensual atavist on our hands."

A beeping interrupted his thoughts. He tapped his linkvest connector. Odd how it didn't tell him who was calling.

"Mr. Lincoln." The olive-skinned man's image filled his vision, blotting out the mountains.

"You again. I'm not buying."

"We're not selling—"

"Fine. Good day."

He cut the connection, adjusted the climate controls

on shirt and pants, stepped off the porch and headed for the log bridging the stream. On the other side, he followed the path into the woods.

Six months later, Lincoln leaned back, pushed the plate away. In the distance, the Eiffel Tower rose in slim splendor over the roofs, another of the few Old Works not yet considered superfluous. As he gazed at the tall metal tower, he was reminded of another relic. He pulled the penny out of his pocket, tossed it onto the table.

He looked up to see a tall negroid-variant 'zeke in faded blue shirt and ragged blue cotton pants step through the gate of the outdoor cafe, followed by a stocky anglo variant in striped pullover shirt and ill-fitting baggy tan pants. Lincoln watched as the negro lifted an arm like it weighed several pounds and pointed to him. Both stepped over to his table with an awkward gait.

"How's life, my sib?" the black asked, a slight slur to the words.

"Slow and dull." He regarded the pair for a moment. "Quasi?"

"Greetings, nestling of Cradle NA-210. This is Lashonde."

"Really? Could've fooled me. Please, sit. Have some wine. Get your bodies tipsy. Lashonde, why a male genotype?"

Lashonde took the chair to his right, letting her/his hands rest in the lap. Quasi sat opposite her and laid the 'zeke's hands and forearms on the table like dead fish.

"Emergency," the Lashonde 'zeke said. "No females available at the body station, so I took this."

"Doesn't become you. Interesting 'zeke for you, too, Quasi. People of that color used to be lynched for no reason."

"I am well aware of humanity's history. How was your Africa trip?"

"Peaceful. I could almost imagine I was back in the nineteenth century living among Masai tribesmen, participating in their ancient ways. If I overlooked the TerraSphere connections in the chief's vestments or the subtle use of modern materials science to build their weather-impervious huts with cleverly disguised power sources."

"I imagine the continent must be returning to a garden now that three-quarters of the humans are gone," Lashonde said slowly, enunciating each word.

"Yes, but remember that three-quarters of the animals are clones of zoo-bred specimens." Lincoln tapped the penny. "But you guys didn't become 'zekes just to talk about my Africa adventures."

"By doing this, we thought it would be easier, uh, to uh, talk to you." Quasi's face remained mostly slack, making it difficult to tell if the nervousness grew out of the topic or the body. "Uh—I'm, we're to tell you," the face looked away, then back, "we—the Cradle has, uh, filed a Sundering petition—"

"A Sundering petition."

"Because of your recalcitrance, it was decided we should, should leave you behind and move on."

"Whose idea was this? Benafar?"

"He initiated the discussions, yes," Lashonde said. "There, there was no opposition."

"I see." Lincoln picked up the penny, touched one edge to the table, then spun it. He watched as it slowed, began to roll back flat. He spun it again. "And when did the Cradle accede leadership to Benafar?"

"Benafar is merely the most outspoken," Quasi said. "Look, ten years have gone by since our Age of Ascension, and here you are, still romping in your physique like a child. The tradition, my sib, is leaving behind the corporeal body and joining mind to the TerraSphere, becoming free as thought—"

"You sound like old Cradlenanny on a propaganda spiel."

"The rest of us want to go on with our lives. We can't, though, 'cause one Cradle-mate is being hard-headed—"

Lincoln jabbed a finger onto the penny, pinning it to the table. "Can't—"

A beep from a hovering waitron interrupted.

"Do the new arrivals desire anything?" the mechanical voice asked.

"Um—" Lincoln indicated the menu icon floating above the table. "Hungry? Thirsty? You will be if you stay like that very long."

"Uh, nothing, thanks," Lashonde said.

"No," Quasi said.

"Bring me a tankard of boiling water," Lincoln told the waitron. It glided off.

"Can't you guys, you fields of thought, put up with a 'zeke? I'm not hurting anything, nobody's being held back from doing what they want. Let *me* decide when I'm ready to Cross Over."

Lashonde's 'zeke let out a long breath. "Nothing exists out here the Sphere can't sensate. Nothing."

"The TerraSphere is a safe place, where risk and danger are erased—"

"Risk and danger are unnecessary. We drive ourselves to discover new things, new concepts. The Sphere is our world. We have access to everything, all knowledge, all experience, all the things that have happened in the past. We are more now than our bodies would ever allow us."

"Ever hear the term 'spoon-fed'?"

"It's a new world, Lincoln," Quasi said. "And you *are* holding us back—"

"A new world. That was the selling point, wasn't it, a century and a half ago as the TerraSphere coalesced from interconnections of the electronic networks being assembled then." He tapped the penny with his finger. "You know what they called one of the aspects of the network? Virtual reality. 'Virtual,' you understand. Mimicking, only mimicking, the real world. Leave your Earthly bodies, never suffer from disease or degeneration ever again. Let your mind go and sensate things you never thought possible. They were saying that then, we're still saying that now. And lose a little of yourself, your humanity, in the process."

"Mr. Historian," Quasi said. "Did you know over-population nearly tore this planet apart? Loss of resources, degradation of environment, famine, disease, war—"

Lincoln cupped his right ear. "Hark, do I hear the hoofbeats of the Four Horsemen of the Apocalypse?"

"Will you get serious?" The body leaned forward. "Our minds are still human, with all the power that suggests. It is not body that defines us, but mind, the unique pattern of intellect that forms when we are mere chemicals and cells falling into place. Once mature, the mind is its own structure; the body is redundant. All Descartes said was 'I think, therefore I am,' not 'I shit' or 'I burp' or 'I fart.' "

Lincoln burst into laughter. He pushed himself erect and regarded his cradle-mates. He could not, however, remember their original physical characteristics; all he could see were these near-dead forms staring back with only a glint in the eyes suggesting something actually was alive inside. "Have you ever seen the original *Mona Lisa*? The painting, I mean. I did. Yesterday afternoon. Used to be you had to wait in long lines, then you could only look a few minutes before the next person shoved their way forward. As you say, though, the decline in the Earth's population . . . I stood there fifteen minutes looking at it. Connecting with the artist, the original creator, who did his work in the Out-World. All of them. Matisse. Van Gogh. Monet. Manet. Picasso. Dali. Stendon. Urquahrt. Nagato. Uli. Pollock—"

"All of those images are in the field. You can study

them all you want, frontways, backways, inside, outside. Plus call up the artist's shades—"

Lincoln snorted. "Someone's guesswork on how they behaved. Have you been to the Moon?"

"Will you stop changing the subject?" Lashonde said. "Through the Sphere, of course. Nothing much to do—"

"'Cause you're not really there," Lincoln said, spinning the penny on the tabletop again. "No one's been there since *Apollo*. And no one at all's been to Mars, like humanity'd dreamed for hundreds of years before that. Just robots, that's all. I walked on the Moon barefoot. Left the weirdest footprints."

"What was the point?" Quasi said.

"To prove it was fake."

"You requested a parameter-change just for that?"

He looked at the stupid expression on the 'zeke's face. "I find it necessary, nay imperative, to separate the real from what we imagine as real. Moon or paintings, I think we're missing something by not seeing, experiencing the original. That's all this is ever about."

"It doesn't make any sense, Lincoln." Quasi's voice had a plaintive quality to it, surprising in someone having so much difficulty operating a body.

Lincoln sighed. "All right, never mind. When's the Sundering?"

Lashonde moved the hand of the 'zeke across the surface of the table. "A complication has stopped the petition."

"Complication?"

Lashonde's 'zeke glanced at Quasi. "Your PADDs have filed a protest."

Lincoln sat bolt upright. *"What?"*

"They claim ousting you is a blot on their genetic history." Quasi straightened, letting his hands slide off the table to his sides. "The Cradle's action slanders them and their foredonors because it deems your behavior antisocial and, by inference, calls into question the stability of the donor personae. So the brief says."

Lincoln rubbed his chin with his hand, then smiled. "Very interesting. Wonder who they are."

"Please, don't make this worse." The Lashonde face made a quick flicker of muscle movement. "First you embarrass the Cradle, now you're thinking of a heritage search. An *illegal* heritage search."

Lincoln shrugged. "I'm considering no such thing. Just curious, that's all. So what's next?"

"Judicial bloc North America has scheduled a hearing," Lashonde said.

"When? I'll make sure I'm there."

"You aren't allowed to participate."

"Well, that's not fair."

"Fair? Fair? You want it to be fair? Then give it up, Lincoln." A Quasi-hand jerked like he'd wanted to make a gesture. "Cross Over. The Sundering will then be canceled."

The waitron glided over and placed a tall tankard of still-boiling water on the table. Lincoln dismissed it with a wave of his hand. Then he poured some of the hot water on Lashonde's 'zeke's hand. A moment passed before it jerked away. "What—"

"Been a while since you felt pain, eh?" He poured the rest in Quasi's lap, who barely moved in reaction.

"Really, Lincoln, this is childish. The Sphere can simulate this just as well."

"*Do you ever sensate pain, though?* Things that hurt? A cut from a sharp edge? Heat blistering your skin? Freezing until you shiver so much you lose control? Real physical pain, the kind you'd do anything to get relief from?"

"We can avoid pain—"

"Then you ain't human."

"I'm beginning to be sorry I came—"

Lincoln stood up, pocketed the penny, put his hands on the table, and leaned toward Quasi. "Try to remember that random sensation, Quasi. Codify it, put it into memory. When you go back Across, try to remember it, duplicate it, line by line, nanosecond by nanosecond. I don't think you can." He straightened, stepped away from the table. "And I don't think you ever will. Waitron, these people are paying for my lunch."

Sensual stimulation: Diving in what was left of the Great Barrier Reef, the medi-ship responding to a real emergency after a shark attack nearly tore an arm off. Hiking through the Amazon River System International Protected Rain Forest with a tribe of aborigines, living as they did, eating what they did, but they stood back staring as he let an army ant corps lacerate his feet and legs. Orgies in Japan. Riding an elephant-clone in India and being mauled by a tiger-clone (by design). Driving a copy-car of ancient design and wiping out in the third lap, forcing robo-rescuers to struggle for twenty minutes to extricate his 'zeke.

"Petition to Sunder Lincoln Jones from Cradle NA-210 accepted, with the proviso said action and all inferences therefrom apply only to the Defendant and not to any parental/donors or foredonors. Responsibility is the Defendant's, and he alone must bear that burden."

Lincoln's first action after that was to volunteer for a full-scale reenactment of the Battle of Gettysburg. With live fire from musket and cannon.

"I told you you'd be back."

Slaben grinned at Lincoln. The teen looked almost natty in dark trousers, white shirt, and vivid yellow vest.

"Just in the neighborhood, thought I'd drop in."

"Sure," Slaben said. "Goingta jump?"

"No." Lincoln watched a woman encased in a rubber suit sail off the bridge. "After what I've been through, this is nothing."

"Nearly getting blowed apart at Gettysburg, you mean."

"And how do you know that?"

The teen leaned against the railing, waited until the rubber-woman's medi-ship reported. "You're famous, you have a big following among the Sphericals. We watch you just to see what you do next."

"I wasn't aware of this."

He shrugged. "Didn't want you getting wired about it."

"Well, I'm glad I provided amusement for some-body."

"Amusement, yabba, that's it. You get Sundered, then you almost crash."

"Point-blank grapeshot can do that."

"You're the champion sensator, know that? Little Round Top with the Maine volunteers not enough, hadda do Pickett's Charge, too. On the wrong side—"

"Scariest thing I ever did, believe me. Still, during those moments of utter terror, I was as kin to the orig-inal soldiers as anyone could get." He looked down the canyon. "Chaos, fear, smoke, noise, bullets whining overhead. And you know something, I felt an exhilara-tion that raced up my spine. Every sense sharp as the bayonets, flashing information to my hyper-operating brain, mind alive like it's never been before. Makes me wonder . . . can I actually love war?"

"Buncha people died."

"Believe me, that added reality to the fear. Didn't matter it was a reenactment. It was a battle—and it was real." He turned his gaze to Slaben. "Four hundred fifty-four of them didn't get help in time. Some were class-A criminals, but all were volunteers. Highest death toll in any reenactment for the last hundred years." He took a breath, let it out slowly. "Some of the men died screaming."

"'Member the last time you were here? The girl in the Greek outfit?"

"Yeah."

"She Crossed Over. Almost everyone who was here that day has. I Cross Over in three weeks. I'm preparing myself for a whole new experience. Not you, though. You're still looking for physical thrills."

"You're here."

"I came 'cause I knew you were. I wanted to see the famous Incorrigible 'zeke with my own eyes once more before I go."

Lincoln kept his eyes averted, aware the teen's gaze still was pinned on him. Finally, Slaben blurted, "What are you after, anyway, Lincoln Jones?"

Lincoln looked over at him. Behind, someone else jumped off the bridge.

"I haven't the faintest idea."

"Fuck him." The ancient curse satisfied him for some reason, the words nice and short, to the point and final. The fact that Slaben wouldn't hear it was beside the point. He crossed his arms, stood stoically against the ocean's power. 'Course, not being very far into the water, he could turn and run back to the beach, Waikiki again. Instead, he just stood there, daring a riptide to come and snatch him.

The solitude didn't last long, though. He heard a measured splashing coming up behind him, someone taking careful steps in the surf. The splashing stopped. Seconds passed, nothing. Lincoln rolled his eyes, turned.

"Good afternoon, Mr. Jones." The man stood in full-blown gray suit, water above his knees.

"Oh, Fortuna, why do you plague me?"

"I still want to talk to you. Time is running short. A

meeting of flesh, so to speak, seems the only way. Is something wrong?"

"I'm trying to erase you from my field. Hard to do, though, when we're Out-World."

"Mm, yes, I can understand your difficulty." The 'zeke of the man matched exactly, as far as Lincoln could tell, the Sphere wraith. Now, a flicker of a smile played across its lips. "Unless you drown me."

"I cut my medi-shop contract."

"And I don't have one. Well. You just might get away with it."

"I don't think you need to worry. You're just a pest, not a threat. What can I do for you? Asked, you understand, only to speed up the process of being rid of you."

"Understood. Your PADDs asked that I speak to you."

"Them again!"

"They have been with the Orion Project a long time. Based upon the DNA combos they donated, they assume you might have a hankering to join."

"All their combos have done is make me a crazy sensualist, seeking excitement, providing amusement for the masses while getting me Sundered."

"The mistake you're making, Mr. Jones," said Fortuna, pulling a foot up, then stepping down again carefully, in the process showing Lincoln he still wore his shoes, "is confusing physical stimuli with intellectual fulfillment. You are not entirely to blame, it is what you have been taught. Cradle education is biased toward the nonreality of the Sphere where nothing is out of reach. And what *is* in reach often isn't satisfying. You are aware of this without knowing why. So this leads you to sensory pursuits which you have found hollow because there's no informational underpinnings. The Great Barrier Reef, even what's left today, is a treasure of fascinating things, but you were not taught to seek those. So you were stuck with the merely physical."

Lincoln put his hands on his hips and regarded the dapper little man. "Hell of a speech to give someone standing up to his knees in water."

"We take what we can get."

"Isn't the Orion Foundation that bunch that wants to send a rocket into deep space or something?"

Instead of answering, Fortuna pulled out a flat, clear disk. "What I'd like you to do now, Mr. Jones, is play this. Would you mind attaching?"

"Ah, the sales pitch at last."

"In a manner of speaking. However, I'm not going to say much. I will let the images speak."

"What are they from?"

"The Smoot Deep Space Telescope."

"The three-thousand-meter monster mirror that got taken out by a meteor?"

Fortuna lifted one shoulder in sort of a half-shrug. "The Smoot Scope was destroyed by a rocket nose cone full of concrete sent on a deliberate collision course. The flexible mirror essentially wrapped around the object and was carried off. It's all still in a very eccentric elliptical orbit. No chance of saving it."

"Who would launch a rocket like that?"

"Some group or other during the Five Hundred Five Days' War. Many First World technical installations were targeted."

"Too bad."

"Yes, especially so soon after capturing these images. You're looking about eight hundred light-years away, a relatively isolated star toward Arcturus. We call the star Helios Prime." Fortuna held out the disk and link connectors. He looked at Lincoln, waited patiently.

"Oh, hell, all right. Anything to be rid of you."

What he saw, though, raised the hackles on the back of his neck.

"You did what?" Quasi dropped all pretenses to accents or culture in the outraged shout.

"I volunteered the Cradle for a star migration."

"You—y—you had no right to do that! Not without coming with us first—"

"How could I do that? I've been Sundered, remember?"

"Even more reason this is an outrage! You have no—damn!"

"Quasi, you're going to get us into trouble." Lashonde, the ID window said.

"He called me! To tell me about this brainless thing he did!"

"Interesting term, brainless."

Lashonde ignored the remark. "What did he do?"

"I volunteered the entire Cradle for a migration."

"A migration? Where?"

"To the stars. Or at least one—"

"Why?" Quasi again.

"Adventure. Challenge. A purpose beyond existence."

"That is the biggest load of zekecrement I've heard in a long time." Quasi's wraith exhibited every ounce of his disgust.

"No one in the Cradle is being forced to do anything. All I want you to do is look, discuss, then decide. Here's the basis for my action. Look at these images."

"From where?"

"The Orion Foundation—"

"Even worse. They've been talking about this for years. You can't expect us to fall in with them—"

Lashonde cut in. "What are we seeing?"

"A planetary system about eight hundred light-years away. Sun, six planets. Fourth one is Earthlike. Look in the space surrounding it."

Even though she was a wraith inside an artificial neuron network, Lincoln still heard the intake of breath.

"Are those—"

"Artificial constructions of some sort, space stations, perhaps. The resolution isn't enough to tell us exactly what they are or do, but they are there. And they are *huge*. Meaning a spacefaring intelligent race built them. That's the impetus of the Orion Project now, to send someone out there to meet them. Of course, what we're seeing is eight hundred years old, so there's no guarantee they're still there, or any of this still exists. But the stakes are too high not to go."

"Lincoln, they've been planning this for years," Quasi said in a calmer tone. "First they planned ten thousand ships, then five thousand, then a thousand, and now they're down to what?"

"One hundred thirty-six, a mere speck in space-time. The budget cuts parallel our fading visions and dreams. At first, they were going to send the thousands of ships in random directions, but the Smoot Scope discoveries have changed the destination of the remaining few. The entire fleet will go toward this system in the hope that one or two actually make it. We leave in another three standard months. We'll go as wraiths in offshoots of the TerraSphere because mind-wraiths are much easier to transport than flesh bodies. Each ship's Sphere will be just like the Mother Sphere until, if, we need corporeal bodies. We can drop into 'zekes grown in tanks and do what has to be done."

"Why?"

"Why? Why? You pinned it yourself, Quasi: It's the mind. Always the mind. The Sphere is a nursery, but now it's time to leave it. Lotus-Eaters: that's us, that's humanity now, comfortable in its electronic cocoon, existing for no other reason than to exist. Well, here's something new, something really challenging. Don't you see? Another civilization is out there. Someone else in the universe to say hello to, an answer to all the dreams mankind's had over the millennia. And we can go there! I *want* to go there. And I want all of my Cradlemates to go with me and share the adventure."

In the end, every one of them turned him down.

Benafar even called him crazy, a foreign concept for eighty-four years (he looked it up).

The decision devastated Lincoln. He sat on the hotel balcony, watching the Sun sink slowly into the Pacific, and although he tried to reject it, his mind wouldn't let go of the image that his hopes, his dreams, were going with it, drowning in a growing darkness. He was alone, now, too, like he'd never been before.

He took out the penny again, staring at it as it rested in the palm of his hand. Then he placed it on his thumb.

"Heads, I drown myself, tails I go to the stars."

The spinning coin buzzed as it shot up. It reached the top of the curve and began its downward trek. He caught it in his hand but didn't look at it. With his other hand, instead, he touched the linkvest controls.

"Lincoln?" Slaben had combed his hair, put on a red, collared shirt. "I thought this was an emergency. I was sort of meditating. I'm Crossing Over tomorrow."

"I know, Slaben, I'm Crossing myself in two days."

"Oh, yeah? Congratulations, I guess. What—"

"I want to meet with you Inside as soon as possible." He looked out the window where the Sun finally disappeared in a yellow-and-red glow. Then he hurled the penny out over the balcony railing. "I have a proposition for you."

THE CUTTING EDGE

by Janet Pack

Janet Pack lives in Williams Bay, Wisconsin, with three cats named Brika, Shannivere, and Syri. She works as the manager's assistant at Shadowlawn Pottery in Delavan, WI. She gives writing seminars, and speaks to schools and groups about reading and the writing profession. When not writing short stories and books, Janet sings classical, Renaissance, and medieval music. During leisure time she composes songs, reads, collects rocks, exercises, skis, and paddles her kayak on Lake Geneva.

The intense blue eyes of Dr. Gray Northman, administrator of the prestigious Mid-Atlantic Peace Hospital on Virginia's northeast coast, sought those of Dr. Ronald Jeffrey and held them prisoner. The newest member on the medical staff, Ron heard his pulse hammer excitedly in his ears while nerves left tiny cold footprints up and down his spine. Northman continued speaking to the hospital's key personnel.

"An alternative to our usual micro-laser surgery is available. In rare instances, we've already used molecule-sized machines to determine the kind and size of growths. This innovation will eventually make biopsies obsolete. It's time to take the next step. Dr. Jeffrey studied nanotech surgery with Dr. Sydney Frohmann, the recognized leader in the field until his recent untimely death. Yes, it's relatively new. Yes, it's untried on humans."

The administrator's celebrated penetrating stare left Ron and rested momentarily on each doctor seated around the wooden conference table. "We have to decide on something fast—that malignant tumor's growing so rapidly that in another twenty-four to forty-eight hours we'll lose Amelitia Rujillo."

"Impossible," snapped Dr. Gault, a large older woman of forbidding mien and the hospital's Head of Pediatrics. "We can't possibly approve that type of surgery on the first woman president of the Pan-American Economic Alliance. She's far too important." Her distaste for such radical techniques filled the hospital's conference room.

"We all know each other's capabilities, except those of Dr. Jeffrey." The lean administrator sat back in his chair, prepared to listen. "Tell us about Dr. Frohmann's discoveries in the field of nanotech, Dr. Jeffrey, specifically relating to surgery."

Ron inhaled the hospital's conditioned atmosphere, nearly choked on tension, and somehow forced his voice to respond. To his relief, it sounded almost normal.

"I worked for five years with Dr. Frohmann. It's too bad he died of a brain aneurysm three months ago. He should be telling you about this, not me."

"Wasn't there some speculation after his death

about Dr. Frohmann experimenting with his own research?" asked Dr. Kassarr, Chief of Oncology.

"That's true. If he did, though, he didn't do it in front of me." Jeffery responded. The success or failure of Dr. Frohmann's long years of research lay partly in his being able to persuade MAPH's leaders of the viability of his mentor's remarkable procedures and ignore the man's quirky, irascible, some would say downright wacky, personality. In the past, Ron had almost gotten used to explaining around that. He hadn't faced this situation for months now, and felt rusty remembering the best defenses and stratagems for diverting attention away from Dr. Frohmann's eccentricities and concentrating it on nanosurgery particulars. He straightened his backbone and plunged in.

"Nanosurgery is perfect for this case: minimally invasive, easily controllable, fast, and the machines go as shallow or as deep as we need them to. There's no cutting, no digging. No human fallibility in missing a chunk of malignant matter hidden by healthy tissue or a few cells buried among vigorous ones. Too, there's less chance a few cells might metastasize, cocooning themselves in an almost indestructible layer of protective matter, and wander into other regions of the body where they can begin growing. In that case, Ms. Rujillo would face a similar situation again in a few months or a few years. We need a technique that will thoroughly deal with her malignancy."

"Do we even know what these . . . these *things* are made of?" snapped Dr. Gault. "We can't go introducing foreign matter into Ms. Rujillo's system that might trigger reactions such as anaphylactic shock."

"These things are machines, Dr. Gault, and manufactured to be hypoallergenic. In fact, they've got a much lower allergen ratio than most serums and vaccines. Nanites are crystalline, essentially silicon, carefully layered together to produce a microscopic tool for a specific purpose. They're programmable, and have predetermined lifetimes. This makes them perfect for applications such as surgery."

"I knew that!" the pediatrician huffed.

As Ron warmed to the familiar subject, he no longer heeded the smoldering, curious, or downright unfriendly regards of the doctors surrounding the table. He reached forward to activate the keyboard of the tiny full-function computer he'd brought to the meeting.

"I'm downloading five years of studies to the hospital's main system, under the heading 'Nano Research.' Dr. Gault, I'll print a hard copy for you." Her snort told Ron his verbal arrow had hit the mark. It pulled a tiny half-smile of triumph to his lips as he savored a moment of satisfaction. The lion-maned physician was no friend to him, was in fact an enemy of most experimental procedures. She glared at him. Jeffrey forced her irritation to slide past his attention, and wondered briefly how Gault had ever gotten on the medical staff at MAPH, a hospital long known for innovations. The other doctors concentrated on reading from their own hand-sized computers, or ingested the information from small screens equipped with keyboards that popped out of the conference table for their convenience as Ron continued. "The results you see are from rats, dogs, cats, horses, cows, some monkeys, and a very limited number of apes."

"Didn't an organization stop Frohmann from experimenting on apes?" the dark voice of George Rikard Greene, Chief of Surgery, rumbled. "Think I remember that from some report."

"Yes, the Organization Against Cruelty to Sentient Animals got a Cease and Desist order signed against us. That's why results on primates in general halt abruptly in the studies. No matter that we sought subjects already suffering from diseases or tumors, then did exhaustive medical workups on them. Dr. Frohmann and I saved a number of apes from painful, wasting deaths with nanosurgery, but that didn't matter to OACSA. They were convinced we savaged the creatures from inside, or changed something within them for our own purposes, making them behave differently. They already owned the judge's ear and perhaps ruled his pocket by the time we filed protests. A court battle would have been lengthy and cost money Dr. Frohmann thought better put into research." The young doctor took a couple of breaths to cleanse the anger engendered by memories of that volatile time from his system before continuing.

"Nanosurgery is the only alternative in this situation, considering what we've just discussed about the patient having a tiny, deeply embedded, fast-growing malignant tumor where the base of the brain elongates into the spinal column. She's already lost part of her motor function rather suddenly, and, as Dr. Northman mentioned, will lose her life if something radical and quick isn't done. This is a serious matter and, as we all agree, requires immediate attention."

He used both his voice and his strong, steady hands to describe the process. "The nanites act as carriers and controllers for the actual workhorse, a carefully designed artificial virus. The machines surround the material they're programmed to find, forming an impermeable perimeter where the virus can go to work. Dr. Frohmann and I discovered that leaving a layer of dead cells between the tumor and virus enhances rather than impedes the destruction for some reason we never clearly understood, almost as if examples are shown to the living tumor. The machines direct the virus as far as solving problems, and the latter encapsulates the material of the tumor so no portion of it, especially a group of metastasized molecules, can wander into the bloodstream and eventually begin growing elsewhere.

"When the virus attacks the malignancy, apoptosis occurs, programmed cell death where the tumor material actually commits suicide at the behest of the virus and nanites. Necrotic—dead—material is then removed to the point of retraction, where the nano machines and their piggyback riders gather and are sucked back into a syringe, much the same way they were introduced into the subject's body. The molecule-sized bits of tumor can also exit naturally with other wastes, never leaving the company of the nanites and virus once the programming has been fulfilled. We monitor the machines by computer, making certain every one is out of the body one way or the other. Each is marked, so that's possible. Their paths are easy to follow."

Dr. Kassarr kept reading from his monitor while he spoke. "These machines can't lose their way and end up making trouble on a heart valve or in the brain, can they?"

Ron shook his tawny head. "No. We're talking machines the size of a molecule or even the size of an atom. In this instance, we can rely on the larger molecular size. As I said before, they have a carefully programmed life expectancy. And they only remove the tumor material they're programmed to recognize, remove it more thoroughly than any other type of surgery because they're working on a microscopic level. This technique is the least invasive of any currently available, and the easiest to recover from because there are no incisions, no sutures, no rehabilitation. Just rest and monitoring for the patient, encouraged by increasing levels of exercise as the body returns to normal, usually within a week to ten days." The young doctor sucked in another deep breath and steadied himself for the protests to come. "There are, however, several drawbacks which require consideration."

"I knew it," Dr. Greene growled. "It sounded too good to be true."

"Let's stop this nonsense now," demanded Dr. Gault. "Get her into surgery with Dr. Greene and his micro-laser while we've still got a few hours to spare."

The administrator tipped his graying head to the right. "Continue, Dr. Jeffrey."

Kassarr beat Ron to the point, his brown gaze friendly and understanding. "The mutation hazard is the biggest problem. Viruses used in medical applications can mutate at any moment, therefore losing the focus of its intended work and possibly becoming a threat in itself."

"Right," agreed Ron. "That's a little better controlled with the nanotech directing the virus, but the possibility still exists. Using a virus is one of the most unpredictable factors in this surgery. Another is the plasticity of the brain itself. This prohibits an absolute boundary the programmed machines can use as a marker to register how their work is progressing. There is also no way to say that the nanotech and accompanying virus thoroughly captures every little bit of the malignant material. The only thing I'm certain of is that this technique will destroy more of the tumor than even the steadiest hand wielding a micro-laser. That's not meant as a denigration of your talents, Dr. Greene."

"Thanks," replied the tall man with big hands who could perform wonders in tiny places partnered by the laser he'd designed. "Frankly, this isn't a surgery I looked forward to. Too risky for my technique. That's a bad area to work in." The grizzled head moved slowly in negation. "Rather leave it to someone else's hands, or machines, or whatever. Willing to assist, though." He shrugged off Dr. Gault's glare.

"What are the percentages of success?" requested

Jennilyn Smith, head of Obstetrics and Gynecology, in her peculiar soft voice.

"The lows are 89 to 92 percent," replied Jeffrey. "The best numbers we achieved were 98 percent of the tumor removed. That was figured by additional weight the extracted necrotic tumor added to the machines after Dr. Frohmann and I retracted them by syringe after the procedure.

"There are a couple of benefits I didn't mention. We never had a patient go into cardiac arrest during the operation because nanosurgery is much less stressful on the heart and lungs. Neither does the patient have to worry about the aftereffects of deep anesthesia required for most major surgeries—it only takes enough to keep them quiet. So there's little nausea, hardly any confusion, and almost no memory loss afterward. The patient actually wakes up feeling relatively normal."

"I'd vote for that," said Lianne Wages, Head of Anesthesiology. "Sounds good."

Silence reigned as the medical staff considered the options. With the exception of Dr. Gault, who pointedly stared out the window into the hospital's blooming exercise garden, the medical staff absorbed the information on their screens and highlighted bits for later study.

"We should vote whether to try nanosurgery or not," Dr. Northman stated a few moments later. "All in favor—"

"Just a moment," Dr. Gault snapped. The satisfied glint in her eyes gave Ron a jolt of concern. "Wasn't this Dr. Frohmann also known for his, ahem, oddities?

How do we know we can trust this study?" She dismissed it with a wave of her hand. "It might be just a fiction meant to waste our time and detract from the seriousness of the case at hand. I say we should ignore it, and use more traditional methods we understand, not some theoretical gibberish meant to confuse the issue."

Jeffrey was on his feet before he realized it. "Dr. Gault, that study is mine, too. I was with Dr. Frohmann every step of the way. His personal eccentricities have nothing to do with his genius. In fact, I programmed most of those nano surgeries myself. You're essentially calling me a liar."

The self-satisfied look on the Head of Pediatrics' face confirmed her feelings. Ron felt heat spread across his forehead.

"STOP THIS!" Dr. Northman shot a quelling glance around the table. "Calm down. Let's get back to the important subject—we have a dying patient who needs our undivided attention. Now, who's against Dr. Jeffrey using his skills in nanotech surgery?" Silence followed as a number of hands raised. The administrator counted silently. "Thank you. Those for?"

Predictable, thought Ron. The vote split almost exactly down the lines of those who followed traditional medical care versus the progressive thinkers. He was pleasantly surprised by Dr. Greene's support.

Gary Northman smiled thinly. "Tie. I guess that leaves the deciding vote to me." He weighed the pros and cons for another few seconds, looking hard at the table in front of him before voicing his decision. "This hospital has always been known for its innovative techniques, especially in surgery. We go out of our way to entice those who are best in their fields to work for Mid-Atlantic Peace. We need to think of continuing that reputation, as well as saving this patient's life in the quickest and best way possible for her and the Pan-American Economic Council." He looked up, eyes holding the flame of an old-fashioned preacher's zeal. "It is my belief that both patient and hospital will benefit from the introduction of nanites as a surgical technique. Therefore I'm for trying the new procedure. Dr. Jeffrey, how soon can you do surgery?"

"I—I've got five groups of machines ready to go. They're in storage not far from here, held in cold stasis by a technique Dr. Frohmann developed just before he died. I checked them last week, and they're still viable. The virus will probably take only four to six hours to culture properly—I have a computer parameter that can set up everything quickly as soon as the virus is introduced to the growth medium."

"Good of you ta make my job easier," drawled Cerissa Mathers, Chief Pathologist. "But everybody knows I culture the best viruses around."

"And I'll need someone to watch a second monitor in the operating room."

"I volunteer," Dr. Kassarr said quickly, rising and holding out a hand across the table to Ron. "I have to be there anyway, so I might as well get thoroughly involved. Especially if Dr. Greene backs me up."

The big surgeon agreed. "Definitely. I have to be there, too."

Realizing he'd won more than one friend in the last few minutes, Jeffrey shook the Middle Easterner's compact hand with warmth, then nodded to the Chiefs of Surgery and Pathology. "Thanks. It'll be good to have you helping."

Dr. Northman stood, closing the meeting, leaning weight on six fingers balanced at the edge of the table. "All right. Dr. Jeffrey, do whatever you need to do to get your patient into the operating room as soon as possible. Contact me every hour or so with your progress, and let me know when you're ready. I'll inform the patient myself and get the waivers changed and signed. We'll use the nanotech procedure as our primary attempt. If it doesn't work, Dr. Greene can move in with his micro-laser. Computer, file these proceedings into the permanent hospital record. Let's go, people. We've got cutting edge surgery to perform."

The hours following the meeting overflowed with details. Ron hurried back to his office, pulling a checklist he and Dr. Frohmann had used on apes from the depths of his computer's memory. "Didn't think I'd have to dig this out again so soon," he muttered, sinking down behind the worn desk and scanning familiar columns.

When Dr. Frohmann died so suddenly, Ron had considered his nanotech studies finished. Most hospitals still either didn't want to acknowledge the possibilities afforded by them, or considered manufacturing the tiny machines too expensive. He'd fostered a buried hope when he applied to join the staff of MAPH that its progressive leader would prove of different attitude. He had, in a relatively short time. Ron's excitement balanced his nerves.

Verbally, he made necessary changes describing a human patient, saved it at the top of his priorities, downloaded all the information Dr. Mathers needed to culture the virus into the hospital's lab computer, and expelled a long, gusty sigh. With one simple request for information followed by a surprising tie-breaking vote, Dr. Northman had catapulted his shelved nanotech studies back into the limelight as well as given him the chance to become famous almost overnight.

Ron stared at the pale cream-colored wall for a long moment. *If* everything went well. He didn't want to consider the kind of fame he'd have to live with if the virus mutated beyond control, if there was a glitch somewhere during programming the nanites, if the machines themselves hit a certain frequency of thermal oscillation and disintegrated into their component crystals, if the patient had a completely unexpected reaction and abruptly died. Despite the backups he himself was about to put into place as well as having excellent assistance from Drs. Greene, Kassarr, Mathers, and Wages at his shoulders the whole time, those thoughts made him pause.

But only for seconds. The crises he'd just imagined were nearly the same no matter who did surgery, no matter what technique they used. Only the details were different. Ron welcomed his fears and the adrenaline they provided, closed his small office door, and headed for the lab and a short, intense meeting with

Cerissa Mathers to give her instructions for the virus. Then he dashed for the parking lot and his air-cushion scooter, picked up the nanites in their special cooled storage container at his apartment, and raced back. The latter part of the journey was made noisy and exceptionally fast by a personal police escort ordered by Dr. Northman.

Once back inside Mid-Atlantic Peace, Jeffrey checked in with Dr. Mathers regarding progress with the virus, then with the administrator. "How's our patient?" he asked when Dr. Northman's face appeared in the tiny comm bracelet on his wrist.

"Barely stable," the hospital's business wizard replied. "I hate to rush you, but it's only a matter of time before she starts the downhill slide. She's on the brink now. Dr. Greene is checking on her every thirty minutes, and she's got a nurse at her bedside."

Ron estimated time. "We're approximately five hours away from completion of the virus. I just spoke with Dr. Mathers and she said everything's going fine. I'm beginning the programming of the 'nites in a few minutes. Barring problems, I should finish about the time the virus is complete. I'll integrate and program them in the lab before the operation."

"Good. I'll notify the surgical team, Dr. Greene, and Dr. Kassarr to stand ready in five and a half hours. You're scheduled for Operating Room One." He smiled thinly. "I'm sending lunch to your office via an aide. Otherwise you might forget to eat something before surgery. Luck to us all, Dr. Jeffrey. Out."

"Thanks." Ron smiled at the administrator's thoroughness as he slipped into his office and opened his computer. A few minutes later he heard a knock at the door.

"Lunch, Dr. Jeffrey," the petite dark-haired aide stated, shouldering in and setting the tray beside his elbow. "High protein, low fat, except for the dessert." She flashed him a grin before exiting. "I snitched you a piece of pecan pie and whipped cream before it was all gone."

"Hey, how'd you know that's my favorite?" he called.

"Magic," floated down the hall from the direction of the lift tube.

He felt as though magic had taken hold of his situation. He nibbled a piece of excellent roast turkey, then dug into the rest of the meal while setting up the programming for the tiny machines. Ron hadn't realized he was hungry. He finished it all, licking the last crumb of pecan pie off the end of his finger, and lost himself in the process of telling the nanites where to go and what to do.

Jeffrey jerked back into awareness when his wrist comm vibrated hours later. He activated it with a command word; Dr. Northman appeared. "We're an hour and a half away from surgery. Ms. Rujillo is no longer stable. Dr. Mathers says the virus is finished and waiting for you. How's the programming?"

"Almost done," he replied. "I'm running the test sequence now." He tapped a key and watched the screen. "Looks good. I'm on my way to the lab for the virus and to do the programming."

"All right. I'm ordering the surgical team in now. The patient will arrive at the operating room in half an hour. Think you can make that?"

"It'll be close, but yes."

"Good. See you there in thirty minutes."

What he didn't say—and didn't need to—was that the eyes of the world were now on MAPH. Ron sucked in a deep breath and let it out, finalized his programming and dumped it into the hospital's computer under his voice code. Closing his own machine and leaving it on his desk, he picked up the protective box holding the 'nites and headed for the lift tube.

Dr. Mathers met him at the lab door. "Don't mind tellin' you I think I've turned out another excellent virus, Jeffrey." She never used titles except in public.

"Thanks." He sat down in front of the lab computers and retrieved his programming. "Let's see how they go together." Ron hooked a special wire connector he and Dr. Frohmann had devised between the computer and the special box. "I'll program three batches just in case." He dumped the information, then nodded to Dr. Mathers and opened the carrier. "Ready." She injected each of the first three tubes with the virus. After waiting a few minutes, they checked samples under microscopes.

Jeffrey grinned with satisfaction and relief. "Perfect piggybacking." He activated his wrist comm as he rose. "Dr. Northman, I'm on my way."

"We're waiting for you, Doctor," the administrator replied. "Out."

Ops One bustled with doctors and nurses preparing

for major surgery. After exchanging his suit for a simple, loose antibacterial coverall, Ron completed the rest of the state-of-the-art decontamination procedures and approached the operating room with his precious box. He slipped a delicate transparent filament mask over his nose and mouth, conforming it to his face, confined his hair under a cap of the same material, and put on slightly-tinted gloves which in seconds hugged his fingers. He glimpsed the hard-set face of Dr. Gault in the viewing area as he pushed into the second chamber. Probably here to see me fail, he thought. With luck, that won't happen.

Amelitia Rujillo, a delicate-looking lady with silver hair in her late fifties, lay as if sleeping peacefully on the surgical table, a scan plate beneath her head to translate to computer screen the operations of the tiny machines. The Chief of Surgery's unique micro-laser was wheeled in and settled near the patient. Jeffrey conferred quickly with Drs. Greene and Kassarr about their duties watching the monitor and the molecule-sized machines. Settling down behind the secondary computer with the prominent surgeon at his shoulder, Dr. Kassarr nodded his readiness.

"Okay, folks, here we go." Hoping the trembling of his hands wouldn't impair his work, Jeffrey reached out for a syringe, loaded it from the first vial in the box, and injected the tiny machines into the patient's carotid artery.

The computer screens brightened suddenly with a swarm of blue dots concentrated to one side of the outline of the patient's neck as the nanites swirled in her bloodstream and became used to the sudden heat. Slowly at first, then in a rush, they surged toward the growth at the base of her brain on the current of Rujillo's lifeblood. First they scooted into smaller arteries, then into capillaries, from there easily crossing that permeable barrier to charge at the growth pulsing yellow on-screen.

An audible gasp came from the operating room team when the first few specks of blue attached themselves to the bilious surface. Ron let out a long breath, unaware he'd been holding it, eyes glued to the monitor and the battle now joined beyond his reach. The malignancy was only the size of a hazelnut kernel, but had demanded a critical toll of the systems controlling Rujillo's body. Silently, Jeffrey urged the little machines on.

"Will you look at that?" Dr. Greene leaned toward the screen he was watching with Dr. Kassarr as the first wave of microscopic machines fell away from the growth and the second took their places. A thin green line remained to mark the original circumference of the cancer, already a measurable difference. "They're just peelin' it right off."

Ron didn't know who started the applause, but it took over the operating theater before he could get it stopped. "Hold it, hold it," he snapped, voice cutting through the sound. "We've got a long way to go yet. Keep your focus." He checked the time by the wall clock. Fifteen minutes into the first surgery ever performed on a human by nanites.

The malignancy was now completely covered by

blue mites, with more on the way. The process increased in speed, the green line showing space clearly now between what had been the original outline of the growth and what remained. For Jeffrey time slowed, dripping like cold honey as his long years of research and struggle crystallized into success.

The growth spasmed as if fighting back, causing exclamations among the operating room personnel. Like a line of miniature bulldogs the tiny machines kept tight hold on their enemy, in control of the offense.

"Half gone," Dr. Kassarr murmured in an awed voice as more space showed clear between the green line and the existing tumor. "Already half gone."

"Anything can happen now," replied Ron tightly, his blue-gray gaze locked on the screen as the nanites with necrotic burdens began gathering to one side of the internal surgical field. "Stay alert."

"I wouldn't miss a second of this show for anythin'," muttered Dr. Greene. "Look at that!"

The tiny machines and their partner virus had reduced the malignancy to the point where it seemed to be dying twice as fast as before. And then suddenly everything stopped.

"What happened?" bellowed Dr. Greene, frowning at Ron.

"They've found something different," replied Jeffrey. "They'll check the programming to figure out what to do." Beyond sight of his colleagues, he crossed his fingers.

The nanites not involved with the main part of the

growth swirled around the upper end. Abruptly they began working, but in a different pattern than before.

Ron caught his breath. "It's a tendril."

"It worked itself deeper into her brain," Dr. Kassarr said. "None of us saw that. No wonder she lost her motor functions so quickly."

The tiny machines that had accomplished their task now outnumbered the ones working. Except for those extracting the tendril, most gathered in the upper right hand quadrant, awaiting the rest before they plunged back into the bloodstream and eventually congregated at the extraction site. There remained very little of the original malignancy to remove. Ron glanced at the clock. One hour into surgery. With micro-laser techniques, it would have taken several, perhaps all day.

A tiny motion on the screen caught his eye as the hum of excited conversation from the surgical team rose in the theater. A block of virus piggybacked on 'nites shuddered delicately. The motion passed from the first group, to another and another. The observant Dr. Kassarr looked up frowning from his monitor as Ron's flying fingers split his own screen and called up the programming.

"What's going on?" Kassarr asked. The staff hushed suddenly, making Ops One as silent as a tomb except for the sigh of the small pumps helping to regulate Ms. Rujillo's breathing.

"Virus mutation." Jeffrey scanned the lines of code, found the ones he wanted, and amended them.

"What're you going to do?" rumbled Dr. Greene.

"I'm sending in a second batch with stronger programming to take out the first. I've got to do this within minutes, or we'll have a massive viral infection to deal with as well as what's left of the tendril part of the tumor." Ron connected the special cable to the box protecting the nanites, administered the instructions, took out the vial, and accepted a sterile syringe from a nurse standing nearby. Jeffrey tapped the flat end to activate its automatic function: the syringe activated, sucking the nanites into the needle. Rising, crossing the short space between his monitor and the patient as quickly as he could, the doctor injected the micromachines a little closer to the tumor site than before.

The new batch glowed red as they surged into her bloodstream, through the capillaries, and to the site where the malignancy was now almost a memory. The vermilion spots ignored everything else, heading directly for the shuddering blue motes.

Some of the latter tried to escape, flying away from captivity. Others attacked, but the new infusion was too strong for the former. One by one, red superimposed the blue, creating an odd purple glow on the screen as the original nanites were overcome. A few reds waited for unmutated blues still working on the last of the tendril, restraining them as they surfaced from the tunnel the malignancy had pushed into the patient's brain.

"What's going on?" one of the nurses quavered.

"The second group of nanites and the new virus killed the mutating group. They've got the originals piggybacked, and will take them to the retraction site." Ron hoped his voice didn't sound as coiled-spring tight as he felt. "With a little luck, I can suck most of them out. That is, if nothing else happens."

Purple indicators streamed into capillaries and back into Amelitia's main bloodstream as the surgical team watched nervously. Their accumulation in a vein on the left side of her neck took an additional few minutes. Jeffrey signaled from his monitor when all but a few swirled in place. Dr. Kassarr stood ready with another syringe.

"Do it."

The swarthy doctor leaned over their patient, inserted the needle, hit the trigger for automatic suction, and watched as the void filled with dark blood. Ron assessed the numbers of the micro-machines as most of the purple vanished from his screen. "What have we got left inside?" he rasped.

"'Bout thirty, close as I can make it," Dr. Greene replied.

"Good. Dr. Wages, how's the patient?"

The primary anesthesiologist checked her readouts. "Blood pressure normal. Breathing with very little assistance. Still on a minimum of anesthetic. From here, she looks very good."

Jeffrey scrutinized the very few colored bits on his monitor. No yellow. No heaving viruses that meant mutation. A minimal number of nanites left in the patient's body—those would be escorted out by the leucocytes, white blood cells that cleansed the system. He heaved a big sigh. "Folks, I think we've done it."

A cheer rose. Someone pulled him to his feet, and a warm hand clasped his. "Dr. Jeffrey," Dr. Northman's voice sounded cool but friendly beneath the din. He was dressed in surgical attire, as if he'd been in the room during the entire procedure. Ron hadn't noticed. "Congratulations. How quickly can you write this up? I'd like to get it into the American Medical Association's *Journal* as soon as possible.

"And by the way, I appreciate your excellent performance under pressure. This was truly your trial by fire. How would you like to head the new nanotech surgical section, working with Dr. Greene and his staff?"

"I–I . . ." Ron couldn't get the words past his constricted throat.

The administrator smiled. "Get some rest first. We can discuss it tomorrow. Nine o'clock, my office." He raised his voice. "Good work, people. I'm going to release the particulars to the media in a few minutes, along with Dr. Jeffrey. In a few hours, I expect to announce a successful new surgical technique, another winner for humanity and Mid-Atlantic Peace—the first nanotech surgery performed on a human. We saved Amelitia Rujillo with microscopic machines!"

HOME WORLD

by Marc Bilgrey

Marc Bilgrey has written for television, magazines, and comedians. His short stories have appeared in numerous anthologies, including *Cat Crimes Through Time*, *Merlin*, and *Bruce Coville's Alien Visitors*.

I was out in one of the fields behind our house weeding tomatoes when I saw Emma walking toward me. The sun was setting and she was framed against a gorgeous purple-and-blue sky, just like the kind I used to remember seeing when I was a kid, back on Earth.

As Emma approached, I wiped my brow and stood up. She was wearing her dirty jeans, work shirt, and boots. She brushed some of her gray hair out of her eyes and smiled at me. "Hiya, Beautiful," I said. "What's going on?"

"Have you forgotten about the meeting in town tonight, James?" she said.

We hadn't been into town in months, not since we'd gone in to pick up some flour and salt. "Was that tonight?" I said. "I thought it was later in the week." After twenty-five years of marriage I had begun to accept the fact that Emma was more practical and always better informed than I was.

"We should leave in a few minutes," said Emma, "I don't want to be late."

"I still don't understand what the point of this meeting is," I said.

"You know exactly as much as I do."

"Why can't they just tell people what these things are all about? What's the big mystery?"

"Sam says he thinks it's about expanding the spaceport."

"When did you see our nosy neighbor?" I asked.

"This afternoon, and how can a man who lives ten miles away be nosy?"

"I don't know, but he manages."

We went into the house, and I put on my jacket. It was completely dark by the time we stepped out again, and the planet's twin orange moons hung motionless in the sky above us.

"When are we going to have dinner?" I said, as we got into our dusty aerocar.

"We'll have something when we get back," said Emma.

I closed the plexdome and turned on the engine. It sputtered to life, and then we lifted off into the air. We floated over the rock-strewn, barren landscape like a crin, one of the planet's few species of indigenous birds.

Soon we were flying over scattered farms, canyons, and tall mountain peaks. Eventually, the buildings of Zeta Town came into view below us. There were aerocars everywhere: in the air and on the ground.

"I haven't seen it this crowded since the harvest festival last year," I said.

"It looks even busier than that," responded Emma, as I set the aerocar down behind Al's General Store.

From there we got out and began walking on Main Street. There was something very comforting about its one- and two-story buildings and stone sidewalks, I thought. It reminded me of old, two-dimensional photographs I'd seen of Earth's American West, circa 1870.

By the time we reached the church a block away, we'd been jostled, pushed, and elbowed so many times I was starting to feel like this was Alpha Central Station, not the Zeta settlement.

Emma and I found seats in the back of the austere church as people filled every available pew and even lined up against the walls. The church was the only building in town made of real wood, specially brought from Earth on one of the first ships that had arrived on Zeta.

A few minutes went by and then Reverend Collins stepped up to the lectern and addressed the gathering. Though he was in his sixties now, he seemed much younger.

After welcoming everyone and making a joke about not seeing this many people on Sundays, he introduced a man, William Evans, who he said was with a company called Plan-Form, and that Mr. Evans had some things to say of interest to everyone. There was some polite applause as Evans stepped up to the podium.

Evans, who was dressed in a dark blue business

suit, looked out at the crowd. "I'll get right to the point," he said. "My company feels that the Zeta settlement has great potential as a center of commerce. It's for that reason that we've been quietly buying up land here, and, as of today, are proud to announce that we're the biggest real estate holder on the planet."

So far I didn't like what I was hearing at all. I glanced at Emma. She had a concerned expression on her face.

The speaker continued. "Up till now, the Zeta settlement has been a quiet, sleepy, little frontier planet at the edge of the known galaxy . . ."

"Tell me something I don't know," I muttered under my breath.

Emma looked at me and said, "Shhhhhhh."

The speaker smiled. It was one of those cold smiles, the kind you see on politicians who are running for office. "Plan-Form," he announced, "intends to bring prosperity to Zeta by attracting new residents with affordable housing. New businesses will come here because of tax and other incentive packages. And with new business will come jobs."

"What do *we* get?" yelled Dan White, a corn farmer.

"Plan-Form intends to expand the spaceport. Also, we will build a community center."

Our neighbor Sam stood up, turned to face the people, and said, "It seems that a lot of us here have been tricked into selling our land to this man without knowing what he intended to do with it. Well, now we know. We also know that this is no man. Don't be fooled by his looks. This is the devil. That's whom we've made a deal with. I never thought the day would come when I'd be listening to the devil in my very own church."

The crowd went wild with applause, cheers, cat calls, and boos. When everyone calmed down, Evans tried to recover. He spoke about progress, about the future and opportunity, but there wasn't anything he could say that would make Sam's words go away.

When he was done talking, a lot of people asked questions and there were a few more heated exchanges.

During the trip home, neither Emma nor I spoke. I looked out at the passing landscape I knew so well. The empty valleys and vast, expansive plains suddenly seemed to be sad places, like innocent mice about to be eaten by a hungry cobra.

As soon as Emma and I were in the house, I went out to the back porch. There, stretching in front of me for hundreds of miles were rock fields and craggy mountains behind them. Emma stepped onto the porch and stood next to me.

"It's even prettier than usual this evening," she remarked, looking out into the night.

"Maybe you'd better take a picture of it," I said, "it might not be here tomorrow."

"Let's not overreact, shall we?"

"We've just been told that everything we've worked for is about to be destroyed, and you think I'm overreacting?" I exclaimed, staring at the shadows in the distance.

"Is that what you got from this?"

"Was there another interpretation? We didn't come here twenty years ago to watch it be destroyed by some outsider."

"But he did say that they would be building things for the community."

"Sam was right. We've sold the Zeta settlement to the highest bidder. We came here to escape from so-called 'civilization.' We're one of the last frontier planets in the galaxy. We wanted a better life away from everything that is wrong with the populated worlds."

"I know why we came here, James. It's just been a very hard life, that's all."

I looked at Emma and saw that her gaze was directed out at the mountains. "What exactly are you saying, Emma?" I said.

"I'm saying that these last twenty years have been a struggle."

"Of course it's been a struggle, that's what pioneers do," I said, looking at her. "We knew that going in. But we've prospered. We're self-sufficient. We live off the land, we want for nothing. And now this man . . . this company is coming in."

"James . . . I want for something. I want things to be easier. I'd like to have some of the nicer things in life."

"What do you mean?" I said. "What do you want?"

"A new outfit, maybe sometimes."

"You make your own clothes."

"And what about the loneliness?" she said.

"I'm not lonely. We have each other."

"I wouldn't mind socializing more, that's all. A community center sounded . . ."

"I can't believe you. After all these years, Emma, I thought I knew you."

"You do know me," she said earnestly. "I guess I'm tired of living so isolated an existence. If there are going to be more people, maybe I could make some friends."

"Is that all it takes for you to give up everything, a stranger throwing around a little money?" I said, walking into our yard.

"That's not it at all," said Emma, following me. "Is it so wrong to embrace change?"

"Yes, if that change is bad." I turned to face her. "Zeta settlement is a world that functions the way it should. We have no crime, no poverty, no disease, no overcrowding. We live in virtually an Eden."

"If you can call this rock Eden, I guess anything's possible."

"I thought you liked our life here."

"I did."

"Past tense?"

"I liked it a lot better years ago when we were both younger," said Emma. "It just gets harder as time goes on."

"I don't think so," I said. "It's gotten better. We've become a part of this planet. I will not stand by and watch all that's wrong with the galaxy take up residence here. All the corrupt people, all the problems that plague everyplace else."

"What are you going to do about it?" Emma asked. "How can you prevent that from happening?"

"I don't think I can. I'm one man, they're a big corporation and have already presented Zeta with a fait accompli. But that doesn't mean I have to go along with it. There are other alternatives. Have you heard of the New Wyoming colony?"

"The one in the Epsilon system?"

"Yes, they're like what Zeta was fifty years ago. Why don't we go there?"

Emma stared at me and blinked. "You're not serious," she said.

"I've never been more serious in my life. It'll be a great adventure. Like when you and I started out. We'll leave with just the clothes on our backs. We'll begin all over again."

"I . . . I don't know how we could . . ."

"Oh, sure, it'll be hard, but isn't that what it's all about?"

"I don't think you've heard a word I've said."

"We'll build a new house," I said. "We'll be homesteaders, like we were here, but there won't be any corporations, no carpetbaggers. You know, after the Civil War on—"

"Just because I'm originally from the Mars colony doesn't mean I didn't study Earth history," she interrupted, frowning.

"We'll be free again, like we were."

"My answer is no," she said firmly.

"What?" I said, my eyes widening.

"I will not leave Zeta. I've worked too hard and you

have, too, to just throw it away and start over. No. I'm staying here. I would hope that I mean more to you than that."

"It's not about you, it's about them."

"Fine," she said, then turned around and walked into the house. The house that I'd built with my own two hands using scrap metal I'd begged, borrowed, or found. The four rooms I'd constructed had served as our home for twenty-two years. Heated and cooled by solar and wind power.

"There are things that are bigger than two people," I said, raising my voice, but if she heard me, she didn't respond.

I spent the next couple of hours walking around our ten acres of land, under the twin moons. I stared out at the valley and thought about how it would soon look. In my mind I saw the housing developments and cities of a dozen other worlds. Everything I'd spent a lifetime getting away from.

I thought about the speaker at the church, all smug in his expensive suit, preaching to a congregation powerless to do anything about it. I knew that soon there would be citizen committees formed, petitions drawn up and circulated, protest marches down Main Street, but in the end nothing would matter. Zeta was a planet with a big target on it, only there were no hostile aliens taking it over, just businessmen. Eventually the open spaces would vanish.

All I had to look forward to in my old age were memories of the lost wilderness. Stories to tell a generation yet unborn that wouldn't know or care about what had come before them.

When I finally wandered back to the house and into the bedroom, Emma was already asleep. I got into bed next to her. After a while, I closed my eyes and had dreams of running from land clearing machines that were trying to devour me in their massive metal jaws.

I got up early, and, without waking Emma, dressed, went out to the aerocar, got inside, and flew off into the sky.

It was a beautiful sunrise filled with red, yellow, and gold light. I sailed around the mountains for a while, then over ancient craters that had probably been made when the planet was new.

Eventually I landed at Sam Rand's place. He greeted me as I stepped out of the aerocar. He was dressed in his overalls and scuffed boots and was holding a pitchfork. There were more deep lines in his face than I'd remembered seeing before.

"Hey, James," he said, leaning the pitchfork against a fence, "bet I can guess what's on your mind."

"Same thing that's on yours," I said, as we walked up the road on his property.

"Doesn't seem a whole lot one can do."

"I'm going to New Wyoming in the Epsilon system," I said.

"The colony, eh? What's Emma say about it?"

"She doesn't like the idea."

"What are you going to do when you get there?"

"Stake a claim, begin all over. It'll be like it was here, before . . ."

"I see," he said, rubbing his chin. "And why are you telling me this?"

"Why don't you come with me? We'll do it together."

"Well, that's quite a thought," he said, smiling.

"Unless you liked what you heard at church yesterday . . ."

"You know I didn't," he said, "only I've put down roots, I've been here longer than you, James."

"I know. That's why I figured it's got to hurt real bad."

"That it does," he said, looking at the ground.

"You have nothing holding you here since—"

"Since Ruthie died, you mean? Yeah, well, I've got friends here, James. This place is in my blood."

"But Zeta is going to be destroyed," I said. "At least the Zeta you and I know. They're going to suck the life out of her. Rob it of its natural beauty. When they're done with it, it'll look like any stop on the space lanes. Like anyplace and no place."

"That's what I'm afraid of, yes, sir, but just pull up and leave? I don't know if I'm ready for that."

"Okay," I said, walking toward my aerocar. "I just thought I'd ask."

"Wait a minute, James," he said, catching up to me. "Would you go to New Wyoming without Emma?"

"I believe I would," I said, the thought being spoken for the first time.

"I guess once a frontiersman . . ."

"I see you understand," I said, then got into my aerocar, took off, and headed in the direction of town.

When I was high above the mountain peaks, I set the controls on auto and just coasted for a while. I half hoped for some revelation, an answer to my question, but nothing came. Instead, my thoughts drifted to Darr, a planet I'd visited when I was eighteen. I'd volunteered to be in the Galactic Help Core and that's where I'd been sent. Darr was a tropical planet with a preindustrial civilization. It was my (and my fellow volunteers') job to improve the natives' farming, well building, and their health and medical needs.

Whatever difference we created in their lives was short-lived. In only one year, I watched as outworlders discovered the planet, poached its animals, and depleted its natural resources. The only thing that had made any of it worthwhile was meeting Emma there.

She'd come three months after me, relieving an earlier group. The attraction had been immediate. Under a blazing hot sun, I recited poetry to her. We talked about philosophy, the future, and then love.

After we left the jungle world, we went in search of a life that meant something, that was worth living. Our quest led us to over a dozen planets and as many jobs. Satisfaction eluded us. Everyplace was too built up, too populated, or simply bereft of that undefinable quality we were seeking. Then we heard about Zeta. The moment we arrived, we knew we'd found what we'd been looking for. Zeta was a place where we could end our wandering and begin anew, together.

"Where've you been?" asked Emma, when I got home a few hours later.

"Thinking, mostly," I said, as I went into the bedroom, opened the closet, and took out a suitcase. I filled it with clothing and then closed it.

"W-what are you doing?" she asked, standing in the doorway.

"I'm leaving," I said calmly. "I'd like you to come with me."

"To New Wyoming?"

"That's right. I just went to the spaceport. In a couple of hours there's a transport leaving that's going as far as the Oceanius system. I reserved two seats for us. From there we can take a jumper that will get us to Marinia, which will—"

"I told you last night, I will not go to New Wyoming or anyplace else. I don't want to start over. I thought I made myself clear."

"You did, but I wanted to ask again," I said. "Well, in that case, I'll be going alone."

"I can't believe you would do this," said Emma, shaking her head.

I picked up my suitcase and went to the door. I kissed Emma as tears filled her eyes. "When I get established, I'll send for you," I said.

"You mean if you live long enough to get established," she retorted bitterly.

I left the house and got into the aerocar. As I took off, I saw Emma staring up at me, like a child watching a lost balloon.

The spaceport was only the size of two or three barns. I saw no one except a lone man behind a counter at the far end of the building. I went to one of the chairs in the middle of the room and sat down. I wondered how long Zeta's spaceport would be like this. One day soon it would be rebuilt, turned into a massive complex filled with throngs of people, restaurants and stores, like something in one of the middle star systems. The solitude felt strange. I realized that I wasn't used to being away from Emma.

Since getting married, we'd always been together. I tried to think of even a night we'd been apart—yet couldn't. I wanted to call her and somehow change her mind, but I knew better. When Emma made a decision, she stuck to it. She had often accused me of the same thing. Time passed slowly.

I began to think about what life on New Wyoming would be like. I knew it would be harsh, like it had been here. I wondered who my new neighbors would be. I tried to imagine the landscape. Would it look like Zeta?

Later, I looked out the picture window and saw a spaceship land. It was a couple of hundred feet long, circular with a triangular end. A more modern design than any I'd seen before. This was the ship that would take me on the first leg of my journey.

I thought about New Wyoming again. The days I would spend out in the fields, tilling the soil in the old-fashioned way and the nights in my new house. I thought about freedom, a new land, a new beginning, about living a dream.

A worker came over to me and said, "The transport for Oceanius is boarding now."

"Thanks," I said and stood up.

As I walked out of the building and onto the landing field, I replayed in my mind what I'd heard at church the night before. I questioned whether I hated the destruction of the wilderness and encroachment of civilization more than I loved Emma.

I stood on the landing field and looked at the spaceship. Little multicolored lights embedded in its side blinked on and off like a Christmas tree. I slowly turned around and began walking back to the spaceport.

I went through the building then exited out front and got into my aerocar. I lifted off the ground, turned the vehicle toward home and accelerated.

When I landed, Emma came running out to see me. As I stepped out of the aerocar, she said, "Your dinner's ready."

"How did you know?" I asked.

"I didn't know," she said. "I only hoped."

DREAMLIKE STATES

by Kristine Kathryn Rusch

In 1999, Kristine Kathryn Rusch won three Reader's Choice Awards for three different stories in three different magazines in two different genres: mystery and science fiction. That same year, her short fiction was nominated for the Hugo, Nebula, and Locus Awards. Since she had just returned to writing short fiction after quitting her short fiction editing job at *The Magazine of Fantasy and Science Fiction,* she was quite encouraged by this welcome back to writing. She never quit writing novels, and has sold more than forty-five of them, some under pseudonyms, in mystery, science fiction, fantasy, horror, and romance. Her most recent mystery novel is *Hitler's Angel.* Her most recent fantasy novel is *The Black Queen.*

When Carter Monroe was six, he and his twin brother Desmond had the same dream. They dreamed that they were alone in a large city. All of the other people had vanished—been taken Somewhere Else—by aliens, Carter thought, although Desmond believed they had been taken by God. The boys, left behind, took what they wanted from shops, ate out of cans, and tried to find a way to make the television station broadcast.

The boys awoke at separate times and did not discuss the dream with each other, although both told their mother. Forty years later, Carter could still remember the look on his mother's face when he started recounting the dream. Her narrow features moved to stark surprise, then to good-natured laughter.

"Don't play no more tricks like that on me, boys," she said, and nothing they could do ever convinced her that they hadn't made up the story to spook her.

But they hadn't.

And Carter saw that moment, that disbelief in something he truly knew had happened, as the beginning of his life's work.

Dream science had always been the most fascinating—and marginal—part of sleep science. By the time that Carter got his MD, at the turn of the century, anyone who went into the science of sleep with the idea of studying dreams was scrutinized more than any other sleep researcher.

Dream study was considered frivolous, a by-product of the more important research. Since most sleep research was funded by pharmaceutical companies, the bulk of the work focused on chemical ways to prevent narcolepsy, insomnia, and jet lag. Researchers who concentrated on the Rapid Eye Movement periods of sleep usually did so with other goals in mind—the ways that REM sleep affected the development of the brain; the brain's chemical mechanisms for preventing movement during REM; and the ways deep sleep differed from REM.

Most of this research involved studies of newborns and infants. Children under the age of two had much higher incidence of REM sleep—in fact, most of their sleep was REM—and they seemed to act out their dreams, a trait lost as the child gained the ability to move in the real world.

Carter found all of these facts fascinating, but as details, not as the central part of the study. Two of these details formed the foundation of his work. The first was the result of infant study: the fact that the brain waves of an infant in REM sleep hardly differed from his waking alpha waves. The second was a quote that appeared in the journal *Neuroscience* in 1992, the year that Carter decided he needed to specialize in three areas: psychology, neurology, and physics.

"Wakefulness," the researchers R. R. Llinás and D. Paré wrote, "is nothing other than a dreamlike state modulated by the constraints produced by specific sensory inputs."

Carter placed the quote on his wall, and within weeks had modified it to a simple line.

Wakefulness is a dreamlike state.

He knew that scientifically the difference between being awake and dreaming was that a person who was awake received input from his senses, and a person who was dreaming received input from his neurons.

Human beings, he knew, accepted information from the senses as real, and information from the neurons as not. But what if they were both real? What if the places people saw in their dreams were as real as the places people walked when they were awake? And was it possible to travel physically from one to the other?

Those were the questions he wanted answered, but he knew better than to pose them in any grant proposal or research paper he presented to private industry. He focused his public work on two different areas: helping schizophrenics through the use of drugs (he believed that schizophrenics "saw" their dreamworld while walking in the real world—again, an opinion he kept to himself) and finding ways to prevent sleepwalking (so that he could investigate why the infant acted out his dreams and the adult did not).

He also founded a sleep clinic for various sleeping disorders, but he made sure his researchers collected information on dreams for him. In the series of three hundred questions he asked of the sleep clinic's patients, the most important one was buried in the middle: *Have you ever, while asleep at the same time, shared a dream with someone else?*

To his surprise, over half the respondents said yes.

Forty years after Carter had shared a dream with his brother, he wanted to try again. Identical twins, he had learned were the best subjects for this type of research, and he was lucky enough to be one. Studies of twins had shown him that twenty percent of all twins had shared a dream, and eighty percent of all identical twins had shared more than one dream. Twins who had used psychotropic drugs, particularly LSD, had claimed to have the same trips, and identical twins tripping in the same room at the same time would have the same kind of trip, even if they didn't share the exact same images.

He had repeatedly gotten identical twins in his lab to share dreams but, as his research associates had pointed out, the lab was an artificial environment and the twins had more in common than any random two people placed in a lab. The associates pointed out that twins might simply have a propensity to share mental imagery. Put them in the same environment and give them the same stimuli, and twins might actually have the same dreams.

Carter thought the idea a stretch, but his research associates were adamant. He would not have good, publishable results until he got random people in separate rooms to dream the same dream.

He thought that was possible. He even thought he knew how to do it.

He had, over the years, combined his neurological knowledge, his psychological training, and his understanding of physics to make a working model of the dreamscape. Dreams, he had learned, followed a pattern. Each dream had its own logic, rather like each country in the world had its own culture. The logic was never violated.

Sometimes, however, one dream overlapped another, making the dreamlogic seem as if it had been violated when, in actuality, the dreamer had changed dreams—or locations.

Thinking of dreams as a wakefulness-like state— the inverse of the quote he'd had on his wall so long ago—made him apply different rules and regulations to it. Watching babies go through their REM sleep and moving with images only they could see made him realize that dreamlogic was an inherent part of being human, a part that humans, raised in Western European traditions were taught to deny.

He experimented with various things. Psychotropic drugs made the dreams more intense, but did not improve incidents of sharing. He tried Native American dreamwalking on his own time and found that while it was close, it wasn't quite what he was seeking.

What he was seeking was simple. He wanted a way to make the dreamer's world no longer private, the way the real world was never truly private. The true difference between wakefulness and dreams, he thought, wasn't the way that the brain reacted, but the way that others did.

If he shouted in a crowd of people when he was awake, they would hear him. The same would probably happen in a dream. The difference was that days later the crowd from his wakeful state would remember his shout, while the crowd from his dream (if he could find them at all) would claim they never heard him.

Dreams were solitary experiences; being awake was not.

He did not know if that was because the ability to share dreams became as frozen as the limbs did, or because dreams all took place in the head. What he really wished, and what he knew he could not do, was talk to the waking infants after their rambunctious dreams. Did they share the experience? Did newborns in a hos-

pital nursery all dream of the same landscape—with
each other in it? And then was that tendency to share
dreams denied so much as they got older that they forgot how to move fluidly through each other's dream
landscapes?

Did the importance of his forty-year-old memory
lie in the shared dream? Or in the relatively advanced
age at which he and his brother had that dream?

Or was the importance truly his mother's response—her laughter and her denial?

The older he got, the more he thought it was that
last.

Carter had three research assistants with impecca-
ble credentials and just enough courage to believe that
anything was worth one attempt. Two of these assistants—Shira Montgomery and Amos Kelly—had been
with him for years. The third—Glen Goodwin—had
been on his staff just six months, but had proved to
have an ability to see the corners of the world that no
one else was willing to admit existed. He asked them
to assist with his own private experiment, the one that
he hoped would lead him to greater things.

He asked them to watch as he tried to invade his
brother's dreams.

To set up the experiment, he agreed to abide by set
standards of behavior.

For six months, he did not contact his brother—a
wrenching, painful experience made worse by two
things: the first was that he and his brother hadn't been
out of touch for their entire lives; the second was that

he did not explain to his brother that he was severing ties. One day they were speaking, the next day they were not.

Carter then moved into the lab. He turned in his cell phone and his beeper and whenever he left the office, he was tailed by one of the three assistants, who made sure he did not contact his brother while away. He couldn't have contacted his brother in person, since Carter's lab was in Maryland and Desmond lived in Southern California. But the assistants guarded against the phone call, the chance meeting, the surprise visit. They also refused to put Desmond's increasingly baffled calls in to Carter.

Finally, on a day randomly chosen by his assistants, within no predetermined time perimeter, Carter had to submit to the sleeping portion of the experiment. He would sleep in the lab, use the control he had learned with all his experiments, and cross the boundaries of time and space to visit his brother.

He would pick a time in the evening when he assumed both he (on the East Coast) and his brother (on the West) would be asleep.

When he awakened, he would record the dream and its imagery, and he would remain in the lab. His assistants would then call his brother, ask him to report the dream he'd had the night before, and record the conversation.

It was an experiment that could only happen once, and it was one that would not hold up to scrutiny in any public paper or major research journal. But it would answer questions once and for all for Carter, and it would lead him to the next step in his publishable research—guiding others to shared dreams.

On August 24, 2016, at the behest of his three treasured assistants, Carter Monroe fell asleep in the experimental dream chamber of his lab. He found it easier to sleep than he had expected given his state of nervous excitement. But the room had been designed to encourage sleep—and to encourage sleep among the nervous.

The room was small and very dark. It was warm, but not hot. It smelled faintly of the ocean mixed with the crisp air of the mountains. The bed was soft, but not too soft, the sheets smooth, and the blankets thick and luxurious. A faint comforting sound, chosen by the sleeper (in Carter's case, he chose the sound of a babbling brook), eased him into sleep as gently as an infant being rocked by his mother.

Carter did not realize when he fell asleep, but he knew when he started to dream. And it was a familiar dream, the landscape he had seen often as a child—a gold-and-orange sunset on a perfect summer's day.

Much as he loved that dream, he did not want to stay there. He wanted to choose another, familiar landscape, the empty city he had once shared with Desmond, when the rest of the world had disappeared.

First, though, he had to get Desmond and that, he knew, was the trick of it all.

Trick. His mother's word. Was it a trick? Or was it something else? Carter pushed the thought away. He did not want to analyze while he was dreaming. He wanted simply to be.

He recognized this feeling from his dreamwalks, the feeling of being in control of himself in a landscape where the rules of physics—the ones his senses understood—did not always apply. He did not have to take an airplane or a car to his brother's house. One moment he was in his lab, the next he was standing beside his brother's bed, watching his brother sleep.

They had diverged over forty-six years. Different life experiences, different hopes, successes, and failures, had made them individuals instead of two forms of the same person. Still, his brother, curled in a fetal position, clutching his pillow beneath his head, looked so much like Carter himself that Carter was startled. Perhaps that was the dream image. Perhaps the brother he had not seen for nearly a year no longer looked just like him.

Perhaps.

The bedroom was stark. Just a bed and end tables, a lamp and an alarm clock. His brother—a geneticist with one of the major California private industries—had learned something from Carter's sleep research: always make sure your sleeping environment was used for sleep only.

Desmond slept alone, just as Carter did. Neither of them had married. Both, they liked to joke, had been married to their work. Their other, older siblings were married and had children. Carter and Desmond were nothing like them and never had been. They did not entirely understand the need for companionship, for a "real life." They thought there was more to living than the expected, and constantly sought it out, whatever it was.

Carter sat on the edge of the bed, and the mattress did not sink beneath his weight. He knew then that he was still in the world of dreams, where physics as he understood it, did not apply. He toyed with waking Desmond up, and then decided that would not work. The results his brother might report to his research assistants might be as vague as "I felt my brother's presence, and when I woke up, I thought I saw him for a moment. Then he was gone."

Instead, Carter used the skills he had learned dreamwalking. He remembered how it felt to be six—they had both lost their front teeth that summer. Little reedy boys who were growing out of their hand-me-downs so fast their mother had no idea what to do.

He shrank himself down to his six-year-old self, reached out, took Desmond's hand, and dragged him into the landscape they both had once shared.

The city was more desolate than Carter expected. It was a cinematic New York of the 1970s—no Trump Tower, no speed trains, a filthy, dirty, and empty Times Square. The buildings, which had seemed full of treasures to him as a child, seemed too dingy to hold promises now. They were dark and frightening, made more so by the lack of humanity around them.

Desmond stood beside him, adult and awake now, eyes blinking at the harsh artificial light from the ancient neon. "Carter?" he asked.

Carter nodded.

"What are we doing here?"

"Experimenting," Carter said, but his voice came

out petulant instead of excited, accentuated by the lisp caused by his missing teeth.

"I remember this place," Desmond said.

Carter watched him.

"I don't want to be here."

"We can try on clothes on Fifth Avenue," Carter said. "We can go to the television station and see if we can make it work."

But Desmond stood in the middle of Grand Central Station—how they got there, Carter did not know. It was not part of the original dream—and looked around him at the emptiness.

"Where did they all go?" Desmond asked. His voice echoed in the vast expanse.

Carter shrugged. "I suspect they were never here in the first place," he said. "This was our secret spot. We never invited anyone in."

Desmond looked down at him then. "Where have you been?"

"Working."

"I called you and called you and called you. Are you dead, Carter?"

"Of course not," Carter said. "If I were dead, you would know."

"If you're alive, why are you six?"

"I'm always six in this place."

Desmond held out his hands in a gesture of confusion. "But I'm not."

"That's because I brought you here," Carter said.

"I don't want to be here," Desmond said. "Let me go."

Even though his brother wore his adult form, he seemed diminished somehow, smaller than Carter had ever seen him.

"I thought this was our safe place," Carter said.

Desmond shook his head. "I never felt safe here. I was the one who was always trying to find a way out."

A newspaper blew past them through the canyons of Madison Avenue. The city had a stale odor, like that of an abandoned house that was filled with dust.

This place didn't feel safe to Carter either. Perhaps the safety he had once felt had not come from the place, but from the fact he had shared it with Desmond.

"Let me go," Desmond said, and Carter, unwilling to put his brother through any more anxiety, did.

Carter woke with a feeling of unease mixed with a sense of elation. He had to calm himself, reminding himself that he might have dreamed of Desmond because he had fallen asleep thinking of his brother. Carter was supposed to stay in the lab until someone let him out. Shira appeared and brought him breakfast, but would say nothing. On the tray was a hardcopy newspaper and an e-reader with no internet or e-mail capacity.

Those were there by his request, so that he would have something to do while they contacted his brother.

Amos said nothing when he brought lunch, and at dinnertime, Glen did not speak either. But he had worry lines on his forehead that had not been there the day before.

Carter was worried himself. He did not know if

spending another night in the room would be productive. He had assumed that his assistants would contact his brother that day. Another night might taint the experiment entirely.

Or might add.

After midnight, Carter fell asleep again. This time, he dreamed he was in the nightmare New York alone. He arrived in Grand Central and searched for Desmond until he remembered how to dreamwalk. He made his way to his brother's bedroom, but it was empty, the bed mussed, the pillow scrunched as it had been the night before.

He was about to walk through the rest of the house when someone shook him awake.

Shira.

He blinked at her face, uncertain whether or not he was still dreaming. Then he heard the babble of the preprogrammed brook, smelled the faint ocean air, felt the softness of the mattress beneath him, and recognized these as input from the senses.

The lights were coming up in the room. Her face became clearer: eyes red-rimmed, lips cracked and bleeding. She bit them when she was nervous.

"I'm sorry," she said.

And he recognized then what he had been feeling all day. "Desmond?"

He didn't need to make it a question. He already knew the answer.

"He's dead," she said. "We got one of his colleagues to let herself into his house. He died in his sleep."

Let me go, Desmond had said.

And Carter had.

He closed his eyes, but not to sleep. To shut out a world that was no longer safe. No longer comfortable.

A world in which he was entirely alone.

Desmond's death had its real world logic. He'd never had any friends. He had broken up with his last girlfriend two years earlier. Like Carter, he hadn't been in touch with his older siblings for more than a decade, and his parents were dead.

His only real contact outside of work had been Carter, and Carter had cut off all communications nearly a year before. The decline, Desmond's coworkers said, began then. It was not swift or sudden, but it was noticeable. His dark moods became darker, his emotions vacillating.

He complained of dreaming of empty places, places where he spent all of his time alone.

In the end, said the woman who found him, she hoped he had found a better place.

And when she had said that, Carter thought of sunsets on perfect summer evenings, and the kind of beauty a man could only see in his dreams.

The kind of beauty a man should have shared with someone else.

Someone he loved.

Later that month, Carter sold his lab to his three assistants. He went on a cruise to the South Pacific, a place where days felt like summer and sunsets were always perfect.

He now knew the answer to all his questions. The strictures on shared dreaming were cultural and learned and could be overcome, but at great cost. Just as babies needed an adult to feed and clothe and shelter them against the world, they also needed companions in their dreams to make that reality a safer place. But as they aged, the reality molded to the mind that was strongest, and that strong mind might not know what the other dreamer needed.

Even if the dreamers were close, even if they were twins, they might not have the same reaction to the same landscape. One might find it exhilarating, the other terrifying.

The dreaming world became private before it could become dangerous.

I never felt safe here, Desmond had said. *Let me go.*

Carter had let him go. In the physical world too early, and in the dream world too late.

Wakefulness was a dreamlike state, and Carter wished he could find a way to wake up.

THE LAST BASTION

by Lawrence Watt-Evans

Lawrence Watt-Evans is best known as an author of heroic fantasy, but he has always had a fondness for the darker side as well. He's published one horror novel, *The Nightmare People,* among his more than two dozen books. His works have appeared in *Robert Bloch's Psychos, Cemetery Dance, Ancient Enchantresses, Castle Fantastic, City Limits,* and elsewhere. He served as president of the Horror Writers Association from 1994 to 1996.

T wo human beings stood alone in the observation chamber, looking at projected images of the Milky Way Galaxy. On the central diagram a harsh, hostile orange tint stained most of the gigantic whirlpool of stars, leaving only a tiny sliver of friendly green, covering no more than a hundred stars, at one edge.

"There's nowhere else to go," Wang said, gesturing at the screen. "We stand or fall here."

"But there are millions of other galaxies out there!" Lee protested.

"Oh, of course there are," Wang agreed. "But we can't *get* to any of them. They're simply too far away to reach in a single lifetime. The best minds we have

have been studying the problem for centuries, and there's no way to exceed the fivespace constant."

"That's what they said about fourspace," Lee said, "but even if there isn't, or if we can't find it in time, why do we need to do it in a single lifetime?"

"You want to spend a thousand years in stasis, at the mercy of a bunch of self-maintaining machines? You have more faith in our technology than I do."

"I was thinking more along the lines of a multigenerational journey—boost an oneill or even a small planet into fivespace. It's just a matter of engineering . . ."

Wang shook his head. "We don't have the resources on hand," he said. "If our ancestors had given the matter some real thought, and started preparing, then yes, it could be done, but now it's too late. We don't have the energy sources we'd need to ramp an entire planet into fivespace, we don't have the resources to keep an astellar ecology stable for a journey that long—remember how dark and empty it is in intergalactic space! Not enough light to power anything important, not enough matter to collect for anything."

"You've run the numbers?"

"Of course. To see our descendants safely to M31 would require everything we have, and would have a safety margin so small the odds of completing the journey are fifteen to one against." He sighed. "And just in case, I checked my conclusions with the top theoreticians among the other groups. They all confirm my figures."

Lee grimaced at the mention of the other surviving

individual-human factions; her own clan was Purist, and had always opposed any cooperation with cyborgs and genengineers. Events had forced the alliance when she was still a child, despite its unpopularity, but she had never entirely reconciled herself to it. The others weren't really *human* anymore, by her standards.

But they were still close. They were still individuals, still had human concerns. And they had joined the naturals in fleeing here, to the edge of the galaxy.

The cooperation was so complete now that the galactic map didn't even show the three factions as separate territories; all their systems were shared.

They had all fought so long and so hard to maintain their individuality—and now Wang, the coordinator for their defense, said the fight was over.

"There must be *some* way," she said.

"I've told you my proposed solution."

"I'd rather try that thousand-year stasis. The odds sound better."

Wang sighed. "We don't know the odds on negotiating; nobody's tried it in millennia. The Link may have changed. It's got the rest of the galaxy; why should it insist on taking our pitiful handful of systems?"

"Because that's what it *does,* Wang!" Lee said. "It's *hungry.* It wants data and energy and matter, as much as it can get. It's pursued humanity everywhere we've gone, trying to absorb us."

"The old stories say that it thinks it's doing people a favor by assimilating them," Wang said. "It thinks it's doing it for our own good."

"That's what it *says*. I don't believe it."

"Oh, I think it's sincere, even if I don't want to be assimilated any more than you do."

Lee looked very doubtful indeed, but didn't argue further. Instead she asked, "Have you spoken to the others?"

Wang nodded. "I left your clan until last—I knew you'd be the hardest to convince."

"They've all agreed?"

"Yes. Some of them imposed conditions, but they've agreed."

"They're all ready to surrender?"

"It's not a *surrender,*" Wang insisted. "It's a negotiation."

"It's offering to stay on the reservation," Lee said. "It's offering to become its pets, a bunch of animals in a zoo, a museum exhibit. *I* call that a surrender."

"A surrender would be letting the Link assimilate us," Wang said. "I won't do that."

"You may not have a choice."

With that, Lee turned and stalked away, toward the lift.

Wang watched her go. He understood her feelings, but he also understood reality.

He looked up at the galactic map. That sliver of green was so tiny, the orange smear so vast. . . .

"I still can't believe they agreed to talk this way," Lee said as she watched the ship descend smoothly, sliding gracefully down through the cloudless blue sky. "I thought the Link never let any of its units detach for even an instant!"

"I told you they would be reasonable," Shmit said.

Lee grimaced at the unnaturally musical sound of the cyborg's electronically enhanced voice and fought back a bitter remark. The Link had been *created* by cyborgs, thousands of years ago. Of course Shmit would be more tolerant of the Link than it deserved.

And Lee didn't want to listen to any machine man telling her "I told you so."

The ship settled gently onto the pavement, and Wang and the others started forward. Before they had covered half the distance an opening appeared in the ship's side and a figure emerged.

It *looked* human enough, but Lee knew better. Reluctantly, she began walking closer, but she didn't hurry; let the others get the preliminaries out of the way, she thought. The less time she spent close to the Link representative, the better, so far as she was concerned.

The representatives wore a smooth, formfitting red garment that made it plain the creature was neither male nor female; its skin was a lovely golden brown, its black hair trimmed short. It was inhumanly sleek and beautiful—but it moved awkwardly, unevenly, as it stumbled down the ramp the ship had extruded.

"Welcome to Refuge," Wang began when his party and the Link representative were a couple of meters apart.

The representative held up a hand signaling for him

to wait, staggered, then straightened up. It took a deep breath, let it out, and then spoke.

"I'm sorry," it said. Its voice, as lovely as Shmit's, was unsteady. It cleared its throat and added, "This is *hard* for us—for me. Give me a moment."

"We appreciate your willingness to meet with us under these conditions," Wang said.

"It's important," the representative said. "We know that, so we'll try to cooperate. You've all had years of practice being unlinked; but it's new for us. For me."

"I understand," Wang said, though Lee doubted that he actually did. The cyborgs, with their implants and gadgets, might have some idea what it would be like for a single unit of the Link to be detached and forced to operate independently, but a natural human like Wang—or Lee—could have only the vaguest understanding of the experience.

The representative took another deep breath, then stood up straight and recited, "You understand that as a single individual, I cannot make a final decision for the entire Link if you present me with an option we had not previously considered?"

"Of course," Wang said. "We wish to make our proposals, discuss options, then send you back so that the Link can think the situation over."

"Good. That's what we want, too. What *I* want."

Lee had now joined the group, and got a good look at the representative. Up close it looked considerably less human—wiring was visible along its fingers and neck, there were slits that Lee thought might be gills, and some of the black fibers on its head, clearly not human hairs, moved independently. Its eyes had tiny insets that Lee guessed were added sensory equipment, and the gleaming blue biting surfaces in its mouth were definitely not teeth.

Some of its distant ancestors had been human, but it was not.

"Shall we go inside, where we can sit down?" Wang suggested.

"That would be good."

A few moments later the entire party was gathered around a conference table. Wang had offered to wait until the representative had rested and adjusted to the local climate, but the representative had declined the offer.

"The sooner I get this done and can rejoin myself, the better," it explained. "You have no idea how uncomfortable this is for me. It's like being blind and alone."

"You aren't alone," Wang said. "We're here."

The representative didn't answer, but simply stared at him in astonished disgust.

"It's not the same, I'm sure," Lee said. "Now, can we get down to business? I'm not that much more comfortable than our guest is." She gestured at the others gathered around the table.

They were all individuals, not part of any hivemind Link, and they were all of human ancestry, but Lee was the only Purist. Wang, Mez, and Kita were fellow naturals, their flesh unpolluted with machinery, their genes perhaps cleaned a little but still entirely human.

But Shmit, Maet, and Das were cyborgs, with metal

and plastic built into them. Llur, Saffa, Berene, and Tiril were genens, their genes modified at their ancestors' whims, and each had visible features—skin, eyes, hair—that had never evolved on Earth.

And Ashi and Ho were both genetically engineered *and* cyborged.

A hundred years ago, this gathering could never have happened. The human factions had kept themselves separate. Pressure from the Link had driven them to this mixing, which Lee could only see as pollution.

Wang stood up. "We all know the situation," he said. "The Link wants the entire galaxy, and we prefer to remain as we are, independent individuals not part of a network, free to arrange our societies as we choose. Up until now the Link has pretty much expanded as it pleased, driving us into a smaller and smaller volume of the galaxy, and we've reached a point where we can retreat no farther. Rather than simply give in, though, we've asked you to come here to give us a chance to convince the Link *not* to assimilate our paltry handful of worlds. We asked you to come here as an individual, not part of the Link, partly because of our distrust of you and our fear that if the Link were permitted the tiniest access to Refuge that the entire planet would be absorbed into the system before we could do anything to prevent it, but also—and this part you may not have realized—because we wanted to remind you what it's like to be an individual human being. We think it's a very special experience, one that the Link tends to forget or underrate, and we don't want to see it eliminated from the galaxy. Surely, the Link can see some value in maintaining the few of us here, as a possible resource, a source of diversity?"

The representative stared silently at Wang for a moment, then said, "There's so *much* you don't understand."

"I'm sure you're right, that we don't appreciate how much better and happier we would be as part of the Link, but nonetheless, we want . . ."

"No, no, *no*," the representative interrupted. "That's not what we . . . what I mean at all."

Wang blinked.

"What *do* you mean, then?" Llur sang.

"We need these systems," the Link representative said. "We need them urgently. We don't want to harm you, though—we understand you better than you might think. What we propose to do is to pay you for them."

"What good is *payment* if you're going to absorb our entire world?" Kita demanded, before Lee could say anything.

"It depends what form the payment takes, doesn't it?" the representative asked, lisping slightly. "We propose to pay you with the resources of several star systems, including technology we don't believe you have, that will permit you to launch two or three planets into fivespace, bound for whatever destination you choose."

"You want us out of your galaxy entirely, is that it?" Lee demanded, rising angrily to her feet. "Damn it, you monster, it's *our* galaxy, too!"

"Not anymore," the Link representative said. "Individual consciousness has been driven into this tiny fringe; wouldn't you rather have an entire new galaxy?"

Several voices spoke at once, growing louder as they tried to assert themselves, and in a moment everyone was shouting. Wang held up his hands for order, and eventually silence returned.

"You said you *need* our systems," he said. "For more space? What will you do then, when you've filled it? Follow us to M31?"

"There are millions of galaxies," the representative said, which Lee found an eerie echo of her own words of just a few days before. "You take one, we'll take another."

"Will just one more be enough?" Kita asked sarcastically. "If *this* one isn't big enough for you—"

"We won't have this one much longer," the representative said.

A stunned silence fell.

"Why *not?*" Lee asked at last.

The representative struggled to find the words it needed. At last it said, "There was an experiment. An accident. A few centuries ago. The Link was attempting an upgrade, and the test portion became something else. We call it the Oneness." It pulled a display chit from its pocket and tapped a command; a galactic map appeared in the air above the conference table.

"Here are your stars," the representative said, and a familiar sliver turned yellow. "Here are ours," and a broad expanse of blue covered perhaps a third of the galaxy—but only a third, a huge crescent around one side of the galactic disk, the yellow sliver a patch on its outer edge.

"This is the Oneness," the representative continued, and a great broad ring of red appeared, nested against the blue crescent and centered on the old Sagittarian sector. "And this last portion," it said, as the white patch in the middle of the ring turned orange, "we call the Transcendence."

"The *what?*"

"The Transcendence." The representative sighed, and explained, "the Oneness experimented, as well. The Transcendence came into existence about a century ago."

"What do these names *mean?*" Shmit demanded. "Aren't they just Links that for some reason separated from yours?"

The representative shook its head. "No," it said. "The Link is a group mind. Each of its constituent parts is linked to the whole, but we are still separate minds, even if we aren't individuals by your standards. We share data and sensation and memory, and a given consciousness may not be attached to a specific body, but there are still multiple consciousnesses in the Link, even if the boundaries between them are weak and variable. A fivespace datalink is fast, but it's not instantaneous. We can't maintain a true single consciousness across interstellar distances.

"But the Oneness *can.* We don't know how; we don't understand it. It's as alien to us as we are to you. I was able to detach myself from the Link and come here to talk to you; I don't think a constituent body of the Oneness could do that, any more than you could take off one of your fingers and send it to do an errand. And the portions of the Link that have tried to communicate with it have been absorbed into it."

Lee looked around the table at the faces of the others, and could see that they were all thinking the same thing she was—that the Link was getting a demo of its own programming.

"And the Transcendence?" Wang asked.

"The step beyond the Oneness," the representative explained. "We *really* don't understand that one. It seems to be something that combines space, time, and consciousness into a single entity—and it's the only thing that scares the Oneness, which means it *terrifies* us."

"Wheels within wheels," Lee said, looking at the galactic map.

"So this Oneness is taking the galaxy away from you?" Shmit asked.

"Gradually, yes. And the Transcendence is then taking territory from the Oneness. Waves of expansion, spreading outward—a very, very old story."

"So you intend to push us out of the galaxy entirely to buy yourselves a little more breathing space," Kita said.

"More than that, we hope," the representative said. "It's not your *space* we need—it's your *worlds*. It's mass, in big convenient chunks."

"You have half a galaxy!" Wang protested. "What do you need with a few hundred rocks?"

"You haven't been listening," the representative said. "We *don't* have half a galaxy, not for long. We need to get out of here while we still can."

"I don't understand," Lee said.

The representative looked about as if seeking inspiration, then said, "It's a long way between galaxies. You couldn't make the jump without us because you don't have enough energy, enough technology, to ramp entire planets into fivespace before we overrun your territory, and nothing less than a planet can safely sustain your civilization for so long a journey. Well, we have the same problem many times over. We are the Link—we are all joined into our single community by fivespace datalinks, and without that connection we're nothing—or at least, we aren't what we want to preserve. And a fivespace datalink can't function over intergalactic distances."

"So you'll send a community to another galaxy, and build a new Link there," Kita began.

"No!" the representative protested. "No! We don't want another Link; we want *our* Link, our life. It's the difference between sending your children to safety and saving yourself—we'll settle for creating a new Link if it's the best we can do, but we want to *live,* not die. We want to stay Linked."

"Well, how can you . . ." Shmit began.

"A bridge," the representative said. "A bridge of planets, spaced at distances that allow proper Linkage, stretching out from this galaxy to another. And when it's complete, we'll transfer whatever is left in this galaxy to the other. It'll take thousands of years, of course, but we can handle that."

The sheer audacity of the concept left the humans stunned.

At last, Lee spoke up.

"You have millions of planets already," she said. "You don't need to buy ours."

"It's a long, long way to the next galaxy," the representative said. "And we're steadily losing planets to the Oneness. Even a few hundred could make the difference between success and failure."

"It's more than that," Lee said.

"Of course it is," the representative said. "Believe it or not, we *like* you. You're family."

"The idiot cousin," Kita suggested.

The representative flushed. "Well, yes," it admitted. "Or maybe the dotty old uncle would be a closer comparison. We'd like to see you have a chance at survival, and we really don't want to fight you on one side and the Oneness on the other if things turn nasty."

"And we're your test pilots, aren't we?" Lee asked. "To see if there are any unforeseen problems in ramping planets into fivespace and sending them out between galaxies."

"That, too," the representative admitted. "We don't want to risk detaching an entire inhabited planet from the Link."

Lee nodded thoughtfully. "I like it," she said. "On behalf of the Purists, I vote to accept the Link's offer."

Several of the others stared at her in astonishment.

Clearly, they had expected the Purists to put up unreasoning resistance to anything so radical.

"A bridge between galaxies," Lee said, musing aloud. "That's quite a proposal. I wish you luck with it, so long as it's not *our* galaxy you aim it at."

"Thank you," the representative said.

Lee smiled. "There's one thing that puzzles me," she said.

"Oh?"

"I wonder what method the Oneness will use to reach a new galaxy, when it flees from the Transcendence?"

FORGOTTEN

by Peter Schweighofer

Peter Schweighofer lives in Williamsburg, Virginia, where he works at the Omohundro Institute of Early American History and Culture and continues his free-lance writing and editing projects. He's written material for the *Star Wars* roleplaying game, published several science fiction and historical fantasy stories, edited two *Star Wars* anthologies, and reported for a newspaper in Connecticut.

Grampa gazed past the platform railing, watching the gas giant's clouds towering in the afternoon sunlight. The plumes formed animals, colors, fuzzy words, and fantasy landscapes. He saw the faces of friends long gone whose names and memories had passed into the shadows enshrouding his mind. The vapors often turned back into the bodies of children, dogs, starships, and plants, all playing effortlessly and free in the sky, waving to Grampa, inviting him to join their adventures. He strained to raise his hand and tried waving back.

Someone asked if he was okay out here in the sun, or would he rather go under the veranda for some shade?

He turned to see Sharon, the young friend who took

care of him. She wore a pastel-colored uniform dress—Grampa had long forgotten exactly what the color was called, and had no idea what profession wore such a uniform.

"I'm looking for the companionway ladder to my quarters," he replied. "I couldn't find the command deck or the engineering bay. Is it this way?" He pointed over the balcony at the whispering clouds.

Sonya turned his glide chair away from the railing and back toward the platform. He watched others like him wandering the quaint gardens, patios, and lawns. Some huddled around the fountain, splashing their frail hands in the liquid. Everyone mumbled quietly to themselves like those bubbling waters. Sanitary white building with arches and tall windows rose in the distance. Anyone with half their brain intact would have found the environment similar to some pleasant alpine resort. But those people left here were lucky to possess even half their minds.

Years ago Grampa would have known this platform served as a medical holding facility, an idyllic paradise floating in orbit through the gas giant's habitable stratosphere. Sometimes the trees, flower beds, buildings, and people turned into piles of trash in his mind, a junkyard where folks dumped their debilitating elders. With science focusing on space travel, colonization, and warfare, nobody cared about medical research to improve hopeless human conditions. Here they lived out their remaining days, months, sometimes years, in a miasma of fused memories and blurred images.

Sondra pushed his glide chair past trimmed hedges and onto a shaded veranda. She smiled at him and brushed the hair from his face. He settled his chin into his hands like some pampered but aging dog too old to bound carefree across the lawn. Grampa heard her say how much more comfortable he'd be spending the afternoon here.

She was Grampa's friend, some might say his assistant or nurse. He wasn't quite sure if her name was Sandra, Sonya, or Shannon. One day part of his mind returned, insisting she looked like a friend from his teenage years named Jenny. Grampa decided to call her Jenny as a nickname, entertaining Sondra with a story about his boyhood infatuation with the girl. Then that part of his brain went off-line again, and he was stuck with the impression that her name really was Jenny. Or Sandy.

Grampa liked to think Sharon had a crush on him, too, and that's why she spent so much time making sure he was okay.

She sat next to his glide chair and watched the sun playing off the clouds. Grampa wanted to leave the chair and go touch the light, frolicking with the friendly children and dogs it formed in the distant stratosphere. But he couldn't walk on his own anymore—he couldn't do much of anything without Sandra's help.

Bits of his consciousness and memory kept blinking in and out, some gone for weeks on end, most gone forever. He frequently stared at his bed, wondering what it was for. Grampa forgot how the sky worked and how music smelled. He worried he was speaking some foreign language, like Swahili, blue, or enemy. He might spend all afternoon on the veranda, but would still become frightfully lost in the labyrinth of his mind.

It was a sad fact of life—a fading brain, a body degrading with old age, never to recover. Grampa felt like he waited on a wounded starship. His adversaries had destroyed the engines, and the cruiser drifted aimlessly through space. The atmosphere leaked out very slowly. It was only a matter of time until death. Not that Grampa could recall how time functioned anymore. Sometimes he became angry, running alone through the vessel's corridors, throwing his tools at blown capacitors, molten coupling boxes, and dead power conduits. "Darn these old parts," he'd shout. "The captain should have ordered them replaced long ago." At about that time Jenny would find him and calm him down. Her soft words and a gentle hand on his shoulder eased him into a resigned melancholy, knowing he couldn't fix anything. Grampa slumped back into his glide chair and sadly surveyed his derelict cruiser.

He gazed at the grounds and the people staggering aimlessly through them. Some used glide chairs like him, others pulled themselves along on crutches. A few shuffled along, fortunate to cling to some dignity of independence. The inmates wandered into flower beds, embraced bushes, argued with trees, and asked the fountain for directions. They all wore concerned expressions, like they were looking for something they'd lost, but seeing only the emptiness of their minds. Many searched their flimsy gowns for pockets, hoping to find a watch, some change, or their ticket to the starship away from here.

One woman tottered up to the railing where he'd spent the afternoon watching the clouds play. Her brittle body leaned over and she peered into the dark vapors below. Grampa often saw people looking into the distance there. Maybe they thought it was some ocean, their favorite restaurant, or the way back to their quarters. The woman clawed at the railing, scraped her feet on it, slowly pulling herself over. No attendant rushed to stop her, and only a handful of other patients watched her, muttering insanities to themselves. After a moment her body toppled over the edge and fell into the gaseous plumes below.

Grampa wanted to ask Sharon what happened to the woman, but the words passing his lips made no sense. "Can you help me find the ladder to my cabin? I'm lost in these passageways." When he looked at her face, he saw a tear rolling down her cheek.

He frequently wandered the gardens looking for the companionway ladder to his quarter. Not that he could have climbed it, but he would bridge that gap when he came to it. Grampa's search often brought him to the railing, where he'd sit for hours watching the clouds. Sometimes he found Jenny sitting alone on a nearby bench, taking one of her breaks. Even his blurred senses could tell she wept softly to herself. He moved closer to comfort her, tell her everything would be okay, but it came out all wrong. "What do they see?" he asked, pointing at the edge. "I want to see, too."

She dabbed her moist cheeks with a handkerchief, moved Grampa's glide chair closer, then helped him out and up to lean on the railing. He peered over the edge into a storm far below, its festering red-and-orange clouds fascinating his simple mind, calling to him. The vapors and lightning surged in waves of emotion: love and hate, happy and sad, ugliness and enchantment. The colors and lights filled him with wonder and fear, seducing his heart and rejecting his body.

When the electrical discharges flashed orange, Grampa thought he saw people down there dancing in the storm—among them all those wretched souls who'd jumped. He once knew all about gas giants, atmospheres, space travel and propulsion drives. Grampa imagined the pressure crushing their bodies, lightning blasting them to pieces, and gales blowing the bits to all points of infinity. But then all that faded into some dislodged part of his brain. He only remembered Jenny holding his hand while it trembled with excitement.

He'd prop himself up there as long as his weary arms could manage, staring into the tempest far below. When his strength finally failed, Sharon helped him slump back into his glide chair. Grampa looked longingly at the clouds. "Can I play, too?" he asked.

At that point Sandra always turned his chair away and guided him back toward the gardens. "I'm looking for the ladder to my cabin," he'd mutter. "Please help me find it." Grampa couldn't see her behind him, but he heard her sniffing, like she was sick with a runny nose. Sharon put a gentle hand on his shoulder, whispering that there was no ladder, but she'd take him back to his room anyway.

Grampa's mind turned the trip through the landscaped grounds into a shopping excursion to buy Jenny a new dress for some holiday—exactly which celebration he couldn't recall.

The despondent patients around him transformed into vibrant young shoppers purchasing gifts for their loved ones. A passing nurse looked like an attentive sales girl. Trees and bushes became clothing racks displaying party dresses, evening gowns, even those frilly skirts designed to float seductively in zero-gee. He reached out and ran his hand through one shrub's leaves, feeling the shimmering silk of the dress, glancing at the price marker. Grampa fumbled through his shabby gown, looking for his ident card and finding only a tuft of lint. He handed it to the tolerant sales girl. "I'll take this one," he told her.

When Sharon helped him back into his bed, he smiled at her. "I bought a new dress for you," he said. "I had it gift-wrapped and delivered to your apartment. I hope you like the flowers, too." Shannon patted his head and thanked him. Before leaving, she wiped away the tear rolling down her face.

Grampa felt most helpless in that nest of sheets, blankets, and puffy things synthetically soft to the touch. Sondra often fluffed them, but they never offered quite enough comfort as he liked. From his window he could look out at the clouds, but he felt isolated from them. He couldn't touch them in here. The sun's sharp light couldn't penetrate the dingy viewports, couldn't disperse the fog of artificial illumination from square ceiling panels.

When the lights powered down, Grampa cowered in fear among the shadowy forms surrounding him: billowing plastic curtains, gas tanks and tubes lurking in the corner, electronic monitors staring with glassy, empty faces. They watched over him like silent mourners at his funeral looking down into his grave. He choked on unseen odors: stale air, old grease, ammonia leaking from somewhere.

Grampa dreamed that Jenny came to rescue him, sweeping him off his feet for an evening of dinner and dancing. She'd wear the dress he bought her, and he'd compliment her as the fabric shimmered over her body. During dinner she'd keep one hand affectionately on his knee, reassuring him with a smile over a glass of wine. They'd order one dessert, sharing the rich confection like two lovers. As he fed her a mouthful, he'd watch her lips linger on the sweetness as if she were savoring a kiss.

Finally, some part of his mind woke up and realized he was trapped on that dying starship. He wrestled in the tangled conduits, squinted against the sudden emergency strobes, and threw himself against the myriad enemy arms restraining him.

Grampa looked in the darkened viewport and watched a wretched old cripple thrashing around in his

bed. "Who is that man?" he asked Sharon. "Why is he
so angry?"

She only shushed him and tried calming his nerves.
Grampa relaxed as she stroked his hair and whispered
gentle words in his ear. He felt she was with him in
bed, holding him close, to wake with him in the morning and start a new day together.

Sandy stood by his side when he stumbled from
sleep, senility, or dream—he still couldn't distinguish
between them. Grampa never quite figured where his
consciousness went. He just knew he wanted to find
the ladder back to his quarters, to run off and play with
his friends in the clouds. He often mumbled such sen-
timents to Sonya. She looked at him like he was sick
and there was nothing she could do. But she always
knew how to cheer him: Jenny pointed to the window,
out at the puffy stratosphere where the air didn't choke
him and the light shone pure and steady.

Several times Grampa noticed a huge metal creature descending from the sky and landing on the station's docking platform. People emerged, many
smiling, some crying. They surrounded the deteriorating inhabitants and shoved things into their hands, then
took them back and opened the gifts for them. They
decorated a shelf in Grampa's room with these offer-
ings: sonic shavers and cheap chronometers. He had
no use for clocks, since he couldn't tell time anymore,
and if he could, it would only frustrate him. He frequently thought the numbers ran backward, or in some
random order, or turned into letters which spelled out

cryptic messages: "Go to Mars," or "Gardens no dog Sandra under."

He'd long since forgotten how to shave. Jenny did it for him. Sometimes Sharon shaved him.

The visitors did not shave Grampa. Few came close enough to touch him. Some haunted the perimeter of the room, staring blankly at his bedridden body. Others wept when Grampa said anything, then excused themselves and hurried away. Strangers carried on animated conversations with him like they were old acquaintances, chattering at him despite his cryptic responses. Once a sweet little girl climbed onto his bed and kissed him on the forehead, saying she loved her Great Grams. She obviously mistook him for someone else.

After the people left, Sandra came and took the numerous shavers away, though she began crying softly to herself as she left. He thought she was taking away his guns, and that was fine by him; Grampa had seen enough of the war humans brought to space. He figured they reminded Jenny of her parents—who might have been killed by guns during some battle—and that was why she wept.

Grampa supposed it was just easier this way, leaving folks like him on some beautiful, deserted cloud-world at the edge of known space. Nobody would miss them if the enemy slaughtered the colony, or if the rest of the galaxy blew up, or if they just waited here forever. Maybe they had all become immortal and didn't know it. Grampa hoped not—he wouldn't mind being immortal, but not like this.

His body transformed into that crippled starship, no

weapons or engines, the air leaking out slowly—incapable of anything but watching himself corrode from inside. Grampa could accomplish little on his own. Sharon bathed him, changed his clothes, tidied up that thing in which he slept, and helped him relieve himself. Grampa struggled to continue feeding himself, but only because he didn't want a nutrient tube surgically inserted into his stomach. Eating by himself remained Grampa's one last wisp of dignity. Nobody would feed him, shoveling food-mush into his face like an infant.

At least his glide chair afforded him some mobility. Grampa enjoyed sitting in the gardens, ignoring the other inmates as they floated about him. He gazed over the flower beds and shrubs—beyond the fountain and the railing—and lost himself in the clouds. They didn't care if he mumbled incoherently, wandered around the trees, or lived out delirious fantasies in his head. The tall plumes simply smiled back at him and danced in the sunlight. Grampa yearned to leap from his chair, run across the lawns, and join the friends he saw playing there—jumping, laughing, singing—savoring life in one endless, ethereal picnic.

Instead he pushed himself around in the glide chair, peering under bushes, searching the fountain, asking everyone he met—even some of the trees—if they could point him toward the companionway ladder back to his cabin. Eventually he'd find himself at the railing, gazing at the clouds again. He didn't always see her, but Grampa knew Jenny sat nearby, watching him, weeping quietly to herself.

During those rare moments when he became slightly more lucid, Grampa often wondered how Sandra managed among so many people like him. Some had already died inside and were just roaming, mindless husks of flesh. Maybe Sonya spent her nights crying in her quarters, like Grampa often imagined her, weeping away the stress and sadness of working with folks like him. Perhaps she was dead inside, too, but he didn't think so—her smile and warm brown eyes showed some kind of soul lived in there.

Grampa turned away from the sunlit plumes dancing beyond the railing. Sharon sat on a stone bench nearby, blinking her eyes to hide her tears. "Did someone leave you here, too?" he asked. "You always look sad . . . bad reports from the command deck, the enemy surrounding us, nothing working in the engineering bay, no hope for relief, no chance for retreat."

Eventually Grampa got so worked up he tried pulling himself from the glide chair. Jenny came to his side, trying to calm him down and ease him back into the chair. Grampa touched her cheek, wiping away the moisture there. Her arms steadied him, and he looked into her eyes, silently pleading to her. Grampa pointed out to the clouds, to the faces and memories he saw out there. "Can I go play with my friends?" he asked. "I'm damaged. I can't do it without your help."

Sharon touched Grampa's wet face, then guided him to the railing. He slumped over it, steadied by her hands and what remained of his suddenly focused willpower. Grampa gazed into the swirling vapors below. His friends from the clouds had all descended into the storm to play. They ran with the gales, laughed at the incredible pressure, and tossed bolts of orange energy to each other. Someone sang a childhood song, its words mumbling in the back of his mind. The storm intoxicated him with awe and fear, a euphoria of raw emotions he hadn't enjoyed in many years.

Grampa decided he was going to touch those storm clouds, no matter what it took. If his friends could do it, so could he. Grampa had some idea he'd die, but his mind could no more comprehend the concept of death than it could understand the humiliating delirium called life.

He suddenly felt Jenny beside him, holding him up against the railing, patiently standing at his side. His body's weakness pulled at him, threatening to drag his frail form, his mind and his spirit back to the glide chair. With each breath the atmosphere gradually leaked from his body. "Help me evacuate the ship," he begged Sharon. "If we escape the enemy now, we can return with more cruisers and stop this senseless slaughter." Grampa pulled at the railing, trying to climb over the edge and reach his friends.

Jenny put a hand on his shoulder, not holding him back, but comforting him. She asked what he was doing. "I'm just looking for the way back to my quarters," he said. Tears blurred his vision of her. "Where do you go when you can't find your home?"

Sharon looked back over her shoulder, surveying the well-kept gardens and the hopeless souls lingering there. Grampa saw tears well up in her eyes, too, at this sad sight, a limbo where memories and identities wandered aimlessly out of people's minds.

She helped him get one feeble leg over the railing, then swung one of her own legs over. The two straddled the edge for a moment. Grampa reached out to hold Jenny's hands.

And they fell together.

Grampa felt like he'd just jumped out the air lock into open space, with the remaining atmosphere rushing past him, dissipating into the void. He peered down, watching the fierce storm leap up to meet them, its spiraling arms spread to catch them in its vapory embrace.

While they plummeted, emotions surged through Grampa's heart: fear of death, anticipation of freedom, fascination with the gale raging around them, Sharon's hands holding his. Her eyes sparkled with the same uncertain hope and inexplicable joy he experienced.

Grampa prepared for death, wondering if anything waited for him beyond that final, conscious barrier of life. He glanced over Jenny's shoulder at the wind and lightning tearing through the pressure-dense clouds. He expected at any moment they'd crush, rip, and blow him and Sharon to oblivion. But her eyes gave Grampa the peace and courage to face what he expected . . . or whatever unimaginable end awaited them.

He closed his eyes, allowing his addled senses to tumble around him. Instead of falling down, Grampa felt like he was climbing, pulling himself up that companionway ladder to his quarters. Familiar impressions surrounded him: the smell of his service locker, a utility bag stuffed with tools tossed on the deck, holographic pictures stuck on the bulkhead wall. He collapsed onto his bunk with the satisfaction of successfully completing the day's work. Grampa wrapped himself in his warm military blanket. Here he was free from life's problems and limitations. He didn't care when his cabin dissolved from his consciousness, because he could finally embrace its memory without fear of losing it.

On some level he felt the pressure crushing his weak body, compacting his fragmented brain into a neutron star. The winds filled him, and he drank deeply of their crisp, pure scent. The electrical discharges flashing all about them energized him, blasting through the fog haunting his mind. But Grampa wasn't destroyed. His consciousness—his soul—remained, his perceptions and memories becoming sharper, more vivid. He looked into Jenny's eyes, and suddenly everything became clear.

The clouds transformed Jenny into the girl he remembered from school, the one on whom he'd had a crush. All the feelings of blissful infatuation filled him: giddiness, idealized euphoria, the vague yet certain expectation of joy. The vapors clothed her in the dress he bought her during his delusional shopping trip in the garden. The winds played with its hem and tousled her hair like a warm morning breeze. The pressured haze and orange lightning transfigured her into an angel surrounded by an aura of golden brilliance. Her arms reached out to save him, draw him back from the darkness of his life into something more wonderful and delightfully mysterious.

Jenny touched him, and details of her life illuminated his mind. He read it all in her eyes, heard it in her smile, felt it in the gentle touch of her fingers. He knew she watched her parents die like those back on the platform—their lives slowly deteriorating, trapped in useless bodies with disintegrating brains. He realized the infinite love and patience within her to have endured that torture, then stay to comfort others trapped there. It might as well have been purgatory.

Grampa focused on Jenny's hands holding him, infusing him with a shimmering light that cleared the gray from his mind and returned memories long lost. Now they flooded back to him like the million voices of a triumphant choir: pride swelling in his chest at his technical academy graduation; reconfiguring the power conduits around a blasted coupling box; his granddaughter's infant hand holding his index finger; approaching a massive starcruiser in an insignificant personnel shuttle; sharing dinner with his family, the smell of roast lamb wafting through the kitchen. He saw them not as if he were losing their impressions, but experiencing them for the first time, fresh and unexplored, all at once. He embraced them like meeting old friends after countless years apart . . . and picking up right where they'd left off.

The intense pressure became innumerable warm hands patting him on the back, embracing him, welcoming him home. They surrounded Grampa, inviting him to join them, a cheering crowd hoisting him to their shoulders to celebrate the victory.

The wind rushed through Grampa, calling his name in myriad voices, the sounds of people he once knew, still knew, and would know. They gave him the comfort of strong friends reunited, the excitement of meeting them for the first time, a life's worth of experiences ahead of them. His old buddies encouraged him to join them for another drink. Shipmates congratulated him on a job well done. Children giggled as their light voices climbed over him. Someone whispered seductively to him, a long-lost lover, or perhaps even Jenny.

Grampa looked into her face, smiling, glowing, framed by her golden hair. Beyond them the storm's plumes formed a stratospheric landscape. In the distance all their friends enjoyed a picnic among the hills and fields of illuminated clouds. The gale's cries formed music, the lightning laughed, and the pressure surrounded them in the pleasant humidity of an early spring morning.

Grampa turned to Jenny, smiling at her gentle, brown eyes. "I'm Charles Anthony Marlowe, engineer's mate first class."

"Hi, Charles. I'm Danielle Jennifer Hawkins, nurse."

"Please, call me Charlie," he replied.

As they floated off to picnic with the others frolicking in the sunlit clouds, Jenny took Grampa's hand in hers. "Come on, Charlie," she said. "Let's go play."

DOWN ON THE FARM

by Julie E. Czerneda

Canadian author and John W. Campbell award finalist Julie E. Czerneda lives in a country cottage with her family. Her novels include *A Thousand Words for Stranger, Beholder's Eye, Ties of Power,* and *Changing Vision,* all published by DAW. A former biologist, she has written and edited several textbooks, including *No Limits: Developing Scientific Literacy Using Science Fiction.* A hockey and football fan, Julie is currently at work on her next novel.

*T**he satellite signals pulsed to Demeter's surface, regular as rain, collecting like so many puddles in stations nestled within belts of fertile farmland. They were interpreted, enhanced with input from land-based towers, rerouted, and passed along to the tireless machines without flaw. It was archaic but reliable. This far from Earth, on humanity's latest frontier, reliability counted for more than style.*

"Stick your nose in it!" Deighton roared. The wide-eyed, would-be colonist looked up from her crouch, then, doubtfully, at the handful of dark, steamy organic matter in her gloved hand. She hadn't expected this; then again, which of the eager recruits from an overly civilized Earth did? *Education was,* Deighton thought with a bit of exasperation, *always left to those in the field.*

"In it?" came a horrified mutter from someone among those clustered for today's class at Demeter's Colonist Induction Center. Deighton made a mental note regarding pig sty assignments for the remainder of the week. *Should kill or cure him.*

Deighton gestured impatiently. The recruit with the handful took an ill-advised deep breath as she bent her head over her hand. The class, mindful of past experience and determined to succeed, unconsciously leaned forward with her. The delicate, upturned tip of her nose disappeared into the mass. There was a silent, prolonged moment of disbelief—on Deighton's part as well as his class. She raised her head, the beginnings of a triumphant look on her face, a flake of greenish black on one cheek.

"I meant stop being squeamish and take a closer look at it, you fool!" he growled, throwing up his big hands. "What did you think you'd learn about the damned horse at arm's length? Does she need worming or not?"

"Worming?" The recruit turned an alarming shade of green and dropped face first into the manure. Her classmates rushed forward to help her, exclaiming in equal parts sympathy and disgust.

Patterns set by schedules and plans generated the season past were implemented. Spray, like a surgical tool, pinpointed the blush of green that marked resur-

gent weeds and coated them with deadly dew. A hand's breadth away, new seedlings glowed under a mist of nutrients, receiving a boost of phosphorus, copper, and sulfur to help them match those growing in richer soil just ahead. Satellite signals pulsed down unceasingly, telling the machines where they were within mere centimeters.

The lone human in the lead machine, a jockey on a five-ton metal monster, spent the time writing letters home. She was in token charge of the flock of twenty, floating in meticulous formation across the waving grass ocean, immense boom sprayers held out as if wings. A human presence was a holdover from the colony's first days when the machines might have encountered something not covered by failsafes or programming. Now, she was there in case something unimaginable went wrong. But nothing ever did.

Classes were over for the day. Taking advantage of the late-lingering light of the northern prairie summer, most of the Center staff had jumped into trucks and headed to the sandbanks of the nearby Green River to swim and relax.

The newest batch of recruits, not yet entitled to planetside liberties, had all showered, one twice, and were tired in that bone-deep way that encouraged philosophy. As usual, they gathered at the fence line to gaze lustfully upon the fields surrounding the Center, to where machines flashed and gleamed, slicing soil and cradling corn, humming in C major chords.

"That's real farming," one burly recruit breathed, eyes round with wonder. "That's where I plan to be."

"A jockey? Give me a break," his smaller companion dug a sharp elbow into his ribs. "The future's those guys."

The pair turned as one to the huge bay doors where yet another freshly emptied harvester growled its way into the beginning twilight. Ag-techs in their pristine whites clucked and fussed over the immense machine as though over the birth of a champion calf. Unimpressed, the harvester continued toward the field, halting its slow inevitable course only once, to let a stray chicken cross. Deighton's pretend farmyard was never perfect.

"Yep. *That's* farming." They paused in silent communion, no need to remind each other of what was definitely *not,* in their opinion, real farming.

Still the thought couldn't be totally contained. "Have you checked out tomorrow's schedule?" the young woman asked bitterly. "Scouting for smut. On foot. And in the barley, no less."

Shudders oscillated down a dozen backs. The evening air was settling, leaving no doubt that the day's unusual humidity would mean a rough night's sleep and an early return to the heavy heat in the morning. And barley hairs had a way of creeping under pant legs, no matter how tightly they were tucked into boot tops.

"Don't know why they haven't spent the cash and put in automated samplers like we have at home," grumbled one. "What are they waiting for? Demeter's been settled long enough, hasn't it? The government

promos were all raving how perfect this world is for
ag-biz—how soon it will be exporting pharmaceuticals
and fresh produce to the stations, let alone be self-
sufficient. I don't know about you, but I signed up for
my fifteen years here to make some serious credits, not
pretend to be some twentieth-century farmer."

Nods of agreement. Then the young woman said
boldly, "We won't be stuck here much longer."

"Maybe you don't think three and a half Dem-
months isn't long, but I do," the other recruit responded glumly. "You know the drill. We're in for a
full season. Everyone from colonist prospect to temp
worker has to pass Induction training—"

A third, hitherto silent, disagreed sharply. "Haven't
you heard the scoop from home? We aren't the only
ones who think making techs shovel manure and chew
canola is a waste of time and resources."

"Hold it down! Here comes Deighton."

Deighton, also showered but inclined to look fresh
from the barn regardless, contemplated the evening sky,
ignoring the recruits' retreat as easily as he dismissed the
ceaseless machines surrounding his island of peace. He
also ignored the stars beginning to pockmark the darken-
ing arch with unnamed constellations, looking for and
finding what he was after, head strained backward until
his shoulders ached. Satellites, like pendulum clocks,
rolled around Demeter, always where they should be, always transmitting, dependable as rain in spring.

"It's coming," he whispered to the moving spots of
light, feeling unusually discouraged. There had been
news today—the kind that traveled in low voices,

avoiding com systems and certainly never leaving a paper trail. Not good news and not unexpected, at least by those like Deighton whose labors had added Earth-scents to the evening air. "Too damn soon."

"Pardon?"

Deighton dropped his gaze, trying not to scowl at the small, earnest face lifted to his. At least she'd cleaned off the evidence of this afternoon's blunder. "Nothing, Ms. Peirez. Just talking to myself."

"May I speak to you for a moment—"

"If it's about what happened today—" he began warningly. *Last thing he needed tonight was a complaint about his methods.*

"No, sir," she said quietly but firmly. "That was my mistake."

Thinking he knew where this was going, Deighton sighed. "You want out. I'm sorry, Ms. Peirez, if that's the case, but settlement fees are nonrefundable." Among other things, those fees helped finance each little move forward in technology for the colony. Potential colonists contracted for short- or long-term stints on Demeter—and paid up front for both travel and the time it would take to turn them into productive members of a society with quite different demands than the tame world they'd left.

Left being the operative word. Demeter was Earth's first, full-scale attempt to expand humanity's reach. No one was granted full immigrant status here until they'd proved their worth and their commitment to stay. There were too many waiting their turn at this fresh start to waste valuable time or resources on anyone who'd take their skills back home on retirement.

"No, sir." This with an element of surprise. "I'm on a twenty-five-year immigration track. It took some doing, as you can appreciate; there are a lot of robotics specialists who'd kill to be out here, to get a chance at this human-machine interface tech. There's nothing like this back home." She waved in a vague general motion that seemed to encompass the barn as well as the stars above. "I've no intention of throwing away my chance." She took a step to one side. Deighton realized it was so the lights from the barn shone on his face and she could see his expression. He wasn't sure why, until she went on in a determined, jumping-off-the-cliff voice. "What I wanted to ask you is: why? Why are you making us do this? You must know how unpopular it is to force everyone coming here, regardless of their specialties or training, to learn this—antique—farming methodology. Don't give me that government line about training us to survive as pioneers. Sure, all the brochures call Demeter the frontier, but what's that mean, really?" Her voice grew even firmer. "Demeter City is three times the size of my hometown already. From what the staff says, there's nothing on Earth we'd want that isn't here now. This is Earth, as far as anyone can tell."

"Oh, it's not Earth," Deighton countered, inclined to be amused. "Granted, you'd be hard-pressed to find any differences in this particular biome. The prep crews were quite thorough."

Demeter had qualified for colonization based on

two key factors: its Earth-similar physical environment, from atmosphere to gravity, and the relative youth of its biology. The Demetran fauna consisted of three phyla, none with bone or appreciable size, while the flora, slightly more abundant and varied, still depended on good timing and rainwater for procreation. From orbit, one could see how the prep crews had ribboned the colony's agriculture between preserves of native life, preserves kept inviolate by molecular disintegration fields powered from Demeter's own core. Within these fields, Demeter's life could continue to evolve as it would—without further human influence.

That these sentry fields protected the spreading leaves of alien vegetation, from bananas to maple trees, was equally important.

"I've seen it," she agreed. "Which makes me—and not just me—wonder why we have to spend time here before heading to our real assignments. Blanchard Robotics has a job waiting for me in the city. What's the government thinking: that we'll be mysteriously cut off from tech support or ships from Earth won't stop here anymore? That's nonsense. If the planet's secured, why can't we get on with settling it? We know our jobs, Mr. Deighton."

"We'll see if you know any more, then," he said with what he felt was admirable restraint. "Good night, Ms. Peirez."

Deighton turned and walked away, leaving her standing, mouth slightly open.

* * *

The next day, Persephone blazed downward in all her glory. It was as hot, humid, and uncomfortable as any of the recruits had feared. There was barely enough room between the rows of waxy barley stems for a person to stand with both feet together. The plants were just tall enough to discourage straddling. The fifteen recruits followed Deighton down the row like a chain of condemned conga dancers.

"Here," the instructor announced, stopping the advance by simply planting his big boots on a spot absolutely indistinguishable from anywhere on the hundred hectares stretching in all directions. There was a moment of collision and confusion that quickly subsided under his scowl. The Induction Center's farmyard, fondly remembered by the overheated and already weary recruits as a blessed oasis, was over the horizon, as was the transport that had dropped them at the edge of the field two hours earlier. The sole thing taller than the humans and grain was the distant sequence of thunderstorms, luminous white towers connected to the ground by dark walls of rain.

The sudden silence was balm to Deighton's ears. He stilled his own breathing to better appreciate the sense of being supremely one with the world, to better hear the rustling as small hot breezes tossed the hairy barley heads this way and that, reflecting tawny gleams amid the green.

"What do we do now, sir?" asked the recruit whose poor luck had put him directly behind the instructor in line. He had the look of someone feeling doomed no matter what.

"What do you think you should do now, Mr. Redding?" Deighton replied quite reasonably, blinking sweat from his eyes. There was an abominable itch on his inner thigh that he'd wouldn't have scratched to save his life. It lent a certain fierceness to Deighton's expression as he waited for an answer.

Mr. Redding merely gulped. One of the keener types near the back waved a hand. "Establish our position and begin sampling, sir. Is that right?"

"Does Mr. Redding agree with that?"

Mr. Redding would have agreed to running naked through the grass if it would get him away from Deighton's gimlet stare.

"You know the drill, people."

Deighton settled his hip against the walking stick he'd brought with him and watched the ensuing scurry of activity. The recruits quite competently called up the positioning data on their belt comps, children's toys on Earth. New recruits frequently found it charming that Demeter relied on such basic tech.

There was little discussion. The shimmering heat haze and the coating of dust had turned the formerly individual recruits into a pack of brown automatons. Meters and other devices were waved above the plants and soil with almost comical precision. Results were plugged into belt comps for later analysis. Then, out came the nets, and, one by one, the recruits stopped moving of their own accord and looked to Deighton.

He grunted. *What were they teaching in biology back home these days?* Deighton took a net from the nearest student, the unfortunate Mr. Redding again as it happened, and stepped carefully two rows to the west. Then he swept the net in four graceful arcs, back and forth, just kissing the top of the barley heads. Finally, he shook the contents of the net deeper inside and used one hand to close the soft white netting.

"Oh," came a soft chorus of comprehension and nets began beating their way across the field.

"I caught something. I caught something!"

Deighton, almost dozing in the heat, pushed back his broad-brimmed hat to better appreciate the spectacle of fourteen relatively mature human beings rushing to peer into a net held against the emotion-swelled bosom of, yes, Mr. Redding. "I should hope so," Deighton muttered to himself.

The Something turned out to be a cabbage butterfly—a component of the transplanted prairie ecosystem now thriving on Demeter. Deighton watched it flutter away as fifteen recruits meticulously recorded its existence here and now, idly wondering if any had ventured far enough from their homes to see one on Earth. This was the catch of the hour, the other recruits unimpressed by the dozens of tiny green aphids and black shiny thrips that shared the inside of their nets with fragments of barley hair. But they dutifully recorded everything, which was a good start.

The next sampling site was a kilometer away. The recruits, though hot, were buoyed by their success and chatted with enthusiasm for the first while. Then the toil of placing feet one before the other and balancing a pack took more of their attention.

The next site was markedly different to Deighton's experienced eye. He waited, hip braced against his walking stick, for anyone else to notice as the recruits began their tasks.

They hurried through the measurements and sampling, then spread out, nets like giant butterflies themselves in search of prey. They'd learned the fun part. He sighed.

"Mr. Deighton, what's wrong here?"

The quiet voice from behind made him start. It belonged to Ms. Peirez, the wanna-be robotics specialist. He was pleasantly surprised.

"What makes you ask?"

She bent over the nearest row of plants. "They're farther apart. There are gaps—here—and over there. Some of them," her voice came up muffled because she had gone on all fours to better inspect her suspects. "Yes, some have leaves just on the outside."

Deighton was delighted, but kept his face skeptical. "So?"

"Well, that's not right," she insisted. The others, sensing something going on, started to gather around, nets in hand. "What's wrong?"

"Check the nets," someone suggested. The recruits hurried to do their counts, inputting the numbers. A quick stat analysis found no difference in the numbers of insects. A similar check of soil content found only minor fluctuations. Deighton settled himself to wait.

Either they would care enough to find out, or they would give up.

Although there was no place to sit down without crushing the barley plants, the recruits managed to squat in a rough semicircle. Suggestions, some valid and several that made Deighton roll his eyes, flew back and forth.

The ideas slowed, then stopped. They called up last years' harvest map and found a slight decrease in yield, but no other clues. Flasks of water were shared in glum silence. The rustle of the grain was the only movement. Thunder grumbled, safely distant.

Deighton thumped his stick on the ground. Fifteen sets of eyes leaped to him as though they'd forgotten he was there. He thumped the ground a second time. Ms. Peirez shook her head. "We tested the soil."

He smiled. "But you didn't stick your nose in it."

She looked quizzical, then got it with an answering grin that showed startling white teeth in the mask of dust. "Who's got the shovel?"

Twenty centimeters down were the culprits. The recruits stared in awe at the dozens of small yellow larvae squirming on the sieve.

One looked to the horizon, frowning as though it helped her see farther. "Are they native?" she asked nervously.

Before Deighton could form a reply, Ms. Peirez retorted scathingly: "Honestly, Iris. You sound like some tourist. The sentry fields have been in place for fifty years. The terran biomes were sterilized and seeded before you were born."

"Demeter's wildlife is closely monitored," Deighton said more gently. "As is ours. You are all aware of The Plan."

They nodded, several impatiently. Deighton wasn't surprised. It rarely mattered to recruits or, frankly, to politicians on either world that all of the Earth-species so carefully installed on Demeter were being very gradually biogeneered to fit in with the native life-forms already successful here, a deliberate convergent evolution. The Plan was not part of the colony's present; it belonged to the futures of their progenies' progeny. *Fair enough,* Deighton thought, *since their willing ignorance simply made it easier for those in charge of The Plan.*

The Plan's intent was simple: to ultimately blend what humanity had brought—and what humanity was—with Demeter's own. The Plan's purpose was equally plain, if less broadly announced: to ensure both would survive when, not if, the sentry fields dropped.

In the meantime, in their lifetimes and those immediately to come, the two biological heritages would not mix. Deighton tipped a few of the yellow squirming things into his hand, watching them worry their heads into the deep creases of his palm. "Wireworms," he identified for them. "The larval stage of click beetles. Those have likely been in the soil here for a couple of years. Nasty. They'd have fed on the germinating seed as well as shredding the stems of the seedlings." He tipped the sieve back on to the soil. "We'll notify the pest manager to spray this area with parasitic nematodes. And it would be wise to use coated seed next year. Should be okay."

The recruits smugly entered the existence of wireworms here and now into their belt comps. There was a smile on more than one weary face. But Mr. Redding looked decidedly anxious. "Yes?" Deighton prodded.

"Even when Demeter gets auto samplers, they don't get into the soil that deep," the recruit said earnestly. "I know. My parents have a farm in Northumberland. How can we test for these things?"

"Good point." Deighton shared his approval with the entire group. Not a bad day at all for a change. He reached into his own backpack and pulled out a potato. "See this? It's the latest in automatic samplers. Put it in the hole," he ordered, "and record its location." He winked. "You see, wireworms aren't easy to spot with electronics and meters. But they love tunneling into potatoes."

There were no complaints as they started toward the next sampling site. Deighton led the way with a sense of elation that had everything to do with hope. He hadn't had such a successful day in far too long.

What he hadn't told Ms. Peirez, what none of these recruits or any others would be told, was how tenuous their hold on this world was. Nothing stayed the same that lived, a principle truer here than anywhere. Those who lived on Demeter would have to stay intimately aware of its life, remain in touch with the plants, animals, and microorganisms that sustained the world. Technology alone couldn't do it, being designed to resist change rather than prepare for it. The knowledge to recognize and survive change was safe on Earth, stored in millions of minds, but here? Deighton found it all to easy to imagine it fading away, stored in sterile unchanging databases, romanticized in folktales, tucked into jokes told in city nightclubs, "What does a farmer wear to dinner . . ."

Deighton gripped today's small success tightly.

Funny how the world went, Deighton thought. On the same day as his first victory with this batch of recruits, here arrived the end of all his work, standing in a pair of polished cowboy boots; a polite young disciple, so innocent of harm that the wound he was causing refused to splatter him with blood.

My life's blood? I'd love to plow him one. "Why didn't Xiochung come and tell me himself."

A sigh and look that suggested the messenger was perhaps less innocent than Deighton imagined. "You'd have hit him."

Deighton considered the idea. "Yeah." He paused. "So the rumors are true. Interspacial's stopped funding the Induction Center. They'll pass recruits straight to assignments without local training—with only what they can stuff into their heads before leaving Earth." *As if* that *was worth anything.*

"You knew it was likely, Mr. Deighton," the messenger said with a hint of regret in his mild voice. He was nonimmigrant track, a meticulously neutral civil servant who thought no one noticed the treats he always had in his pockets for the heavy horses. "The Center's a major headache for Interspacial. They could fill all the ships they have with paid-up recruits, ready to come, but we make them wait while we take each group through here. That's a third of a year delay—worse, the Center can only handle a max of ten ships at a time. People on Earth? They just don't see any purpose to what you do here."

Deighton growled: "Don't forget the other end."

"I don't, sir. Senior Ag-tech Brandon and others on Demeter's Settler Council are agitating for more bodies as fast as Interspacial can ship them here."

"If they'd let us expand when—" Deighton ground his teeth together. There'd been no local support for additional Induction Centers; a decision he'd naively assumed due to lack of funds. Now he suspected he saw the results of a pent-up demand building over years and a lack of political will to resist.

The messenger held out a thick sheaf of paper with a disk limpeted to it with tape. "I was told to give you these, Mr. Deighton. This is the shut-down procedure. The forms you'll need to finalize the administration—" He paused, squinting at Deighton's barley-dusted coveralls and skin, and turned the sheaf over to protect the precious disk. Deighton took it as though it could bite. "Will you need any help, sir?"

"No. Thanks. As you said, I knew it was likely." Deighton politely saw his fate out of the trailer, then balanced the paperwork, electronic and otherwise, on the top of a barely stable tower of reports. His thick fingers tugged one out seemingly at random. The impatient Ms. Peirez.

Seemed she would get her wish.

* * *

The messenger's delivery wasn't secret. News spread through the Center faster than the wind—encouraged by unsubtle broadcasts from people-hungry Demeter Town. Within the hour, the recruits had tossed their bags and other belongings into the back of the bus that had brought them from the spaceport. As they abandoned the Center, the staff stood and watched, looking more confused than distressed, left behind by events and hoping for a revelation. Only the ag-techs had been oblivious; their schedules turned with climate and ripening grain rather than the comings or goings of others.

This was, Deighton mused, *Demeter's first rebellion.* What a shame for Interspacial and the colonist-recruits that rebellion was part of nature, and The Plan took nature thoroughly into account.

Deighton patted his pocket, ensuring the safety of the disk. The messenger for Xiochung had thought it procedures, perhaps an electronic version of the mess of paperwork he'd been assigned to dump on Deighton's lap.

It was, in fact, a code set. There were seven individuals, four on Demeter and three on Earth, who possessed it. Deighton assumed there were other sets, for other situations. Only this one mattered to him.

There was a room beneath the horse barn, small enough to be mistaken for an old-fashioned root cellar by anyone who had grown up on a planet with such things. Deighton walked by the stalls, patting fa-

vorites, before he quietly took out his keys and un-
locked the door.

The room was a kaleidoscope of present and past,
as was the colony itself. Inside was a simple chair,
made from bamboo and straw grown in Demeter's
welcoming soil. On the floor was a braided rug, an ar-
tifact Deighton had brought with him from Earth, un-
raveled at the edges where generations of puppies had
worried at the fabric. The walls were cluttered with images he'd brought as well, having taken the time to
visit his grandparents one last time before boarding the
ship. There were photographs of farmers, uniform in
their crinkled eyes and easy stance. Deighton remembered how some had been portraits in frames, others
cutouts pinned with round-headed tacks. His grand-
mother had overlapped and linked the latter together
with farming cartoons and articles in yellowed, fragile
newsprint. She'd had a cluster devoted to tractors and
combines; another to children and livestock.

There was a crate that served as a table. On it was a
chipped mug, still containing the remains of coffee, a
curdled circle of milk floating on top, left from his last
visit. There was a second door, marking the entrance to
a storeroom designed for potatoes and currently filled
with boxes of auto samplers intercepted before they
reached the city. There was a time and a place for
everything in The Plan.

Deighton sat in the chair, planted his feet in their
big boots on the old rug, put his elbows on his knees,
and dropped his face into his hands. He drew a deep

slow breath in through his nose, savoring the combination of horse, hay, and human sweat.

With the code set, he had his orders, he reminded himself, and couldn't disagree. He had read of apocalypse and found he could imagine it better than most authors—yet had never found the words to express it himself. Others had. The Plan's true goal had nothing to do with frontiers and everything to do with home. No one but those most intimately involved knew the Earth's time as that home now had a limit, that within the seeable future Demeter wouldn't be the farthest frontier. It would be all there was.

Up came his head, determination firmly written on every crease in his skin. It was time.

Deighton lifted the coffee mug from the crate, setting it carefully on the floor away from his feet. Then he tilted back the crate itself. It moved smoothly on the hinges that held it to the floor along one side and stayed tipped when he released it. There was a single green-and-brown lever underneath, with a slot to one side to receive the code disk.

Deighton dropped in the disk, then wrapped his big smelly hand around the lever. He took a moment to look around the room, meeting the eyes, and he imagined, approval, of the generations of dirt farmers that looked down at him. Then he pulled the lever back with one smooth jerk.

Only when it was done, did his hand tremble.

There were 167 satellites orbiting Demeter. Each had an extra chip hardwired by hand into the transmit-

ter/receiver; it didn't appear on any spec sheet or plan. The prep crews had installed them. What the chips did was simple enough. First, pass along the signal, then fry.

The only rain that fell the next day was water.

Without incoming positioning data, the great farming machines obeyed their failsafes and shut down wherever they happened to be. Jockeys found themselves stranded in the middle of fields, including a very puzzled letter writer. Warehouses and shipping points were ordered shut down as well, until food distribution could be reorganized to meet the crisis. The Demeter Settler Council and Interspacial urged calm. But every satellite remained silent, so every piece of automated equipment remained still. Interspacial promised replacements within two months.

In the meantime, every able-bodied person was to report for service in the fields. The crops had to be tended—ripe ones harvested before they spoiled. The Induction Center was to plan and coordinate the efforts of all. New Centers were being organized as quickly as possible to disseminate knowledge and tools. Demeter surged with optimism, determined to successfully overcome its first crisis.

Deighton leaned in the shadow of the gate, the sun-etched lines around his eyes and nose deeper than usual. The sleeping giants in the fields were being wrapped in protective sheeting by equally silent ag-techs, but that was the only sign of peace. Behind him, the Center was a hive abuzz with tractors and trucks, combines lurching in unpredictable directions as the staff hurried to learn how to drive them in advance of their students' return. Chickens wisely took to the back corners of stalls.

When the first load of recruits climbed out of their bus and stood blinking uncertainly, Deighton recognized his class of only yesterday. From the look of them, there're been enough time for some serious beer sampling before the uncomfortable ride back.

He grinned, then cupped his big hands around his mouth and bellowed:

"Don't just stand there—there's work to be done! What do you think this is? Home?"

SET IN STONE

by Andre Norton

Andre Norton has written and collaborated on over 100
novels in her sixty years as a writer, working with such
authors as Robert Bloch, Marion Zimmer Bradley, Mer-
cedes Lackey, and Julian May. Her best known creation is the Witch World, which has been the subject of
several novels and anthologies. She has received the
Nebula Grand Master Award, the Fritz Leiber Award,
and the Daedalus Award, and lives in Murfreesboro,
Tennessee, where she oversees a writer's library.

If some mad god had deliberately set out to create a
planet utterly alien from all that was normal to the
crew of First-In Scout S-9, he or she could not have
been more successful than with this one. A man had to
force his offworld eyes to report matters that brain patterns found too grotesque to believe.

A dull throb was spreading down from Kannar's
temples, reaching out for room in neck and shoulders.
This place was just *wrong*; yet, along the starways, one
could never rightfully judge anything, no matter how it
appeared—

"Get scruffing, you Gart!"

That sharp mind-beam smote like a blow, though it
was a prodding he had come to expect during the past

three years. Yes, he was a Gart. Not many of them could be left by now, as Garthold had long since been wiped from the maps. As for his kind, they were the least blessed of all their kin. Kannar no longer grasped at memory, which grew—mercifully—ever fainter with each recall.

Fifteen planet years ago . . . The young man plodded along through the dense gray sand, weighed down by his heavy pack but careful to avoid the thick pad-patches of yellow-green growth. Fifteen cycles past, he had been at Herber, a child selected by rigorous testing intended to prove his fitness for special service to Garthold's need.

Two hellish days and a burning, blood-filled night had put an end to that life, though some Veep among the invaders did think to keep Kannar and some of his fellows alive for use in "experiments." More trials were visited upon them by their new masters, during which many died, while others were rendered mindless and thrown into the Pits. What quality the alien overseers believed Kannar possessed had brought him into the Quasing Exploration Service—not, of course, as an equal, but rather as a living test-beast for the unknown perils of distant worlds.

The boy's thick gray skin itched now, as it had ever since Captain O'ju had ordered him to gather a liver-red growth for the science officer using his bare hands. His masters had given Kannar no treatment for the fiery result; they had merely watched its progress detachedly, as yet another investigation.

"You damned dirtworm—gun it! We want to get this crawler going before dark!"

As that order rang in Kannar's head, he could see below him the land vehicle in question, its curved nose almost touching one of the standing rocks. No trees graced this world of Henga, or at least the Scouts had observed none during any of the preliminary flybys; but rising upright in rough circles which, in places, clustered thick together, were the stones.

Those formations had presented the planet's first great mystery. Though to the eye they were only crude pillars of a granitelike stuff, they could not be touched, nor even approached closely enough for any to attempt to set hand upon them. They were, it seemed, impregnably shielded by some unknown force against close examination.

Kannar did not quicken his pace. He knew too well that nothing he could do might protect him from the vicious attentions of O'ju waiting for him down there. The accident with the crawler would, of course, be blamed on him, and then . . .

Overhead, the green-fired orb of the small sun was now close to the broken line of the horizon, and the slate-colored sky had begun to darken. Even as no trees grew here, neither did any birds or flying things soar aloft—in fact, the sole life-form that seemed to have been grudgingly bestowed upon Henga was a variety of malignant vegetation.

The youth drew up beside the land transport and grounded his pack on the sand thick underfoot. The captain, always careful of his tools (human and otherwise), waited until that storage bag was safe; then, wielding his laser like a club, he aimed a blow at its bearer.

Kannar dodged as best he could, stumbling backward toward the stone against which the crawler was now nuzzled. He struck against something he could not see that gave a little on contact with his body, then pushed him away. The combination of that shove, the irritation of his skin, and the throbbing in his head broke through the control he had held so firmly. For a moment, the scene around him wavered; then he could clearly see the weapon threatening him in O'ju's heavy-gloved fist. No longer was the gun held for use as a bludgeon—now it faced him muzzle-end first, the inescapable death-dealer it had been cast to be.

The laser grew in the boy's sight, looming larger as his superior approached. Why didn't O'ju simply fire? Certainly his captive slave possessed no defense.

Defense—?

Through the pulsing pain in Kannar's head a thought struck. The fear that had held him motionless, an easy target, suddenly gave way to a clear memory of his half-forgotten life and the training that had protected him in the past. He was *Gart!*

Moving in one of his old defensive tricks, the youth landed belly-down in the sand, partway under the stalled crawler. Blinding fire burst around him; then there was darkness.

"Scout Six, to the fore!"

Kannar lifted his head an inch or so. The effort was almost more than he could sustain.

"Scout Six, report!"

The order was a further goad. That voice from the

impenetrable blackness—the Scouts must be on night maneuvers.

"Scout Six in, sir," the boy mouthed through the grit that masked his face. He tried to lever himself higher and pierce the stifling night by sheer force of will. Unable to see, he tried to listen, to catch more speech or any identifying sound.

Then he began to cough. It was as though the dark had invaded his throat and was striving to reach his lungs. One bout of the chest-racking spasms left him weak and gasping until he felt that no more breathable air remained to him. Kannar flailed out in near panic, fighting to beat away the smothering blackness, but his weak efforts were futile, and he ceased to struggle and sank into oblivion once more.

Yet even his inner night was without peace, lit by a fitful lightning of dream-flashes and broken bits of memory that skittered away whenever he tried to focus upon them. The boy whimpered and huddled in upon himself, seeking forgetfulness again.

When the young Scout roused the second time, it was into real night-dark, not the curtain that had been drawn across his mind before. The first of Henga's three pale moons was climbing the sky, and there were stars—*stars!*

Though still aware of a heavy stench that made him gag, he had awakened clearheaded enough to know where he was and to realize the source of his lungs' torment. He managed to drag himself upright. Within arm's reach was one of the thick patches of moss, and in the reduced light, he could see the sparks that arose from the mat of vegetation.

Even that poor illumination showed Kannar more: a body—or rather a portion of body, for the head and shoulders of that sprawl of flesh and bone had been reduced to blackened rags melted into the sand on which it lay. O'ju. But—who had turned a laser on *him?* The boy clenched one of his own scaly hands reflexively. A gun was lying on the ground almost within reach, yes, but *he* had certainly not dropped it!

Suddenly the Scout froze. There had been movement close to him—the motion of something small, perhaps only a little larger than his two hands clasped together. As it neared the phosphorescent plant-stuff, he could see its form more and more clearly.

The creature had eight legs, the two at its fore-end being held aloft and tipped with large claws. Its body shared the puffy plumpness of the moss and was a dull gray, near the color of the sand across which it was scuttling. It made a detour around the dead but seemed to be following a purposeful course.

Then it halted by the laser. Both fore-claws swung down and fastened upon the weapon, which was raised until it rested on the round back of the thing. Task apparently completed, the being swung about and headed back the way it had come.

Kannar drew a deep breath, wrenching his mind back with an effort from the curious action he had just witnessed to the ugly scene at hand. He could do nothing for O'ju, and repair of the crawler was beyond his skill. No Gart had ever been allowed knowledge of

Quasing technology. But the youth was aware that the land vehicle sent out some type of signal to guide searchers, and that sooner or later the surviving Scouts would make a flyby from their camp. They would find a dead man, the second-in-command of their mission, an inert crawler, and—a *Gart*. To them, the answer would be very simple.

The boy licked dry lips, then spat grains of sand. Many ingenious forms of death had been invented by his masters—even death-in-life. He could not hope for a clean ending if he remained to be found.

The creature with its perilous burden could still be seen, heading toward a wider space between two of the rocks; it was plainly seeking what it considered a safe place. The Scout made a swift decision. What might be a haven for one born of Henga could be a lethal trap for an offworlder, but perhaps the ending he could find there would be quick. The youth was bleakly convinced that a death of this world was infinitely preferable to any the ship's crew would deal him.

The native had crawled between a pair of the stone pillars, keeping an exact distance from both. The offworld boy was considerably larger than his guide, and the field of power generated by the rocks might well repel him. He could only test it.

Doggedly, Kannar moved forward on his hands and knees, his out-suit crunching on the sand. With every breath he drew, he expected to be smitten by some force beyond his comprehension.

But the opposition he feared did not come. Instead, once he had passed completely through the portal-pillars, he came into a place where there was more light and a feeling of freshness in the air. The boy reached what was roughly the center of that uneven circle and hesitated. At last he hunkered back on his heels and strove to scan all the surrounding rocks with a slow turn of his head, a crouching shift round and round. Nothing he could see differed from what was before him at every view: the silent stones deep-rooted into the sand. But the being he had followed, though the weight of the laser was plainly sapping its strength, was still going purposefully forward.

Now it faced the most massive of the rocks, and there it laid the weapon upon the ground, seeming to have accomplished a set mission. As Kannar watched, unsure of just what was taking place, he saw a movement at the foot of every stone within his range of sight. More of the puff-bodied creatures rose from the sand in front of those pillars. As the first native stood a little to one side, each of the newcomers advanced in turn. None of them attempted to raise the gun, but rather scraped their forelegs across it length- and width-wise, the tips of their claws grating on the metal of the offworld weapon.

The late arrivals trailed away discreetly and vanished as they had appeared; however, the creature who had delivered the laser remained where it was. The young Scout saw no signal given, heard no sound break the ever-noiseless night, but the burden-bearer now began to dig. Throwing goodly clawfuls of sand from side to side, it worked with such speed that, in a short time, a hole appeared. Into that opening it pur-

posefully tumbled the laser, then covered the weapon
with the same haste. An instant later—

Kannar caught his breath. The stone before which
the gun had been entombed began to glow, and—
though he was certain nothing like this had been there
before—a line of some sort of crystals appeared,
zigzagging down the rough side of the pillar. The glittering bits shed a soft light, too, and their radiance
grew brighter with every second.

The creature gave a sudden spring forward, plaster-
ing its full body-length against the rock and across the
crusting of crystals. The watching boy became aware
of a new scent in the air; unlike any he had encountered on this world, yet the odor was pleasant, and
deep memory stirred within him. *Holiday—feasting—
well done!* Why did he now think of a trophy award?

His hand reached forward instinctively, but he was
not close enough to touch the pillar, even if such contact were allowed. The native being had dropped from
the stone, and the vein of mineral formations was fading fast. Then the limited light around him began to
fail, as well, until the dark ruled utterly. Unbearable
fatigue descended upon Kannar, and he slept.

The Scout awoke suddenly. Light had come again—
the light of day—and—sound. A flyby. The search pattern might not take the ship directly over this stone
circle. A flyer had gone down during the first general
exploration, and the theory had been offered that the
protection surrounding the rocks might also extend into

the air above. But, if that hope failed, the rock ring afforded no place to hide.

The boy swallowed, painfully aware of a dry throat and the pinch of hunger. The others need only leave him where he was, and their purpose would be fulfilled: another Gart would be accounted for, and with very little effort on their part.

Kannar could see between the stones clearly. The crawler still stood, nose pressed to one of them, and nearby lay the splotch that had been O'ju. The flyer was setting down well away from that point. Three men emerged from the cargo door, rendered clumsy by heavy protect-suits. Each carried not a laser but a blaster, and they advanced in a broken pattern as though to discourage or evade attack.

There was nowhere to run now, the youth knew. The strength that had sustained him through his years of being a Gart in bondage was gone. He could do no more than wait and hope he would die quickly.

A crackle sounded in the earphone he still wore. Captain O'Lag had reached the land vehicle and looked upon what lay beside it. The harsh stridency of his voice seared Kannar as his commander voiced the filthy destiny due a Gart.

"No laser." That was O'Sar, the science officer.

But O'Lag was no longer studying the stalled machine and the corpse at its base. His bulging eyes burned yellow with rage as his gaze swept through a gap in the stone circle, pinning the boy to the spot like an insect specimen on a board. The captain stopped his

volley of curses almost in mid-word, and his blaster
shifted as he sighted through that opening at Kannar.

On impulse, the Gart abandoned his hugging of the
sand to pull himself upright and face his superior who
stood outside the ring of rocks. It did not become one
who had been Second Cadet Officer at Herber to
cower before the enemy. Sometimes how a man dies
matters, and death would be swift and sure when
O'Lag pressed the button—

Fire came. So blinding was the flash that Kannar
staggered back, though he did not fall. He heard sizzling in his earphone, then such cries as brought back
nightmare memories of the invasion of his own world.

Fire had come—yet he was not consumed! The
youth blinked, fought against the brilliance that
seemed to cloak his eyeballs. Though the shrieks had
died away, he could now smell the stench of cooked
flesh, the acrid tang of metal heat-seared. But he still
stood—*lived*—and soon he began to see again, at first
as if through a mist, then without hindrance.

No blaster-burn was visible on the stones facing
him, between two of which O'Lag had fired; no reek of
death any longer poisoned the air. Without the circle,
however, lay two crumbling forms, their ash mixing
with the sand, and the crawler with a great hole melted
into it. It looked—Kannar rubbed the back of one hand
across his eyes and cleared his vision enough to see
true—it looked as if the captain had aimed not at a
trapped Gart but had rather turned his weapon against
his own men and their machine.

Noise again; the flyer was taking off. The vessel was

equipped with out-mounted blasters. Did the pilot now intend to avenge this disaster with air-to-surface fire?

Yet though the vessel made a circuit of the standing stones, it did not approach closely, nor loose any deadly bolts from its belly. It did not linger long but winged away toward the camp.

He was still alive: Kannar accepted as fact something he would have thought impossible. Yet Death was not far off, for so great was his thirst that the dryness in his throat choked, and hunger gnawed him like a beast. Because there was no more need to make a parade of pride, the boy allowed himself to slide to the ground, facing the opening in the rocks so he could still view the carnage that lay beyond.

What he saw there was as much beyond reason as his own survival, if he could believe what dimming eyes told dulling mind: both the near-consumed corpses and the blasted crawler were sinking steadily into the sand. But even so strange an event meant nothing to him now. The last link with humankind—for the Quasings had to be deemed at least physically human—had been broken. The youth turned his head slowly and stared up at the dense gray-blue clouds that showed Henga's green sun through their drifting mass like matrix rock revealing a precious jewel.

Time seemed to have stopped for him. His memory had been buried even as had the dead Scouts and their vehicle, and he was being consumed by hunger and thirst. A man could not take long to die thus. . . .

It was as though a hand had been laid on his scaled

cheek, moved to touch his lips. Kannar raised his head
to follow, to hold that touch—and then he was crawl-
ing toward the stone pillar before which the laser had
been entombed. He gasped and coughed rackingly as
he dragged himself forward, barely able to breathe or
see; but though all other senses were nearly gone now,
he could still smell, and there was a *scent*—

His fingers touched the roughness of the rock, and
for an instant he hunched his shoulders, waiting for a
blast of defensive energy he would be helpless to
counter. When no attack came, he looked up again.
Then he saw it—a glow welling up from a crevice in
the rock between his hands. Those crystals with the radiance of gems—they gave forth not only light but that
scent, which promised help ever more strongly.

The boy's painfully swollen tongue touched the
bubbling stuff. It gave— No words existed in any
galactic language he knew to describe *this!* Warmth,
comradeship, all he had lost long ago were restored to
him in a moment, more richly than before they had
been torn away. He licked the feast, which did not cloy,
until he was thoroughly sated.

It appeared that Kannar had partaken of a true ban-
quet. First his body had been tended, and he was not
tired anymore but refreshed and avid to enjoy what
might be offered next. That was the main course. And
for the after-sweet? A gift to mind and spirit: thoughts
were what he drank now. This planet was indeed more
strange than any he had seen or heard of.

What his kind had taken for pillars of lifeless stone
were the Old Ones, who stood rooted in the very flesh

of their world, who had seen stars be born and die. To them knowledge came, though some of that a human could not understand. With them in partnership lived the skaat, the creatures who served as hands when such aids were needed. And even the winds and the clouds brought messages, for what any thought became a part of all the world.

Old Ones—?

Welcome, star son. The words rang as clear in Kannar's mind as if he had heard them with his ears. *You are now blood of our blood, substance of our substance.*

The boy had been minded of a prize awarding when the gray creature had claimed its crystal-feast after burying the laser. He felt so now. Everything that had been Herber in the days before the ending of Gart was here, and he was entering the great Gate of the Victors where all his comrades waited to greet him.

Kannar knew that he had much—oh, so much!—to learn, but those of this place were anxious to share. And he did have something of value to offer in return: his memories of Gart, his knowledge of other worlds, different beings.

A flurry of activity commenced in the space near the Old One who had made him welcome. The skaat—a number of them—were digging speedily, and a hole of some depth soon appeared. Without hesitation, the youth took two steps forward, then lowered himself into the scooped-out place, which engulfed his body to the knees. Sand was shifted quickly back to cover him.

Rest now, star son, the stone-born voice rang in his

mind. *When the Change is done, we will have all the time of the stars to learn from one another.*

A gentle night closed upon Kannar as though curtains had been drawn, and a sudden drop of sweetness dewed his lips. He drew it in eagerly, then slept.

RUINS OF THE PAST

by Jane Lindskold

Although she has frequently volunteered on archaeological digs, Jane Lindskold has yet to find anything
more spectacular than bits of broken pottery and
stone. The author of over thirty short stories and several
novels—including *Changer* and *Legends Walking*—she
lives in Albuquerque, New Mexico with her husband,
archaeologist Jim Moore. She is currently at work on
another novel.

I f the credit line on her tattered plasteel card wasn't
already run so far into the red that all that remains is
the faintest blush of rosebud pink, nothing would have
tempted Lillianara to climb Vorbottan Mountain to the
crest where the old ruins stand.

"Stand" is perhaps too strong a word. In all the
sprawl of great stone blocks, hardly one stone remains
upon another. Those that have not been brought low by
gravity's conspiracy with time have been knocked
apart by treasure hunters. The ancient civilization
which built the ruined city had used ample amounts of
gold in its circuitry, more than enough to prompt thorough destruction lest a cable or cribox be missed. That
the gewgaws and gimcracks sometimes found amid the
rock dust and litter would fetch their weight in plat-

inum rather than mere gold had assured that the very sands would be sifted.

That had been more than a century ago. Certainly at this late date there can't be much left to scavenge, but Lillianara can't think what else to try. Next dawn the extension—the third extension—her creditors have granted her will end. Unless she can settle her debts, her freedom will be revoked; she will become life-chattel of the Agency.

That's the problem with third extensions, Lillianara muses as she toils upward: there isn't anything left when they end.

She'd been so certain that she would find a way to settle the phenomenal debts left to her upon her late husband's death that she'd gratefully accepted a first extension with its merely financial penalty. When that first extension had ended, she'd had little choice but to accept a second extension. This one permitted her personal inheritance—to that point immune by law from seizure—to be used as collateral. When she failed to settle the debt by the second deadline (and that flood is looking more and more suspicious, never mind that others had been harmed as well), her choices were prison or a third extension. At that time, the third extension had seemed by far the lesser of two evils.

Too late Lillianara had learned that the same forces which had conspired first to ruin their small business, then to prod Jofar into suicide would not be content with Jofar's death. They wanted everything related to him ruined as well and she, Lillianara, is all that is left.

She struggles up the mountainside, glad that the tor-

turous climb in the stinging cold keeps her from thinking about what a life-chattel's existence could be like,
but eventually she must stop for breath.

Naive, some have called her, especially those who
knew she was taking on the Agency, but Lillianara
isn't so naive that she doesn't realize what the first as-
signment would be for a young, pretty woman. When
she is no longer pretty—though thanks to contraband
life-prolongation drugs she will be young for a long,
long time—then she can look forward to a series of
other jobs. Never one specialty for long, however; it is
dangerous to give chattel a chance to learn too much.
When the Agency personnel office ran out of things for
her to do, she'd end her life repairing radiation shielding or riding herd on a hot engine.

With that in her future, maybe she should just jump
off the nearest cliff. But Lillianara can't make herself seriously contemplate the option. She's a fighter. Suicide
may have been Jofar's way out—the ultimate surrender
to something he had fought all his life—but it isn't hers.

But maybe climbing up to the ruins is just an elaborate form of suicide. It has been a long time since
anyone found anything of interest at the crest of Vorbottan Mountain. A long time since anyone had come
back at all.

Alastar has sinews of steel and muscles of iron—
not literally; those who had created the android had
progressed far beyond such primitive materials—but
the effect is much the same. The fluids pumping
through her hydraulic systems resemble liquid gold

touched with the iridescent shimmer of oil. Her skeletal structure is made from super-collapsed metals. Her skin is impregnated with hordes of nanobots, programmed to restructure her outer appearance within rather wide parameters; those who had created Alastar came from a wide-reaching, intergalactic culture only dreamed of by the humans who had followed.

From her hidden fortress within the ruined installation, Alastar watches with interest as the human female labors her way up the mountainside. The human is swathed in clothing against the cold, but every so often she pauses and Alastar has an opportunity to estimate her appearance.

Height and build: average. Condition: average to slightly below average; there is an abnormality to her base metabolic line. The climber's lack of training gives Alastar a pause. Most of those who have challenged the mountain called Vorbottan these last hundred years have been supremely fit. They have also come in company. Why is this woman alone? Why is she so poorly equipped?

Variations in human coloration fascinate Alastar. The race that had created her had been much more homogeneous—as indeed humanity might become in a few thousand more years. This woman is of medium complexion. Her eyes are light—gray or pale blue. Her hair, judging from what peeks out from under her hood, is also fair. Alastar considers and makes a few adjustments to her own appearance.

How long has it been since a treasure hunter came

to the ruins? Alastar counts and the numbers she uses are strange in shape and in sound.

Twenty years? Thirty years? No. The hunter thirty years ago (thirty years, seven months, four days, six hours, two minutes, seconds counting . . .) had turned away on the lower slopes, frightened perhaps by the storm clouds that roiled gray and black and indigo blue above the mountain's crest.

That one had turned away, as had many before him. The woman climbing now keeps coming; she has reached higher than most of those who have attempted the climb since Alastar's second awakening. Most are unable to pass the ridges that form the lower tiers. A few have ventured higher, but none who have passed the final tier have climbed down again. Alastar had polished their skulls and keeps them in her private chamber. She had made a point of learning each of their names and talks to them during the long, lonely watches.

They, of course, have remarkably little to say in reply.

Even thirty years ago, Alastar would have begun the discouragement before the treasure hunter reached the second tier. A lightning bolt, perhaps: brilliant indigo outlined in eye-searing white. A gentle earth tremor. A robotic bird screeching out of the sun, pecking at the climber's eyes or hands.

But it has been a long time since a climber has challenged the mountain. In the pulsing center of her gold-squirting heart, Alastar admits that even an android can grow lonely.

She will talk with this one, hear the rise and fall of the stranger's voice. It will make it easier to imagine the woman's replies when she is dead and her skull has joined the silent entourage in Alastar's parlor.

Lillianara pauses, wiping the sweat from her forehead before it can freeze on her skin. The fabric of the tattered jumpsuit she wears over long underwear is torn in several places and the cold leaks inside. Her gloves, newly stolen for this very journey, and her barely used boots are holding up somewhat better.

Looking down the mountainside, she realizes that she is so far above the populated lands that the cities of the plains have ceased to look like toys. From this height they are reduced to a faint waver of heat and discoloration against the pale green of the flat river valley. Almighty humanity looks mighty small and insignificant from here.

Winter ice melt flows freely down the sides of the mountain, welcome despite the hazards it adds to her climb. It means that the one small canteen Lillianara had been able to scavenge can be kept full. She wishes that her food could be as easily replenished, but up at this height very little grows. Indeed, the sides of the mountain look as if something has cut them bare of growing things.

Records made by early explorers show a different mountain, one covered with evergreen forests, looking soft and gentle. Those forests had been so thick that no one had even guessed at the presence of the ruins until a chance study of satellite photos had revealed them.

The first treasure hunters had flown directly to the top of the mountain, sliced apart rocks with cutting beam lasers, blasted more stubborn formations with concentrated chemical explosives. The second wave of treasure hunters had done much the same, though they had added screens and shifters and densitometers to their kits, for by then the goodies were harder to locate.

A third wave had never arrived. One afternoon in hot midsummer, a storm had blown up out of nowhere and taken residence on the crest. Its swirling tides crushed expensive skimmers and atmospheric flyers like origami cranes between a child's fingers. Vehicles attempting to speed up the mountain slopes met avalanches and earthquakes.

Would-be treasure hunters rapidly discovered that only small groups of climbers had a chance to gain the summit and then only if they climbed without any electronic or mechanical assistance. Those who actually reached the top had been carefully watched via remotes. They were seen arriving at the crest itself, giving a cocky wave to their distant observers, and then vanishing into the shifting mists that now cloaked the ruins.

Not one ever returned.

Lillianara looks down upon the cities of the plains. It is full daylight now. She had begun her climb in darkness, knowing that she had to mount high enough that the Agency goons wouldn't come after her. She is safe now, after a fashion, safe from everything but starvation or death from exposure. Safe, that is, if one forgets whatever strange power now guards the ruins.

Lillianara can't forget, but going forward is all that is left to her. Snapping her canteen back into its holster, she sets her boot toes into the crevices in the rock and continues climbing.

The skull of the one who had awakened Alastar sits in the place of honor at the center of her mantelpiece. Faceted sapphires replace eyes that had been much the same color in life. Other sapphires are placed with loving care into the bones rimming the eye sockets, along the curves of cheek and jaw. Large diamonds alternate with more sapphires to make him a crown.

Alastar bows to the begemmed skull as she hurries through her parlor on the way to the buried chamber where are housed devices for manipulating the immediate weather.

Brushing dust from the infrequently used control panels, the android considers the array with glee. First she sets the controls for sleet and freezing rain, then changes the setting when she considers that the climber might fall and so deprive her of conversation. Still, the imperative to protect what remains of the installation is strong. Alastar must take some action.

After careful consideration, she sets a hot, dry wind blowing down the slope. It will stir up dust and make vision difficult, melt ice and turn dirt into mud. That it will also warm limbs cramped and weary from cold the android puts from her mind.

Now that the protective imperative has diminished to bearable levels, Alastar departs, considering what she might serve for tea.

* * *

In a deep recess, its massive body encrusted with rubble, rock dust, and mold, an entity watches Alastar make her choice and disapproves. The watcher is an ancient device, as sophisticated in its own way as the android, though not as refined. For its purposes it does not need to be.

Long ago, on a distant, younger Earth a man named Juvenal had asked: *"Sed quis custodiet ipsos custodes?"*

"I will," the watcher would have replied, unaware of the irony contained in its own response. "For when the guards themselves cease to guard, then I take over."

It stirs and the dust shifts, billowing into the cramped space. The watcher splits its perception from the interior screen on which it has patiently observed Alastar's every motion since she had been awakened. It had listened to her interminable conversations with the skulls, but had never been tempted to alleviate her loneliness. Indeed, it had never even recognized the state, nor that the state was a danger. The watcher is a limited device, but all the more deadly for those limitations.

Now, looking about itself for the first time in centuries, it realizes that it is completely entombed in rubble and settled debris. It feels no surprise, nor does it feel despair or frustration. Those who had created it had not seen a need to give it the capacity to experience such emotions.

Using shielded probes, the watcher analyzes the situation. Having found a spot where a mere three meters of rubble separate it from a buried corridor, the watcher opens its mandibles as far as they can part. A few centimeters of stone shift to fill the new gap. The mandibles close. Crushed rock drifts down. This time the mandibles can open wider.

With the infinite patience of the machine, the watcher—no longer merely a watcher but now an enforcer—sets about the task of freeing itself. All the while on its internal screen, it observes Alastar and sternly disapproves.

Lillianara is too far gone to either welcome or question the warm wind that blows down the mountainside toward her. Long before its coming her entire universe had been reduced to moving hands and feet, following the simple imperative to climb up without falling down.

She accepts the wind as she accepts the sharp edges of stone that alternately provide her with handholds and tear her clothing. The wind is merely something to contend with, something that adds to the parched sensation in her mouth. (She has forgotten about drinking, though water flows around her).

Occasionally, she talks to Jofar. Her tears for him are long dry. Now what she feels for him is closer to hate.

Previous groups who'd reached this high up the mountainside had trained extensively. They had carried small bottles of concentrated oxygen to sip as a remedy for the thinness of the atmosphere. Lillianara has neither training nor oxygen, but buried in her subconscious mind is the certainty that *down* means death while *up* holds a chance at life. More remarkable things have been done under the pressure of that primal imperative.

Hand up over a rock edge. Grasp. Find nothing. Grope. Flatness. Grope. Nothing. To the left side. Flatness. To the right side. Flatness.

Flatness?

Push up with feet so numb they feel like wood. Gain a few centimeters. Grope. Flatness. Faint curiosity. Sense it would be good to get onto the flatness. Knee into small indentation. Push body up. Grope. Find handhold, something smooth and cylindrical. Pull. Pull.

Flatness. Collapse. Darkness.

Pain brings Lillianara to herself. Her feet and hands are thawing and with that thawing comes a throbbing ache. She will never know how close she came to frostbite. Only the synthetic fabrics of her clothing and the toughness of her long underwear had saved her.

Her mouth is like powder. Twisting her neck to one side, she laps water from a muddy puddle, chokes on the sediment. Laps eagerly again. The same drugs that extend her life span beyond the average human four score and ten have granted her a limited capacity for regeneration. That regeneration, however, takes its toll. Lillianara is starving.

She sucks down mud to fill the gap in her stomach, but she cannot digest such slime. Retching jolts her from her belly onto her hands and knees. Her tortured fingers scream protest. Pain cuts through the muddle that substitutes for thought. For the first time she realizes that she has reached the crest of Vorbottan Mountain.

Triumph provides a thin warmth that helps her drag herself to her feet. She leans against a long, slender pole, remnant of some fence or scaffold. This must be what her desperately grasping fingers had found. Impulsively, she kisses the pole in irreverent salute. Her lips nearly freeze to the metal.

Joy cannot substitute for food. Lillianara shakes the last crumbs from her provision bag into her mouth, swallows them with the assistance of a bit more muddy water. She wonders if bacteria can survive in this cold. Realizes that they can and resigns herself to eventual distress.

Blinking frost from her lashes, she looks around. All is like yet unlike her expectations. Here are the huge blocks of building stone, barely one upon another, but the paths between them have been swept clean by the winds. Rubble sits in tidy piles wherever two or more stones intersect.

Remnants of earlier treasure hunting expeditions are remarkably absent as well. She had counted on finding a broken shifter or a discarded atomic torch or at least a shovel. Nothing of human making remains. Surely it can't all have deteriorated or been blown away?

Lillianara feels a prickling along her spine, a sense of being watched. She is also amazingly aware of the cold, enough so that she almost longs for her former numbness, even knowing that such heralds death. Stomping her booted feet to warm them, she faces into the area where blocks of stone are most thickly clustered. Surely there she'll find shelter of some sort, maybe an abandoned cache or an old warming stove.

Tottering along on weary legs, Lillianara fights back the thought that coming here had been an elaborate form of suicide after all.

Alastar neatly arranges the human trash as a lure. Her eagerness for companionship wars constantly now against the imperative to protect the ruins. She hides from herself the knowledge that what she has placed as a lure also contains the means for the treasure hunter's survival. She manages only because the traps she has set are so very deadly, so very fatal.

Sitting in her parlor, acutely aware of the faceted gaze from her collection of polished skulls, Alastar balances a tray on her silvered knees and listens for an explosion. Distantly, as from far below, she hears rumbling. She ignores it and all it implies, even as she ignores the nagging sensation that perhaps her trap is not fatal enough.

Or too fatal.

If she'd turned right rather than left, she'd never have found the cache, that's what Lillianara tells herself as she huddles over the heat cast by the compact ceramacrete camp stove. Such a small thing—left versus right. Right would have been wrong. She hears her own giggle, high and rather hysterical, and feels a trace of disgust, followed almost immediately by indulgent compassion.

Stars above, but she's been through enough to warrant a full nervous breakdown let alone a giggle or two.

Impatiently, she kneads the tube of ration concentrate she holds suspended from her teeth over the heat. Her arms had proved too shaky for extended effort, but they are strong enough to tell her that the goo in the tube is still rock hard.

Food must wait a little longer, but heat, though, heat is a sensual pleasure, a decadent delight forgotten hours before. She feels a flush traveling up her cheeks, revels in the warmth soaking her torso. Almost, almost she could do without food at all.

Eventually, the concentrate softens enough that she can gulp it down. It tastes rather like very dark molasses threaded with strong hints of vitamin tablets. Disgusting in any other circumstances—its creators had meant for the goo to be mixed with flavor packets—absolutely delicious now.

Lillianara feels her mind begin to clear with each sticky swallow. Once again she marvels at her luck, but this time her wonder is mixed with a certain degree of suspicion. She rigs a piece of wire to hold a second concentrate tube over the heat, freeing herself to investigate the contents of this fortuitous haven.

A camp stove, itself almost empty but with a partial container of fuel nearby. Food concentrates stacked in a box. A plasteel jug for liquids, with a built-in micro filter. A battered atomic torch. Various odds and sods heaped in a pile. Even without digging into the pile, Lillianara can identify a shovel, a broken shifter, a couple of pulleys, some rope. There even seem to be a couple of ancient relics: a block scratched with what she vaguely recalls as the aliens' ideographic writing, the base from a small statue.

None of the stuff in and of itself is out of place. Indeed, all of it belongs there, part of the expected gear treasure hunters would have brought with them. Still, there's something wrong about it, something that doesn't fit. . . .

She's finished her third tube of concentrate and is rummaging through the food box looking for the flavor packets when she figures out what's wrong. Although everything here is reasonable in and of itself, it doesn't belong together. The food concentrates alone were manufactured over a century's span. The stove is comparatively modern, but the fuel tin is date-stamped at least forty years before the stove could have been manufactured.

Because of Jofar's research, Lillianara is more aware of time than most people. What is gathered in this little cave must be the remnants of several expeditions, not just, as she had thought originally, a cache left by one. That either means that someone survived up here long enough to scavenge the goods and set up housekeeping in this spot or . . .

She considers.

Or someone put this cache together precisely for her.

The latter explanation makes more sense. Although the cache contains food and heat, there is no evidence of bedding or clothing. The tools are a jumble of junk and useful gear. True, it could have been something of

an intermediary cache—a stopover meant to shelter the
unknown scavenger in an emergency or to hold over-
flow from some other hiding place.

Lillianara shakes her head. She simply can't believe
it. Maybe it's egocentrism, but her gut tells her that this
cache was meant for her. Why?

That stumps her. Why should the mountain try to
save her life after presumably killing so many others?
Puzzled, she begins to sort through the cache with deliberate care. Somewhere between moving a shovel
and shifting a coil of rope, she drifts off to sleep. The
little stove burns on, warming her rest.

When Lillianara awakens, dawn has come and
gone. The sun is already high over the mountain.

"I've missed my third extension," she says to the
chill air. "No matter what I do, no matter what I find,
I'm doomed."

Alastar is fascinated by the treasure hunter's behavior. When the woman awakens, she ignores the tanta-
lizing hints of ancient relics that Alastar had so
carefully planted. She passes over the broken statuette
with a noncommittal grunt. She glances at the tablet
inscribed with runes and then ignores it.

Mere human trash holds the treasure hunter's attention and even that she handles with great care, checking all sides of each piece in the light of the torch
before lifting it, inspecting it, then sorting it by some
arcane system of her own. In this way she finds two of
the lesser traps and disarms them. Alastar wonders if
she recognized them for what they were. The android

can't be certain; she'd been careful to use explosives brought by earlier treasure hunters.

By late in the day, the treasure hunter has re-arranged the cave to her satisfaction. Only then does she venture out into the open air. Seeing her flinch from the cold, Alastar chides herself for not providing a substitute for the ragged jumpsuit. Almost immediately, her imperative to eliminate the intruder rages in indignant response. She can no longer wait to see if the human will set off one of her traps. She must do something more.

Rising, the android steps over the tray that had slipped from her polished knees. The skulls wink at her as she goes by or perhaps the gems set in their eye sockets merely vibrate in response to the now om-nipresent rumbling from below.

Obsession and curiosity, Lillianara finds, provide almost as good a distraction from her own problems as the climb had done. By midday she had become cer-tain that the cache had been constructed as a trap. Twice she had discovered explosives connected to a piece of gear, set to go off if the tool—a shovel in one case, a crowbar in another—was picked up.

After that she'd taken a closer look at the statuette base and the rune plaque she had ignored in her more immediate search for food and warmth. These, too, were booby-trapped. Why go about trying to kill her in such a clumsy fashion? Certainly there are easier ways. Local legend is full of tales of would-be treasure hunters blasted by lightning from the sky or shaken off the face of the mountain by localized tremors.

True, any one of the four explosive packs she had unhooked would have gone up with sufficient force to shatter stone and turn her into a bloody smear, but there had to be more efficient ways of killing her, even if the means to create lightning bolts and earthquakes no longer exists. Why not just rig a trip line over the entry to the cache or wire something to the "on" button of the stove?

Feeling like the girl who had slid down the tube worm's hole and found herself in a land where everything was reversed and logic no longer applied, Lillianara decides to use the last few hours of daylight to begin exploring the rest of the ruins of Vorbottan's crest. Returning to the cities on the plains means ignominious slavery; therefore, she is exiled here. If she needs to accept insanity to survive, then she is quite ready to do so. It beats sitting in the cave watching her fuel dwindle to nothing.

When nightfall comes, the enshrouding mist reflects back a slight natural phosphorescence clinging to the fallen building stones. The reflected light clothes the ruins in a dim, bluish glow that seems to diminish the light of the atomic torch by which Lillianara picks her way across the frozen mountaintop toward the cache.

During her questing about the ruins, she has found very little of interest, but what she has found confirms her impression that the cache was a deliberate creation. Nowhere else are there any remnants of the treasure hunters. The only visible reminders of their presence are the sliced-apart stones, the masses of rubble. Everything else has been effaced, even the monument put up by the Second Wave to commemorate the First. Nor are there any portable alien artifacts. That makes the two she found in the cave not only anomalous, but downright unlikely.

When she sees the soft, silvery glow blossoming against the darkness, she doesn't need to check her direction to confirm that the light is coming from the cache.

Where else would it be?

"Down the tube worm hole, Lillianara," she mutters to herself and hurries toward the light. Where else can she go? Her other choices would end in freezing to death.

An angel all of silver stands before the door, a flaming sword held within her hands.

That's Lillianara's first impression. The second is hardly more reassuring.

Tall and slender, a figure stands in the entry to the cave. Although feminine, what stands there is definitely not a woman, but a creature whose form weds aspects of woman and wasp.

The creature's elongated ovoid upper body pinches down to a tiny waist before swelling out again into a matching lower ovoid. Various sets of appendages sprout from both ovoids. The upper possesses two long, slim "arms." A set of wings, very like those of a wasp or bee fan gently behind the upper torso. The lower torso possesses two sets of "legs." Looking at the joints, Lillianara would bet that the creature can become bipedal or quadrupedal depending upon need.

Immediately, Lillianara is reminded of an artist's reconstruction of one of the alien races that may have built the ruins: slim, insectoid creatures, much like the one before her.

However, this creature's head differs from the usual representations of those aliens; it is also what lends the impression that this creature is somehow a "she." The features are nearly human, all but the eyes which are great violet mirrors set slantwise below a pale brow. These have neither whites nor pupils, but are faceted like those of an insect. A wispy mane of white hair, as fine as milkweed down, falls to the creature's wasp-waist, somehow failing to entangle the wings.

As Lillianara halts, an involuntary scream rising to her lips, the creature raises what Lillianara had taken for a flaming sword. This proves neither flaming nor sword, even as the creature has proved itself to be no angel. It is a rifle of some sort, the barrel made of transparent glassteel through which rioting eddies of red and yellow energy course like contained volcanic fires.

As the alien aims the rifle with ready assurance, Lillianara is caught by the expression of sorrow and pain on the creature's delicate features. The full, womanly lips pout as if holding back a sob, and the violet eyes shed silver tears.

"Your name," the creature says, and her voice is like a quartet of alto flutes. "Your name!"

"Lillianara," the woman replies, too astonished to do otherwise. "Lillianara of Klee."

A bolt of copper light jags forth from the rifle barrel, but Lillianara has not stood placidly waiting for the creature to shoot. She has leaped—forward, not back—rolling into the creature's legs, hoping to knock her off balance.

It is like crashing against two steel fence posts. The shock makes Lillianara gasp in pain. She hears another shot, rolls again, this time into the cave, hoping that the insect-woman will not fire within and risk setting off the explosives.

Of course, they could have been removed.

Groping for a weapon, Lillianara's hand falls on the shovel. She wheels, panting in the thin, cold air, expecting to find the creature coming in behind her or perhaps the barrel of the rifle pointing into the cave.

Instead, the creature stands outside the cave, leaning on the rifle. Her perfect lips are smiling now. In a voice that sounds oddly familiar—only later will Lillianara realize that it is a variation on her own—she says:

"My name is Alastar. For this moment, at least, I do not need to kill you."

Lillianara swallows a sarcastic reply, but she doesn't lower the shovel.

"Thanks. Just out of curiosity, why do you need to kill me at all?"

The lovely alien face again expresses almost human sorrow.

"It is my imperative. I am created to protect this installation."

Lillianara wonders if she is seeing things. She has heard that altitude sickness or starvation can cause hallucinations. She gropes for one of the concentrate tubes. Alastar makes no move to stop her.

"Your imperative?" Lillianara asks, trying to match the alien's casualness, wondering if this is the being who set up the cache in the first place.

"I am an android," Alastar replies. "An intelligent entity created for a purpose. My purpose was to protect this place and to serve those who dwelt here. I . . . slept . . . for a long time until the digging of one of your people freed me. Then I resumed my duties."

"Your creators built this place?" Lillianara gestures vaguely toward the ruins. As long as Alastar is talking, she isn't shooting. That has to be an advantage.

"My creators, no . . ."

Alastar pauses. Lillianara has the impression of vast amounts of data long unused being retrieved, sorted, evaluated, translated, and all in the time it takes her to swallow a few inches of concentrate.

"My creators and others," Alastar says. "Allies. Trade partners. This place was built as a supply dump for various goods. This world would someday have been colonized, but colonization was not a priority."

"Oh." Lillianara bends and switches on the stove. Welcome heat wells up. "How long ago?"

"Your race was considering farming as a new and exciting concept."

"Oh." Lillianara doesn't bother to ask how Alastar

knows so much about humanity. Apparently, the android has had little enough to do in the century or so since some treasure hunter had inadvertently awakened her. Doubtless she's tapped various communications transmissions.

"One return time," Alastar volunteers, "they did not. I was left alone. Eventually, something must have happened, some terrible disaster. I can only surmise what this may have been, but it was severe enough that my body went into repair shutdown. For some reason—perhaps damaged sensors perceived that the danger persisted—I did not awaken when repair was effected. Not until the treasure hunter found me and the danger of his appearance was assessed as greater than the danger that had kept me in shutdown did I awaken."

"So you've been waiting for your makers to come back."

"I have been guarding the ruins of this installation. It is my imperative."

"I haven't," Lillianara offers hesitantly, "done anything to hurt your city. I haven't taken anything but the items in this cache—and they're all of human manufacture."

Alastar nods agreement, but a frown now wars with her gentle smile. Her arms jerk as if attempting to raise the rifle into firing position.

"True. But you are an intruder."

"I'm a refugee," Lillianara says, thinking fast: *Explosives wired to clumsy traps. A cache that is both lure and refuge. Alastar doesn't want to kill me. Give her an excuse to let me live.* "A refugee is not the same as an intruder."

"Explain."

"A refugee is someone seeking safety from enemies."

Knowing she is pleading for her life, Lillianara tells how Jofar had discovered a drug that would prolong human life. In the process, he had made enemies of those who would reserve such things for a select few. These enemies had conspired to get him into debt, a debt from which his only release would be to trade them the secret of longevity.

Jofar had refused. Telling Lillianara nothing of his plans until it was too late to change them, he had arranged to destroy all his records and research, along with their limited supplies of the drug. His final act— perhaps heroic, perhaps merely cowardly—had been to destroy himself along with his work.

Lillianara relates the entire hateful, painful story, moving from Jofar's achievements to her own futile struggle against the debt that Jofar had somehow overlooked she would inherit. She omits only that she had fled to Vorbottan Mountain out of some vague hope that she might find there something of value she could sell to settle her debts.

The android stands perfectly still as Lillianara talks, soaking in every word, every inflection, but Lillianara can't tell if she is convincing Alastar. She thinks that maybe, just maybe, the listening is a good thing, but to her infinite humiliation, the woman realizes that her body isn't convinced, that she's trembling under that calm, insectoid gaze.

Only when the ground vomits upward thirty meters away does Lillianara realize that the trembling is not her own.

When the enforcer erupts from below, scattering chunks of rock as large as houses to all sides, Alastar can no longer ignore the fact of its existence. She had been doing a fairly good job to that point, though the vibrations from beneath and her own security routines had warned her of its presence.

She hears Lillianara shout in fear and surprise. What would the human see?

A great mechanical monster shaped something like a crab, though its antennae are countless and possess a disturbing tendency to telescope up and down through the enforcer's shell as they collect data, then retreat to safety. The two main claws hold missile launchers at their joints. The spiked protrusions along the edge of the shell are lasers. The legs—eight in all, and lacking a crab's rear swim fins—can be detached for independent action or swivel to fire.

The enforcer had not been created by the same race that had created Alastar, but by an allied race with a simpler view toward matters of security. These had been willing to entrust the administration of the supply base to Alastar as long as one of their own creations remained to keep her focused on her task. Androids like Alastar had a capacity to adapt. This was viewed as one of the androids' greatest strengths by their creators and one of their greatest weaknesses by everyone else.

Indeed, without that capacity to adapt, Alastar

might have deteriorated from inanition. Neural nets, whether artificial or natural, tend to decay if they are not used. Alastar has kept her mind alive through conversations with her collection of skulls, through learning about humanity. In the process, she has become something the enforcer views as a threat to the installation.

Alastar knows all of this, feels also the stiffness in her joints that means an override program has been activated. The override prohibits her from physically acting unless the enforcer can be convinced she has not gone renegade. There is only one way she can do that. Given what she had just learned about Lillianara, the android feels sadness and regret.

As from a great distance, she hears Lillianara shout again, realizes that she is being addressed, sets up a split access program so that she can deal with the enforcer and the human roughly simultaneously.

In her mind, via tight-beam communication she hears the enforcer growl: "WHAT ARE YOU DOING, ALASTAR?"

"Investigating the situation."

And Lillianara repeats. "What is that!"

"An enforcer, a robotic killing machine set to keep me faithful to my duties."

"Shit!"

The enforcer says, "THE SITUATION DOES NOT NEED INVESTIGATION. THIS IS NOT A MEMBER OF THE ALLIED RACES. IT DOES NOT BELONG HERE. IT MUST BE REMOVED."

Alastar replies calmly, *"This is a human. It claims to be a refugee—to need sanctuary from its enemies."*

The enforcer's claws rise, open, missiles protrude slightly. Dust falls from its joints. Like a row of eyes opening, the lasers come on-line. Alastar notes with some interest that not all of them are as brilliant as they should be.

Lillianara waves her shovel nervously. "Is it after you or me?"

Alastar replies, "Me, but you will not survive me by more than microseconds."

The enforcer states, "SYSTEMS CHECK IN PROGRESS. THE HUMANS ARE THE ENEMY. LOOK WHAT THEY HAVE DONE TO THIS INSTALLATION!"

"Did they do this to the installation? I was in repair stasis. Since I have returned, no human has done any such damage."

A claw waves vaguely to indicate the sliced apart stones. "THEY DID! I SAW THEM!"

"And took no action?"

"THAT IS NOT MY ROLE. MY ROLE IS TO ENFORCE YOUR ACTIONS."

Alastar smiles slightly, recognizing the irony in that she is talking now to preserve her existence much as Lillianara had been talking to preserve her own. There is one major difference, however. Alastar was inclined to be convinced. The enforcer cannot be. As soon as it has completed its systems check and selected which of its many weapons are most effective, it will destroy her.

"Alastar," Lillianara is saying, "do something!"

"I cannot. It is against my programming. If you ran, you might hide. I shall endeavor to point out to the enforcer that it cannot hunt you out and kill you without causing further damage to the remnants of this installation."

Lillianara wavers.

"Hurry," Alastar says. "I do not rate my chances of success as very high, and the enforcer has only delayed this long to check its systems."

"Why didn't you say so before!"

Alastar cannot understand this last exclamation. Simultaneously, she says to the enforcer:

"What is your role when I am destroyed?"

"TO PROTECT THE INSTALLATION."

"And you will then destroy the human?"

"YES."

"Are you certain you can do so without destroying more of the installation?"

Pause.

"Why," Alastar goads, *"did you not protect the installation when I was off-line in stasis?"*

"YOU STILL EXISTED."

"But I was ineffective. Your inaction led to damage to the installation."

"NO MATTER. YOU WERE IN EXISTENCE. MY PROTECTIVE FUNCTION DOES NOT COME ON-LINE UNTIL YOU NO LONGER EXIST."

Alastar feels, despite her frozen limbs, the rifle being wrenched out of her hands. She experiences a certain degree of abstract surprise as from the periphery of her restricted vision she glimpses Lillianara running toward the enforcer. The woman shouts:

"Alastar, where is it vulnerable? Tell me or it will destroy you and you will be unable to fulfill your role!"

Various programming imperatives bounce off of each other. Alastar finds herself unable to speak either through tight-beam or by mouth. Her eyes are slow to track, but they follow Lillianara as she runs across the broken ground toward the enforcer.

The enforcer's missiles oscillate in their tubes as its own programming comes into internal conflict. Unlike Alastar, it has not kept its limited neural nets flexible; it has done nothing but watch Alastar and occasionally scan the surface during the millennia since their creators had abandoned them. It has not even questioned the bombardment that shattered the installation nor that Alastar had been damaged by a member of the allied races in advance of that very bombardment. It has not been flexible enough to wonder if damage to Alastar constituted a threat to the installation.

So now it finds it difficult to switch tracks as the ragged human pounds across the broken ground toward it, a power rifle in her gloved hand.

Lillianara runs. Her fingers fumble for the trigger. She plays the beam of coppery light across the enforcer's shell. The more vulnerable of its sensory antennae are sheared off. The less vulnerable retreat, reducing the scope of the enforcer's vision.

Alastar hears a frustrated whine along the tight-beam.

"RESTARTING SYSTEMS CHECK. AIMING AREA OF EF-
FECT WEAPONS. DECONTAMINATION. PEST CONTROL."

"Lillianara! Get away from it!" the android calls.
Simultaneously, she sends to the enforcer.

*"Countermand decontamination and pest control
procedures. Damage to the installation will result."*

The enforcer balks. "DAMAGE TO THIS UNIT HAS BEEN
DONE. PEST CONTROL INDICATED BY BASE PROGRAM."

*"My duty is to protect the installation. If you dam-
age the installation, I will be free to act against you."*

Alastar can sense the enforcer's programming seeking a way around these conflicting imperatives. She
knows it will find one. Their creators were not stupid;
moreover, computer minds work far faster than organic analogs. Lillianara is no longer within the android's limited range of perception. Alastar hopes that
she has reached relative safety.

The muddle of discussion from the enforcer's internal programming is fading. A single purpose is coming
to the fore.

"YOU ARE A THREAT TO THE INSTALLATION. YOU ARE A
THREAT TO ME. IF I REMOVE YOU, I MAY PROTECT THE IN-
STALLATION."

As the enforcer's claws lift, Alastar resigns herself
to dissolution. The missiles click into firing position.
The enforcer states calmly, all conflict dismissed:

"FIRING FROM DUAL PORTS. PREPARING TO RETARGET
ON INTRUDER."

A brilliant light sears the android's optics. A thun-
derclap forces her audio sensors into emergency shut-

down. Puzzlement fills her brain. She never should have heard the thunder.

Lillianara lowers the rifle from its awkward support against her shoulder. Heat washes over her as the enforcer robot explodes. The rock on which she is perched shivers, but stays in place. She realizes with a certain philosophical detachment that not only is she bleeding from dozens of small shrapnel cuts but she is also completely deaf.

When she finishes blinking the spots from her eyes, Lillianara sees that the enforcer has been reduced to a smoldering heap of burning metal. Alastar stands staring into the flames. When she moves to shift a piece of carved rock out of the reach of the fire, it is with her customary ease and grace. Lillianara wonders how long until the android comes hunting for her.

By the time the enforcer is merely burning embers, dawn is touching the sky. Lillianara's hearing is returning to normal as well. For many hours, she hasn't dared move from her perch on the rock. Gratitude might not be a factor in the android's calculations. Lillianara still has the rifle, but she wonders if her own life is precious enough for her to destroy what she has so recently tried to save.

Eventually, the needs of her body force her to crawl down from the rock. Leaning on the rifle for support, Lillianara limps toward the cache. When she moves, Alastar turns:

"You are out of repair stasis?"

Lillianara laughs dryly. "I never was in repair stasis. Actually, I'm in pretty bad shape."

Alastar appears to consider. "You are leaking. You stopped doing so for a time."

"The blood froze on my skin. I'm afraid that moving opened the cuts again."

"Your energy levels are low."

"I'm starving. I'd probably have frozen, but the flames from our friend there kept me warm."

"Friend?"

"Humor. Irony." Lillianara sighs. "I meant the enforcer."

"Oh."

"Do you mind if I get something to eat?"

"No."

Lillianara staggers a few more steps. Once inside the cache, she sucks down a tube of concentrate. Refreshed, she calls out to the android.

"Alastar, is there any way we can disarm your imperative to kill me?"

"I have been considering that as the stars turned. You preserved me from the enforcer. I presume your motives were self-interested."

"Well, you did seem inclined to talk. The tank didn't."

"Tank?"

"Old-style armored war machine."

"Oh. I thought you might think it looked like a crab."

"It did, didn't it?" Lillianara laughs. "So, do you plan to kill me?"

"I would prefer," Alastar admits, "not to. I am weary of being alone here. However, as long as I remain in the installation, the imperative will be repeatedly triggered."

"Can you leave the city? I mean, it isn't much of a city any longer and the civilization that created it . . . If you've scanned the archaeological reports on the things the treasure hunters brought back from here . . ."

"Yes. I long ago deduced that the creator race are no more. Moreover, recent evidence suggests that the alliance eventually broke down and that the installation was destroyed by those who created it."

"It doesn't seem right that you should be left to guard something they destroyed."

"Fair doesn't really enter into my programming."

Lillianara sighs. Alastar continues:

"But data from the enforcer's final burst transmission suggest that the damage that put me into stasis was inflicted by one of the allied races."

"Oh?"

"And therefore I could argue that they themselves felt my task was ended, that I was no longer needed to guard this place."

"I like that train of thought."

"Moreover, it has occurred to me that if I were to accept that the new residents of the planet were heirs to what remains of the installation, then I could accept new programming from them. Lillianara, my understanding is that your civilization has the concept of personal property."

"That's what got me into so much trouble," Lillianara agrees.

"Who owns this mountain?"

"No one, I guess. The government, maybe, by default. It's difficult to say."

"We should check. I suggest that I accept that Vorbottan Mountain and all it holds are your personal property—you as a representative for the human race. You then would no longer be in financial difficulty, and I would no longer be under an imperative to kill you."

"I like that," Lillianara admits, "but what if no one else does?"

"Then I inform them that it will be my duty to return to my original imperative and destroy all traces of the human race on this planet."

"Severe."

"Yes, but I can make a convincing demonstration."

Lillianara glances over at the smoldering enforcer, up at the odd storm clouds that mask the mountain's crest.

"I bet you can."

Alastar is rather pleased with how everything turns out. Not only does she have interesting companionship, but Lillianara—once she learns that Alastar can look as human as the next person courtesy of nanotechnology—encourages her to get out and see something of the world. Apparently, Alastar's collection of human skulls had not been in the best taste. She wonders why, given some of the things humans keep in their museums.

Moreover, Lillianara's long life makes her an ideal additional guardian for the secrets of the ancient, alien installation. Already she is talking about cleaning out some of the tunnels below and bringing archaeologists in to study what she finds.

Alastar feels vaguely uncomfortable when she considers that she hasn't told Lillianara everything about her new property, but would the woman have agreed to remain if she knew that the installation had been created to store military equipment, that the enforcer was not least among the weapons hidden beneath the rubble?

ANGEL ON THE OUTWARD SIDE

by Robin Wayne Bailey

Robin Wayne Bailey is the author of a dozen novels, including the *Brothers of the Dragon* series, *Shadow-dance,* and the new Fafhrd and the Grey Mouser novel *Swords Against the Shadowland.* His short fiction has appeared in numerous science fiction and fantasy anthologies and magazines. An avid book collector and old-time radio enthusiast, he lives in Kansas City, Missouri.

Ryder North leaned quietly against an old wall near the mouth of a narrow alley that ran between a pair of warehouses. Now and then, he turned his gaze from the tavern door down the street toward the planet Dom's night sky where a softly shimmering ribbon of stars hung visible beyond the dark rooftops.

It was easy to let his attention wander. The waterfront was too quiet tonight. No crowds, no drunken revelers, no fights in the street. Only the eternal lap-slap of the surf against the pilings, the barely perceptible creak of the boards under his feet, the salted breeze whispering by his ear. These made beguiling music, and he listened, and watched the stars, and felt strangely homesick.

Forcing a grin, he rubbed a hand over his stubbled

chin, and chided himself. No one knew better than he—Ryder North was a man without a home.

Footsteps.

North slipped deeper into the shadows. A solitary figure glided past the alley mouth; a cloak and hood concealed his identity. North crept closer to the street to mark how the stranger peered both left and right before pausing at the entrance to the tavern. A brief clamor of music and laughter as a gloved hand opened the door, then the street fell silent again.

North drew a pack of cigarettes from the pocket of his leather flight jacket. A match flared briefly, then died. He leaned against the wall again with the red-glowing stick between his lips. He tapped on the crystal of his wristwatch. The local time appeared dimly blue, then faded.

A moment later, a voice whispered over the transceiver in his left ear. "*The curtain's going up; it's showtime.*"

North stubbed out the half-smoked cigarette. Checking the laser pistol strapped in plain sight on his left hip, he crossed to the tavern's entrance and went inside.

The noise assailed him. Altairan rock music boomed from speaker-chips in every corner. A handful of drunken ocean-miners clustered around a tiny stage where they hooted raucously at some half-starved excuse for a stripper; customers of various ethnic types and planetary species huddled over small tables; a group of rough-looking humans lounged nervously around an ancient pool table, their eyes watchful, suspicious. Everyone talked loudly to make themselves heard over the music.

The place stank, and the filthy floor felt tacky beneath North's boot soles. He shouldered his way to a long, steel-topped bar where a few solos like himself leaned with their backs to the crowd.

He'd seen such dives on a hundred different planets. This place offered one singular attraction, however—a spectacular view that offset its shabbiness. The east wall was a solid sheet of armor-glass. Beyond it, Dom's two effulgent moons lit up the heaving surface of Obsidian Bay and made stark silhouettes of the scores of small barrier islands beyond. For a moment he thought it a holographic trick. The dark vista was real, though, and testament to Dom's strange beauty.

Still, he hadn't come for the view. Remembering his purpose, he set a glower on his face, leaned one elbow on the bar, and crooked a finger. A dour bartender responded. A moment later, with drink in hand, North turned again to survey the crowd.

In a shadowed corner, the caped man sat alone, his hood pushed back to reveal a shock of white hair over a smooth brow. A gray-eyed gaze raked nervously over the crowd, finally settling on North. Giving the slightest of nods, he put both hands on the table. A small black box rested between them.

North picked up his drink. Before he took a step away from the bar, however, someone thrust a pistol against his spine. A harsh whisper sounded in his ear.

"Colonel Ryder North." The pistol jabbed him; the

speaker leaned closer to sneer. "One million galactic goldars for your capture. Dead or alive."

North turned his head slowly. Careful to keep his hands away from his gun, he noted the muzzled, wolfish features of the bounty hunter: a Tauran mutant specially bred for combat in the Orion Wars. His kind had more than earned their *Warhound* nickname.

"Doggie slip his collar?" North asked over the rim of his glass, his tone mocking. He sipped his drink with a calm he didn't feel.

Again the gun barrel stabbed against his spine. "The collar will be yours, deserter. A very tight one placed around your neck just before your Redden Domain judges drop you through a trapdoor!"

The Redden Domain again. It might have been Middengard or the Champakkan Theocracy, or a half-dozen other stellar federations after his weary hide. North had no time for this. His gaze shifted to the white-haired human with the black box. The man was watching North and the Warhound, nervously assessing the situation. He half-rose from his chair.

A familiar voice sounded over the transceiver in North's ear. "*Ally, ally, all fall down.*"

North took the warning and dropped to the floor. A bottle whistled over his head, striking the Warhound in the face. The mutant let out a roar of surprise and pain; his clawed finger tightened on the trigger of a charge pistol. The blast seared over the heads of customers, striking the armor-glass wall, which flared in a brilliant rainbow of color as it harmlessly absorbed and dispersed the blast.

North kicked backward with all his strength, aiming his heel at the Warhound's knee. Like kicking a brick wall, he discovered. He directed a second kick at the creature's groin. Again the Warhound roared, with anger this time, as well as pain.

"*Stay down!*" said the voice over his transceiver.

North crawled rapidly under a table and unholstered his own laser pistol as pandemonium erupted. "Crazy mutant freak!" someone yelled, prelude to a chorus of curses and angry shouts. An energy bolt lanced past the Warhound's shoulder, missing. The Warhound returned fire.

Tables flew. Customers scrambled for cover or escape. Not everyone ran, though. The stripper leaped off the stage. Wiping sweat from her face with one hand, she seized a gun from a cringing miner's holster, sighted, and fired, missing her target and taking out the bartender instead. The Warhound dived for cover, then came up shooting.

Beams of deadly radiance, explosive charge blasts, and lethal projectiles crisscrossed the room. The air sizzled and smoked; the smell of ozone rose, then other smells of charred wood, burned steel, scorched flesh. North kept his head down.

The tavern grew suddenly silent.

Over the transceiver in his ear, his hidden partner's voice spoke with benedictive authority. "*But man, proud man, dressed in a little brief authority, most ignorant of what he's most assured, his glassy essence, like an angry ape, plays such fantastic tricks before high heaven as make the angels weep.*"

North heard the cautious shuffle of footsteps and stuck his head up, pistol ready. A tall figure moved among the carnage, nudging at bodies with a booted toe, at pieces of broken furniture, shaking his head. The light gleamed on his face, his hands, revealing as much circuitry and metal as flesh, and eyes that burned with disgust.

"Thanks for the bottle," North said as he surveyed the destruction. He moved to his friend's side; except for them the tavern was empty, everyone else either fled or dead. Slipping the transceiver from his ear, pocketing it, he made a face. "Now, Yoru, here's an argument for gun control."

The Technalien, a full head taller than North's own six feet, looked around and shrugged. "He that dies pays all debts," Yoru murmured. He stared down at the fallen Warhound.

North mouthed a silent curse. His white-haired contact lay sprawled between a couple of overturned chairs. An unmoving hand still grasped the small box. "Here's a debt we won't be collecting," he muttered. Kneeling, he retrieved the scarred box, fingered a catch, and flipped open its lid. "Damn!" A thumbnail-sized smear of melted black plastic was all that remained of a delicate data chip he'd been hired to retrieve and deliver to the Eridani Compact. The energy blast that had cut his contact down had fried the delicate chip inside its box. "No charge pistol did this," he muttered.

Yoru pointed across the room to the body of the

stripper. "She shot him," he said, "deliberately, then tried to escape in the confusion."

"A Separatist agent?" North cursed again. "The Compact will not be happy."

The chip represented five years' worth of under-cover investigations into Veil Separatist Movements, reports that Compact spies had worked at great risk to obtain. To see it turned to slag in a barroom shoot-out . . . He flung chip and box into the bloody shad-ows.

Sirens sounded. There were few police in Obsidian Bay, and fewer who ventured, even under orders, into this part of the Waterfront. Still, a major incident like this would attract attention. North couldn't afford to be caught.

"We have other worries," Yoru murmured, nodding toward the fallen bounty hunter. "There will be more Warhounds. His kind run in packs."

North sighed as he rose. The night was not going well. His ship, the *Warlock Knife,* was in drydock un-dergoing upgrades, and he'd counted on the advance payoff for the chip's delivery to finance those modifi-cations. With Yoru close behind, he leaped over the bar, stepped over the bartender's body, and slipped through a rear door into the rising wind of a cool night.

A familiar click warned him. In the shadows, some-one released a charge pistol's trigger safety. North froze. He was growing tired of that sound, tired of his whole damned lifestyle, growing angry, too, and tired of people pointing guns at him. Yoru stopped half a pace behind North.

"Are you really Colonel North?" The voice was feminine, nervous. She stepped into the thin light that spilled through the tavern's half-open door. Within the folds of her cloak's black hood, violet eyes looked up at him from a heart-shaped face whose flawless skin was framed in half-hidden locks of bronze-colored hair. There was an unmistakable hardness to her features, however, a certain cast that both attracted North and put him on his guard.

He eyed the expert way she held the charge pistol, aware of the sirens drawing nearer. Then, eyes narrowing, he took a closer look at her face. "Katrin?" The name whispered from his lips. "Katrin Janot?"

Yoru spoke warily. "This woman threw the bottle that distracted the Warhound."

North half-turned in surprise. "I thought you . . . !"

The Technalien shook his head, causing light to glint on the circuitry and bits of metal implanted in his scalp and along his face. "I'm a pacifist, remember? I merely warned you to duck."

"What are you doing here?" North said, turning back to the woman, relaxing only a little. "You didn't save me in there just to shoot me in this alley?"

Hesitantly, she lowered the weapon. "You'd deserve it," she answered. "I came to recruit some help from the roughnecks who hang out here, but you've chased everyone off. The way I see it now, I saved your butt. I still need help, and you owe me."

North stared at her for an amazed moment, recalling the Katrin Janot he'd known years ago. They'd shared a juvenile crush. She'd given him his first kiss, and then she'd slapped his face and laughed. Even as a child she'd been tough, independent.

Yet this was a different Katrin. Not just older, but *different*. Not just tough, but hard in the way war makes people. He read that in her posture, her expression, heard the smoldering anger in her voice, the bitterness that had nothing to do with him. He looked at the gun she held and tried to reconcile this Katrin with the child he remembered.

"Don't worry," she said. "I pay well."

Snapped back to the present, he smirked and rubbed a hand over his chin. To some people, the three most important words in the world were, *I love you*. But to a man like himself, on the run and unexpectedly broke . . . "I pay well," he repeated, ticking his fingers. He raised two more fingers. "How well?"

A too-familiar roar sounded inside the tavern. North and Yoru whirled together. Through the half-open door, they saw a pair of Warhounds standing over their comrade's body. Armored police officers charged in behind the mutants.

"Negotiations later," North said. He eased the door closed while Yoru lifted a heavy trash can which he positioned firmly under the door's handle. North bowed to Katrin. "Do you have a car?"

She holstered the charge pistol. "Better," she answered. "A skip-boat."

North glanced at Yoru. The Technalien rolled his eyes; his kind hated water. But following their new-found employer, they ran without further debate down the alley, driven to greater haste by angry growls, the splintering of wood, the can's crash and clatter, and a lot of feral curses.

Katrin stood in the glass-shielded bow at the skip-boat's control console, cloakless, steering the vessel manually with a consummate skill through the rolling seas. The onboard computer could have done the work, but she preferred to drive. "What made you turn deserter, Ryder?" she asked, breaking a long, uncomfortable silence. "You were a war hero. You had it all."

North didn't answer. He stared straight ahead, mesmerized by the glimmering waves, by the moons that lit their way, by the black, jutting spires of sharp rock. He watched the rounded swells and cliff edges, the glittering beaches of unnamed islands where neither human nor alien had yet set foot.

Dom, though settled, was still a new world in many ways, little explored, a young frontier. He cast his gaze upward again to a milky firmament of stars. Here in the Veil, on the edge of the galaxy, a man could make a new life for himself, get a fresh start, maybe strike it rich with hard work or cleverness or luck.

He could stay here, he thought, settle down. Take another name.

Find a new line of work.

Gripping the taffrail, he leaned outward to feel the sting of clean, cold wind on his face, the play of it in his hair as the boat raced above the water. Yet, it was to the stars his eyes turned.

A nice fantasy, to think of settling down, but after two hundred years, the Orion Wars were ending. Soon the various factions would remember the Veil worlds and return to claim neglected territories or try to stake new claims.

The *Warlock Knife* was his home now. Only among the stars, flying free from sun to distant sun, could he hope to stay one step ahead of governments, police, bounty hunters. Only up there could he escape his past.

He forced a weary smile. Turning from the rail, he reached into his pocket and drew out his packet of cigarettes. As he leaned back and lit up, he admired Katrin's ship again, a sleek little skip-boat, powerful, fast.

Too fast. His professional eye noted modifications to the controls, the customized line of the hull, other curious details. "Why didn't you go to the authorities for help?" he said, affecting disinterest.

Her back stiffened. "Not an option."

He drew on the cigarette and exhaled a stream of smoke. "What kind of cargo did you say you lost?"

Katrin shot a hard look over her shoulder. "Ruby salts," she answered, naming one of the rare minerals mined from Dom's seas. "But I told you, I don't care about the cargo. It's my sister, Annin, we're looking for."

According to Katrin, her sister and a crew of nine had lifted off in an old-style Tychus Leviathan cargo cruiser on a simple delivery run to the *Mephisto*, a Compact warship converted for trade and diplomacy, which was now passing just beyond the borders of the Veil worlds. The *Mephisto* was incidentally the same ship to which he'd have delivered the prized data chip.

Before the Leviathan had broken atmosphere,

though, its gravity induction engines had mysteriously shut off. The ship had fallen back to the surface. There had been no communication from the crew at all.

Katrin had continued her story with a marked reticence as she showed them a blinking light on the skip-boat's console. The Leviathan contained a private tracking beacon that operated on a frequency designed to avoid detection by Dom's authorities. They'd been making straight for it at top speed for the past three planetary hours.

"You ever hear of an induction engine failing?" Katrin had said with quick bitterness before North could question her further.

"Only through sabotage," he'd admitted with a cigarette between his lips. Despite her dodge, he'd realized in that moment why she'd gone to the trouble of saving him. Not out of nostalgia for an innocent kiss or a shared past; she hadn't mentioned that once. No, on Dom as elsewhere in the Veil, a willingness to look the other way and a reputation for trouble were marketable commodities.

The skip-boat shot like a bullet over the waves, its own small gravity engines shoving the water away in great white wings of salt spray that glimmered with prismatic fire in the stark moonlight. Katrin at last surrendered control to the computer. Stretching, she came to North's side. "How's your friend?"

Yoru sat in the stern, hanging his head over the side. At Katrin's question, he turned a pale face toward them, then looked away again.

"Don't get wet," North warned. "You'll short out a cybernetic kidney or something."

Yoru clutched his stomach and groaned. "Now would I give a thousand furlongs of sea for an acre of barren ground."

Katrin's brow furrowed. "Shakespeare from a Technalien?"

North shrugged. "Last year I gave him the Complete Works," he explained. "On a data chip. He ingested it." He shrugged again. "I've lived with his recitations ever since."

They sailed uncharted seas now, well beyond the bounds recorded by any mining crews or exploration teams. The waters turned blacker, sinister, as if some devouring algae reached up from the depths to spread its bloom across the waves. The jutting rocks, so dramatic against the sky, were long behind them. Only a few low islands broke up the vast stretch.

They ate a little from onboard supplies while Katrin muttered curses. Swift as the skip-boat was, it moved too slowly for her. She kept an agitated eye on the horizon. North ceased to doubt that her concern for her sister was genuine.

A guarded friendship grew once more between them over the hours. He watched her, and admired her sureness, her supple strength, the grace of her movements. Entrepreneur, adventurer, smuggler—whatever the years had made Katrin, he found her charming beneath her tough exterior and found it hard to resist the rush of old affection.

He reached for his packet of cigarettes, attempted to shake one out. Empty. His head rolled back on his neck and he let go a quietly despairing sigh as he crumpled the packet and tossed it overboard.

No longer sick, Yoru sat unspeaking in the stern, recording with his internal sensors every sight and moment of their strange new journey.

The first of Dom's two bright moons sank in distant waves.

On the console, the Leviathan's beacon grew ever stronger.

One moon down. The second moon floated, red and reluctant, on the rim of the world. In its dim and bloody glow, an island rose up, the first bit of land they'd seen for a while, with stony, silhouetted pinnacles that strained to prick the lingering orb.

The Leviathan's flashing beacon became a constant light.

Yoru rose carefully in the stern as North strapped on the laser pistol he had set aside. Katrin also rearmed herself. Her face grim with efficiency, she took manual control of the craft once more and guided it onto the shore. Gravity engines whined down to silence, and the boat settled onto soft sand. Taking a moment to bind back her coppery hair, she drew on her cloak and slipped over the side. North joined her.

Yoru moved to the computer console.

Thin, silvery filaments, like spiderwebs, extended from circuitlike veins in the backs of his forearms and inserted themselves into the machinery. For a moment, his fingers played over the console's outward controls. Then, the Technalien grew still.

"What's he doing?" Katrin demanded, suspicious.

North gripped her arm before she could interrupt his partner. "He's merging with your computer."

The Technalien species were the greatest machinists and technicians in the galaxy. Over generations they'd made themselves one with their own technologies, changing and adapting even their bodies until they themselves—man, woman, and child—were as much machine as flesh and blood.

For a moment, every control on the skip-boat seemed to activate. The boat itself rose three feet on a gravity cushion then settled back on the sand. Yoru inclined his head toward North and Katrin. There was a vacancy in his eyes that slowly faded as he separated himself from the computer.

Yoru told Katrin as he joined them on the sand, "All this vessel's sensors were trained forward."

Katrin bristled. "You try running rocks and reefs at top speed with them any other way."

"Like as the waves make toward the pebbled shore," Yoru coolly recited, "so do our minutes to their end." In rougher voice, abandoning Shakespeare, he added, "I prefer to know if something dogs our heels."

"You pick up something?" North asked, concerned. "Another boat?"

"No," Yoru answered. Yet something in the Technalien's voice put North on his guard.

Katrin gripped the butt of her charge pistol and scowled. "Then why the hell are we wasting time?"

She touched a tracker strapped watchlike around her left wrist. The crystal glowed with the same light as the beacon indicator on the skip-boat's console.

"The Leviathan's this way!"

She plunged recklessly across the narrow beach into thick jungle growth. North and Yoru overtook her. When she tried to push ahead, branches snapped underfoot. North caught her arm. "You didn't bring us along for company," he whispered. "If someone sabotaged your sister's ship, we can expect hijackers or worse." His tone hardened. "You've been pretty smart so far; don't disappoint me by being careless now."

"Wisely and slow," Yoru and Shakespeare agreed. "They stumble that run fast."

"You don't understand!" Katrin hissed. "Annin's the only family I have!"

North looked at her for a long moment. He understood all right. On Jaeger, his birth planet, he'd had a family once; a father who stood as a leader in the House of Equals, a mother known for her research in the mutagenic sciences, and a younger brother. All dead now, killed by Redden Domain warships.

He understood Katrin; he understood well feeling alone in a universe that dwarfed any individual. It made you cling to things, made you value bonds and relationships that a quixotic universe could so easily snap.

He felt Yoru's penetrating gaze, as if the Technalien knew what he was thinking. North twitched, uncomfortable under those eyes. Sometimes, he thought his partner knew him too well.

He seized Katrin's wrist, ignoring her halfhearted resistance, and glanced at the tracker himself. Then, with a stealthy tread, he took the lead.

They didn't go far. The jungle ended suddenly, and the ground became hard, sharp rock, smoothly volcanic. A few paces farther, breaths catching in their throats, they stared into the bowl of some ancient impact crater.

The last light from the setting moon glinted on the silvery skin of the Leviathan. The ship lay on its side like a beautiful woman who had fainted.

But North's attention went to the structure beyond the cargo ship. "Are you recording?" he whispered to Yoru. The Technalien nodded.

Was it a city or a single crazy construction? North couldn't decide. It looked like a child's box of blocks that someone had overturned. All the blocks were shoved up against each other without planning or pattern. The structure spilled across the crater floor and up the shadowed side where the moonlight barely touched it.

Katrin's only interest was the ship. She crouched at the crater's edge, pistol in hand, her gaze searching. "No scattered wreckage, no visible damage, no skidtrail," she whispered to Yoru. "Tell me someone's alive down there. Can you pick up any bio readings?"

The Technalien shook his head. "Though it be honest, it is never good to bring bad news." He paused. "I can't run that kind of a scan from this distance."

North led the way down the slope, aware that the moon's remaining light exposed them in a red glow. There was nothing to be done about it. Quickly, the three descended and made straight for the Leviathan.

They found the primary hatch wide open, but the vessel was empty of crew. While Yoru ran a check on the systems, North and Katrin slipped into the cargo holds. Nothing indicated a crash or calamity, nor had anything been touched. The huge containers of ruby salts remained neatly stacked and secured.

There was a ghostly quality to the darkened ship. Katrin remained quiet as they searched the crew quarters and galley. In the engineering section, she slipped her hand into North's until, realizing her action, she jerked it away.

Yoru's voice came calmly over the ship's com-system. "The induction engines were deliberately shut off," he informed them from the bridge. "Minute traces of an anesthetic gas in the environmental filters suggest the ship was sabotaged, as we speculated."

Katrin spoke up. "The computer logs might indicate who . . ."

"Crewman Kitaro Keller," Yoru answered. "His attempt to wipe the logs was . . ." a metallic sound, like a chuckle, that might have been the Technalien or a fault in the com-system, followed. ". . . amateurish."

"But where's Annin now?" Katrin murmured.

North didn't have an answer. He pursued his lips and wished for a cigarette as he led the way back to the open hatch. North disliked mysteries. Right now, the missing crew and that structure out there on the crater floor represented one big mystery.

"Would you call that an invitation?" he asked as the Technalien rejoined them.

While they'd explored the Leviathan, an arching entrance had opened in the nearest cube. The azure luminance that poured out suggested a corridor beyond. There was no hint of a door or a gate. There was just an opening where none had been before.

They crossed the short distance to the portal. At North's direction, they stopped again. His reflection looked darkly back at him from the cube's smooth surface. He paused, taken aback by his own image, all leather and sunburn, small scar along his stubbled jawline, face lean and rough and tracked from too many battles, too many tempestuous years among dangerous stars.

He hated the loneliness he saw on that face, and he despised the ruthlessness. But it was his eyes that sent a shock through him, gray and wary, cold as ice— killer's eyes. He put a fingertip to the image, then stopped as if afraid to examine too closely what he had become. He looked down at Katrin, who stood too close, her shoulder lightly brushing his arm. A tremor ran through him as her gaze turned up to meet his, not a tremor of fear, but of something more dangerous to him. For a brief moment he wondered if a woman like this could possibly save him from himself, from what he had become.

Deserter, she had called him. She didn't know it all.

Yoru touched the wall with his bare left arm. The circuitry that veined his skin coruscated with energy.

North pushed aside his inner demons and turned his mind back to business. "Crystalline?"

"Silicon," the Technalien specified. Maintaining contact with the wall, he closed his eyes. "Old," he added. He opened his eyes again. "It defies accurate dating."

The partners looked at each other, wordless, tense.

Katrin said what they dared not. "The Alphans?"

The Alphans. The First Ones.

Only a few ruins of that nearly mythical, first star-faring race had ever been discovered, most notably on Fenris in the Capella system. Also, half a galaxy away at McNaughton's Refuge. And only a few guesses had been made about their strange technologies. Where they came from or where they went, what they called themselves, what they looked like, no one knew.

But now—the door was open, a light was on.

Yoru ran his hand along the opening. "Traces of human DNA here," he reported. "As if someone brushed . . ."

"Annin!" Katrin breathed. She slipped under the Technalien's arm and rushed inside. Her footsteps rang on the strange floor as she raced down the corridor in the weird blue light.

"Damn it!" North cursed. "Katrin!" He plunged across the threshold after her with Yoru right behind. But Katrin stopped, then turned to face him. Her trembling image reflected and fractured in the thousands of crystalline facets that composed the walls on either side of her, on the glassine ceiling above her head, in the polished smoothness of the floor where she stood.

A hall of mirrors and micromirrors. She jerked her gun from image to image.

To her credit, she never fired it.

Reaching her side, North helped her to holster the weapon, then at a more cautious pace, they proceeded together. He kept a tight grip on Katrin's hand to prevent her from running off again, or so he told himself. He, too, found the multiple images disconcerting. He didn't draw his own pistol, but his hand never strayed from its butt.

Down the long corridor they went and into another that sloped downward at a gentle angle through a tunneled archway. They emerged on a railed balcony overlooking a vast atrium—or perhaps it was a pit— whose shuddering blackness yielded not at all to the tunnel's weak blue light. They paused to stare, to wonder, to fear.

North reached into the pocket of his leather jacket and extracted a match. The tiny fire flared. No ceiling, nor floor could they see on the other side of that rail. A moment of vertigo seized him, and he dropped the match. It fell like a miniature comet into the dark, sizzling, winking out, revealing nothing.

At the farther end of the balcony another corridor waited, beckoning with the same sourceless light as the first. Doors lined this new corridor, dozens of doors on either side. North and Katrin listened for any hint of sound behind them, for any presence. Yoru, scanned and analyzed, his sensors augmenting hearing and eyesight. There were no knobs, no handles, no obvious means to activate whatever mechanism opened those doors, so they moved on with increasing wariness.

Through more corridors they wandered, up spiraled staircases, down short ramps so smooth and sharply sloped they slid on their boot soles. On another balcony above yet another atrium they stopped again. A pattering of droplets struck the railing, and a soft, cool mist kissed their faces.

"Rain!" North whispered.

Katrin touched his arm nervously. "Inside? What power . . . !"

No point in finishing the question. North struck his final match and sheltered the timid flame with a cupped hand. It showed them nothing that made sense. He felt, though, as he shook out the match and dropped it, a growing oppressive fear, and the weight of some ponderous eye upon him, measuring their advance. He saw the same fear on Katrin's face and read it in his partner's uncharacteristic silence.

They encountered the first intersecting corridor. North could no longer be certain of direction, if they were above sea-level or below it. He was certain only, by some primitive instinct or intuition, that someone was with them, near them. He could feel some invisible breath upon his neck, some hand unseen descending toward his shoulder. The hairs on his nape stood on end.

Yoru turned slowly, peering down the crossroads into each new corridor. He had apparently ceased his analyses and scans, and on his face he wore a look of fear that North had never seen before.

"'Tis now the very witching time of night," Yoru whispered, "when churchyards yawn and hell itself breathes out contagion to this world."

North bit his lip and strained to think through the cold, unreasoning dread that filled his mind. Which way to go? Three new corridors. Three of them. *When shall we three meet again?* The thought tingled through his brain, but he dismissed it. He would not split up their party. "This way," he said, choosing the rightward corridor.

An unexpected sound stopped them.

A slow, metallic tread echoing from behind, caused them to turn. A shadow where none should be in such diffuse light loomed around an unseen twist in yet another corridor. A shape attenuated, black and terrible, steadily advanced. Then it, too, stopped.

There was about it some hint of humanness.

Katrin, freeing her hand from North's, took a step toward it. "Annin?" The word left her mouth a bare gasp. Louder, she called, "Annin?" Then forgetting her companions, she ran forward.

North shot out a hand too late to stop her. With a curse, he drew his laser pistol and sped after her, his heels ringing on the crystalline floor. Ahead, Katrin stopped, freezing as if in mid-step, arms limp at her sides.

North's natural caution reasserted itself. Mouth dry, nerves screaming, he gripped his pistol in both hands and crept the remaining paces to Katrin's side.

The shadow had resolved itself. A second woman stood unspeaking in the corridor's dim glow. Wide-eyed, North stared, then blinked suddenly as if stabbed by some splinter in the eye. He looked again, tentatively shielding his gaze as if he faced the brightest light.

"What's happened to you?" Katrin cried over and over, horror on her face, tears washing her cheeks. "Annin, what's happened to you? What's happened?"

North forced himself to look. If his retinas melted, he *had* to look.

Annin might have been Katrin's twin, yet there was about her an intangible, untouchable *something*! She wore a beauty that made her sister drab and plain. Coppery hair like Katrin's shone with measureless luster, a fire, that framed a flawless face and violet eyes. The simple turning of her head sang with a grace of movement that made his senses ache, and the stab of her gaze filled him with rapture. Hers was a mad, mind-stealing beauty, an essential yet utterly alien purity, irresistibly strange, violent in its perfection.

North ripped his gaze away. The image of Annin burned behind his lids. He sucked in ragged breaths, fighting a raging impulse to raise his laser pistol, to pull the trigger and destroy impossible loveliness before it choked and consumed him.

Weeping, Katrin stretched out a tentative hand to touch her sister, her only family. Annin, too, stretched out her hand and smiled. Yet, before their fingers touched, Katrin hesitated, doubtful, afraid.

Interlacing her fingers with Katrin's, Annin spoke, her voice musical, as unnaturally lovely as her form.

"Put aside your fears," she said. "I am well, Sister, and sent to guide you."

"Sent?" North caught Katrin's other hand. "By whom?"

Annin smiled. North's brain rocked beneath a wave of fierce desire. "Come," she urged, releasing Katrin's hand. "It's not far!" She turned, glided away in a delicate, poetic motion, long limbs in a white drapery, small golden sandals ringing.

North cried inside to possess her and followed, unable to do anything else. Beside him came Katrin, weeping, muttering as if driven mad, "What's happened to her? What's happened?"

Up a sloping passage they went, down a spiral stair, through another corridor lined with doors. Yet another balcony, and another atrium, but here, in the solid blackness, North glimpsed a shape, a towering tubelike thing leaning on huge gears that might have been a telescope had a human mind conceived it. He couldn't be sure, nor could he even turn his head for a longer look, for Annin continued on, and he followed like a puppet where she led.

Ahead, another figure greeted them, a man this time, like Annin perfect of face and body, his beauty evolved beyond anything naturally human. North felt Katrin tremble, her knees weaken; he caught her, wrapping one arm around her waist as he struggled to avert his gaze. How was it possible? This man outshone Annin!

"Keller!" came Katrin's terrified whisper. "Kitaro Keller!"

The corridor ended. Into a vast, domed chamber they emerged. The air turned cooler, drying the sweat that had beaded on North's face and throat. How different this chamber was from the nearly featureless corridors through which they had wandered. Spires of polished silica, carefully shaped, rose from the floor. Crystalline cubes, some taller than North, squatted seemingly at random about the room. Within those dark structures North glimpsed shapes, objects of mysterious form. Machines, he realized suddenly with that instinct or intuition upon which he so often relied.

Katrin screamed and fell back, clapping her hands to her mouth. With fear-widened eyes, she stared at a rising column of gleaming glass. Within, the nude form of a young woman, eyes closed in slumber.

Moment to moment, from one heartbeat to the next, that sleeping form changed in subtle and inexpressible ways as they watched. In identical spires, the rest of Annin's crew, men and women, underwent their own metamorphoses, achieving inside their strange cocoons measureless and mind-wrenching perfection, beauty beyond the divine, intolerable to behold.

North flung his arms around Katrin, shamed to discover the long scream that filled his ears was his own. She buried her face against his chest, shaking, blood running from the corners of her eyes.

The horror that North had earlier felt in the corridor returned, chilling him, raising the hairs on his neck. As before, he felt a ponderous gaze upon his back. Whipping his laser pistol up, he whirled.

Annin blocked his aim, placing her milky breast almost against the lens of his weapon. The shock of her beauty paralyzed his finger on the trigger. Yet, beyond her, high on the tallest cube in the farthest, most shadowed corner of the chamber, was another form cloaked in black folds of heavy cloth, hooded, without visible feature, shapeless beneath its garment.

Alien!

All his wandering among the stars, the battles, the missions, the running from authorities, all his secrets and all the secret places he'd been—and at last, that word had meaning! Waves of sheer *otherness* radiated from that form, unnaturalness, a life energy utterly incompatible with his own.

Kitaro Keller climbed onto another cube. Lines of force flared within the cube as he mounted it. Without quite knowing how he knew, North felt sure it was Kitaro's own cocoon, the instrument of his change.

Keller struck a pose of inhuman grace. "Master your fear, Colonel North," he said. "Katrin, be calm. What each of you sense is strangeness, but not evil."

"You sabotaged the Leviathan!" Katrin answered, mustering her courage. "What have you done to Annin!"

"Don't be angry with Kitaro," Annin said. "The Leviathan is unimportant. I've undergone an elevation."

North declined to lower his pistol. "How do you know my name?"

Kitaro Keller looked apologetic; heartrending beauty, almost an innocence, shaped his expression. "Katrin should have mentioned," he said, "I'm a mind-walker, hired into Annin's crew to facilitate communication with other species. This machine," he gestured to the coruscating cube upon which he stood, "has amplified all my potentials, including my once-meager psionic talents. I see all your thoughts, Colonel." His gaze locked with North's as he added, "All your secrets." He turned and lifted a hand toward the alien, who stood silently watching from within its black cloak. "So does our host."

Katrin pushed free of North's embrace as anger overcame her fear. "You hijacked my ship, damn you! You've endangered my sister!"

"Days ago, I heard its mind-call," Keller said, gesturing again to the alien, "like music in my head, like a symphony, irresistible."

Katrin was not mollified. "It told you to kidnap Annin? The entire crew? You anesthetized them!"

The alien stirred. No, shivered. A wave of indecipherable thought flowed from it, striking North like a rushing flood. Yet there was something in it of confusion, discomfort, longing.

"It needed us," Keller answered.

"O brave new world that hath such people in it," Yoru said. North risked another glance over his shoulder. Half-drowned in wonder and concerned for Katrin, he had forgotten his partner.

"I know another quote," Katrin said, her tone dangerous. "Oh, what may man within him hide, though angel on the outward side."

The Technalien ignored her. "Is it an Alphan?"

Annin shook her head. "No, though our host has

adapted these Alphan machines to its own purpose. It is a stranger newly come to our galaxy."

"It finds us unbearably ugly," Keller explained. He tapped his temple. "It shrieks just to look upon us."

"That black cloak hides beauty to the nth degree," Annin said as she moved to the spires wherein her fellow crew members slept like caterpillars awaiting wings. "Beauty that would blind and drive us mad. But there is hope for a meeting of our two races." She placed one hand over her heart while indicating Kitaro with the other. "We are steps in a ladder, each of us changing as our host studies the capabilities of these machines and the capacities of our bodies. It seeks to create in us a bridge between its race and ours." She reached out to Katrin again. "This is a great thing, Sister. I'm pleased to play a part."

Katrin whirled away, shielding her eyes as she screamed at Annin. "It's tampered with your mind! This isn't you talking!"

Annin smiled with a sadness that sent daggers through North's heart. "You don't understand, little one," she said. "But you can." She ran her hand over one of the occupied spires. "You can be a part of this, too."

Katrin drew her charge pistol and aimed it at the alien. "I came to rescue you, Annin! I'm not leaving you here with that *thing!*"

In the shadows, the alien recoiled. Another wave of confusion radiated from it, and something more that shocked North. It *feared!* And he realized that humans truly were as incomprehensibly alien to it as it was to them! He shot out a hand, pushing Katrin's gun downward.

Without warning, a laser bolt flashed past his face. Simultaneously, a second beam lanced upward at the alien shape. A thunderous charge-blast filled the chamber. Crystal exploded. Someone screamed.

Yoru knocked North to the floor as a line of laser bolts tore through the space above his head. Stunned by the impact, North stammered, "Who . . . ?"

A feral roar filled the chamber. A pair of Tauran Warhounds ran at them. Another pair emerged from the corridor.

Godlike upon his cube, Kitaro Keller flung out his arms and poured all his psionic strength into a desperate, horrified command. "Stop!"

The effect hit North like a hammer. The Warhounds howled with pain and clutched their shaggy skulls, but the rearmost raised his gun, and though staggered, fired. Keller's chest exploded.

A numbing loss filled North, then rage. Fantastic beauty—callously destroyed! He rose from the floor, pistol in hand, and leaped atop the nearest cube. Dodging fire, he sighted on the murderous Warhound who had killed Keller, then fired one long beam-generating burn. Screaming, he held the trigger, and scythed the beam into a second Warhound. Like a madman, he continued firing, cutting them both into pieces until his pistol's energy drained away.

"Ryder?" Yoru looked up at him. "It's over. Come down."

A red fog lifted from North's senses. He looked

around. The other Warhounds lay dead from charge fire. Katrin's work. He looked past Yoru for her.

She lay sprawled near one of the spires, her right side torn open. Annin, like some angel, cradled her sister. North leaped down, ran to her, and knelt.

"Katrin!" he whispered.

She rolled her eyes toward him, and through her pain, smiled weakly. "All leather," she murmured, reaching weakly to touch his face, "and sunburn." She hesitated, wincing, lip trembling. "What may man within him hide, though angel on the outward side?" She stared at him, and her hand slipped away. "I remember a kiss. . . ."

He watched the life leave her eyes, and another piece of him died with her.

Annin looked up to the far corner of the chamber. "Our host has fled. I felt his repulsion at our capacity for violence." She looked at North, and he flinched from the intensity of her gaze. "For just an instant I glimpsed its form—I couldn't bear it, Ryder North."

"Come with us," North said, offering a hand to Annin. "You can't stay here."

Annin hugged her sister's body. "I will not last an hour," she said. "I was the first, an experiment. I am . . ." she searched for the right word, ". . . uncompleted. The machinery that sustained me is destroyed. Or beyond our understanding." She gazed up again into that dark, empty corner. "You can't imagine what we've lost." She shook her head.

North knew what he had lost.

Annin arranged Katrin gently on the floor and

stretched out beside her. Spooning her body against her sister, draping one arm protectively over her, she seemed just to go to sleep.

After a while, North and Yoru made their way wordlessly out of the structure. The first hints of dawn colored the sky. A Tauran airship lay parked on the harsh rock next to the Leviathan.

North bit down the anger that had been building inside him. With icy calm, he said to Yoru, "You knew they were behind us."

"No," the Technalien answered, "but I know Warhounds. I knew they would sniff out our trail from the bar to the docks and realize we'd headed to sea. Recall that when the skip-boat landed here, I commandeered its computers and scanned for pursuit. Its sensors revealed nothing. Still, I thought they would come, so I opened a radio channel. If they were not following, no harm was done." He paused; then his eyes narrowed, turned hard. "But if they were, I made us easy to find. I do not like Warhounds sniffing my trail."

North fought to control his anger. Clenching his fists, he marched ahead. But harder to master was his anger with himself, for the Technalien was right. North should have been on his guard. Yoru was his partner, and a man in his position depended on his partner.

Yoru caught up with him, followed him into the jungle and to the beach. They might have taken the airship back to the mainland, but North needed the skip-boat, needed the hours'-long trip, the rolling sea beneath him to numb his heart.

"I am sorry about the woman," Yoru said before he climbed aboard. He settled himself at the console, spread his fingers over it, merged with it.

North took a place in the stern as the skip-boat lifted on a cushion of gravitic force and headed out to sea. When they reached port, he would sell the boat and exploitation rights to the Alphan ruins. They would bring more than enough to pay for the upgrades to his own ship.

The island faded in the distance. As far as he could see, the white-capped waves rolled and rolled, seemingly forever onward to strange shores, new worlds.

North closed his eyes. Without the moonlight, it was just a lot of water.